Praise for the Books of J. C. Eaton

"A sparkling addition to the Wine Trail Mystery series. A toast to protagonist Norrie and Two Witches Winery, where the characters shine and the mystery flows. This novel is a perfect blend of suspense and fun!"

—Carlene O'Neil, author of the Cypress Cove Mysteries,
on *Chardonnayed to Rest*

"A thoroughly entertaining series debut, with enjoyable yet realistic characters and enough plot twists—and dead ends—to appeal from beginning to end."

—*Booklist,* starred review,
on *Booked 4 Murder*

"Filled with clues that make you go 'Huh?' and a list of potential subjects that range from the charming to the witty to the intense. Readers root for Phee as she goes up against a killer who may not stop until Phee is taken out well before her time. Enjoy this laugh-out-loud funny mystery that will make you scream for the authors to get busy on the next one."

—*Suspense Magazine*
on *Molded 4 Murder*

Books by J. C. Eaton

The Wine Trail Mysteries

A Riesling to Die
Chardonnayed to Rest
Pinot Red or Dead?
Sauvigone for Good
Divide and Concord

The Sophie Kimball Mysteries

Booked 4 Murder
Ditched 4 Murder
Staged 4 Murder
Botched 4 Murder
Molded 4 Murder
Dressed Up 4 Murder

The Marcie Rayner Mysteries

Murder in the Crooked Eye Brewery
Murder at the Mystery Castle

Divide and Concord

J. C. Eaton

Divide and Concord
J. C. Eaton

Cover design and illustration by Dar Albert, Wicked Smart Designs

Beyond the Page Books
are published by
Beyond the Page Publishing
www.beyondthepagepub.com

ISBN: 978-1-950461-48-6

To all of our friends in the Finger Lakes,
who put up with frigid temps and endless snowfalls,
this one's for you!

Acknowledgments

Thank you to our friends, screenwriter Claire Hutchinson Porter and screenwriter-agent Terry Porter, for helping us explore the word of screenwriting and filming. And to our incredible beta readers and techies Larry Finkelstein, Gale Leach, Susan Morrow, and Susan Schwartz all the way in Australia, we could not have done this without you.

We are so fortunate to be part of the Cozy Mystery Crew of authors who work together to support one another. We're glad to be part of this crew. You're amazing: Ellen Byron, V. M. Burns, Becky Clark, Mary Feliz, Lena Gregory, Tina Kashian, Libby Klein, Elizabeth Penney, Shari Randall, Linda Reilly, and Debra Sennefelder.

Our agent, Dawn Dowdle from Blue Ridge Literary Agency, and our editor, Bill Harris from Beyond the Page Publishing, have been the backbone of this process. We are indeed in their debt.

To the outstanding staff at Beyond the Page Publishing, we owe you tremendous thanks.

Booksellers, librarians, and readers, thank you so much for putting a smile on our faces every day!

Chapter 1

Norrie's House at Two Witches Winery
Penn Yan, New York

I glanced at the mud Charlie tracked in from his doggie door, but instead of grabbing a mop I popped another K-Cup in the Keurig and plopped myself back in the kitchen chair.

"Did you mill around the Ipswiches' little pond this morning?" I asked the dog. "Remind me to thank Stephanie and the rest of her crew at Gable Hill for adding that feature to their winery."

True, it was needed for irrigation and water to mix for spraying, but as of late, it became Charlie's favorite pastime to skirt around the muddy edges looking for frogs. He was too lazy to make the trek to our pond on the south side of the property.

The dog shook and scattered water all over the kitchen and it mixed with the mud on the floor. I ignored it and waited for my coffee to brew. The mud would still be there after I finished my morning cup. It was an ungodly hour. Seven something. Normally, I'd still be sleeping, but the late-night phone call I got from Renee, my producer, kept me tossing and turning all night.

Usually I toss and turn from winery business. Like yesterday, when the tasting room manager asked if she should reorder the business cards with my name on them—*Norrie Ellington, Owner and Interim Manager, Two Witches Winery.* I said only if she put the word *interim* in bold caps and in a larger font. I didn't plan on babysitting here much longer. I happened to enjoy a wonderful life writing screenplays for a Canadian film company and I intended to keep it that way. I was only here on a temporary basis because my sister's husband, an entomologist at Cornell, received a grant to study some godforsaken insect in Costa Rica. The moment I could return to being the silent partner couldn't come soon enough.

My sister, Francine, said the place would practically manage itself.

What she didn't say, however, was that it was a magnet for murders. No sooner had I arrived than a body was discovered in our Riesling section. As the months went by, it got worse. More bodies cropped up on the Seneca Lake Wine Trail than in my entire New York City neighborhood. As if that wasn't enough to send me packing, I wound up investigating them. Not officially, but somehow I got roped into it, much to the chagrin of our local Yates County Sheriff's Deputy, Gary Hickman, aka Grizzly Gary.

At least March was coming to an end this week, and in late June Francine would be home. I'd started to cross off the days on the calendar. I still had three months ahead of me. Three months of supervising the tasting room, the bistro, the vineyards, and the winery. Of course, we had professional managers for all of those areas, but still, they needed someone to complain to if things went south.

Too bad I had no one to complain to when I got Renee's call last night. Her voice was even more chipper than usual and she spoke a mile a minute. A dead giveaway she wanted something.

"Norrie, we need to move the filming of our final scene in *Windswept Love* to a winery farther south than the Niagara corridor. Winter's been brutal and there's so much snow and ice on the ground it would be impossible for our crew to manage. Then I thought of your winery. I don't know why I didn't think of it before but it would be perfect. Absolutely perfect. We can film the final scene in one of your vineyards."

My stomach churned and I reached for the water on my nightstand. "Um, uh, gee, we have winter, too. The snow doesn't really melt until late April. May sometimes." *I'd have said June but she'd have known I was lying.*

"Our location manager did all the research. The snow in your area this time of year is wet snow and it melts on those fifty-degree days. We can get the two actors and a filming crew in and out of there in no time."

"Like a day or so?"

"More like a week. Maybe eight or nine days."

Eight or nine days? It's one short scene with two actors, not something Anton Chekhov wrote.

"Uh, well . . ."

"I know. I know. It's serendipitous, really. The fact your family owns a winery. Trust me, Norrie, you'll hardly know we're there. It's only the actors, the director, the director's assistant, and the film and video technicians. Seven people in all. And speaking of serendipitous, we managed to get three rooms in Geneva at the Ramada Inn. Someone will have to double up, or should I say triple up. Last-minute cancellation. What's going on there? Everyplace was booked solid."

"When? What dates?"

"Three weeks from tomorrow, beginning on Friday."

I didn't need a wall calendar to tell me what would be going on three weeks from now. It was the annual Wine and Cheese Festival on Seneca Lake. According to Cammy Rosinetti, our tasting room manager, it was the final hoorah before the summer season began.

The longer Renee babbled, the queasier I felt. "There's a huge wine festival going on at that time on Seneca Lake. Everyplace will be crowded."

"Oh, I doubt that will bother us. All we need is a nice secluded vineyard with a view of the lake. We'll take it from there."

"I, um—"

"And you'll get to meet the actors. This is the first film where we've paired up Priscilla McCoy and Gavin Chase. They seem to have a certain on-screen chemistry. Goodness, I don't mean to take up so much of your time, especially so late at night. Mind you, I wanted to call earlier but I was swamped. Completely and totally swamped. Anyway, I'll be in touch about the details, and as I said, we'll be in and out of there in no time."

In retrospect, I should have gotten that in writing. But in all fairness, how did she know there would be another dead body to contend with. I gulped the rest of my coffee and cleaned the kitchen floor as Charlie devoured his kibble. Then I took out my laptop and focused on a new screenplay. One whose setting didn't include any vineyard or winery scenes.

Three hours later, with my stomach grumbling, I trudged over to our tasting room. More specifically, our bistro. It was run by a husband-and-wife team, Fred and Emma, who looked more like college juniors than professional chefs. Oddly enough, they also resembled each other with slender frames and long dark hair pulled or tucked behind their ears. My culinary skills were no match for theirs, and since a warm quiche sounded better than cold cereal, it was a no-brainer. Besides, I had to break the news to everyone that we were about to be besieged by a film crew as well as scads of tourists for the wine and cheese event.

Our farmhouse sat at the top of Two Witches Hill and overlooked the winery building and our wine production lab. Farther down the hill sat the Grey Egret, the winery run by Don and Theo, good friends of my sister and brother-in-law, as well as my confidants and partners in amateur sleuthing. Emphasis on the word *amateur.* Theo was the epitome of the all-American kid turned thirty. Tall, well-built, full head of light brown hair and a smile that could cheer up the dreariest day. His life-partner, Don, on the other hand, had that neat cuddly factor going for him—short, portly, and balding. His smile wasn't too bad either.

Both of our wineries were part of a slightly larger klatch—the Wineries of the West, or as we called it, WOW. Six neighboring wineries who shared resources as well as gossip. We met monthly at Madeline Martinez's winery, Billsburrow. Sometimes to share information, but most times to chew the fat. After last night's phone call from Renee, there would be lots of fat to chomp on.

It was less than a half mile from our house to the winery, and since it wasn't snowing or blowing, I hoofed it rather than starting up my old Toyota. The usual tasting room crew was scurrying about since the door had just opened for tastings and a few visitors were already inside.

I spotted Cammy heading into the kitchen and followed her. Her loosely gathered bun was secured by a bright green ribbon that offset her curly brown hair. Slightly stocky and in her mid-thirties, Cammy exuded a certain warmth that seemed to draw people to her.

"Hey, there!" I said.

She jumped. "Geez, you all but scared me half to death. I didn't know you were right behind me. Good thing I wasn't carrying a tray of wineglasses for the dishwasher."

"Wouldn't be the first time someone dropped them," I said and laughed.

Cammy chuckled. "That someone was you, Norrie. So, what's up? Don't tell me you decided to help us choose the cheese dish for the event. We've got to make our decision pronto so we can get the ingredients."

"Um, not the cheese dish, but something related to that event."

"What? I didn't see any emails from Henry Speltmore about changes to the venue. And believe me, the guy emails us about everything. You'd think as president of the Seneca Lake Wine Association he'd have better ways to spend his time other than sending all the wineries his latest thoughts. Two weeks ago it was about engaging tourists in conversation, and only yesterday we got one about the glacier that formed New York's Finger Lakes."

"Yeesh. Nothing like that. Listen, I got a phone call last night from my producer in Toronto. They want to use our vineyard to film one of the scenes in the movie they're shooting. It's from a screenplay I wrote."

"Wow. That could really put us on the map. When do they want to do it? This summer sometime?"

I grimaced. "Three weeks from now. Smack dab in the middle of Wine and Cheese. And before you say anything, I tried to talk her out of it, but it was too late. Something about a brutal winter in Canada and better snow here. Or was it softer snow? Oh, what the hell. They'll be filming and it will be a disaster."

"Relax. It won't be all that bad. You said they will be filming in the vineyard. That means they'll be out of our way in the tasting room. And Franz won't want them anywhere near the winery lab or the tanks. Not to mention those winemaker assistants of his. Rest assured, they'll do their part to make sure no one gets near the wines in production."

"Oh, I'm not worried about that. I'm freaking out about the whole production thing. You know how people get when actors are within a twenty-mile radius. I'm scared to death those tourists will be trampling the vines to get a better look at Priscilla McCoy and Gavin Chase."

"Priscilla McCoy and Gavin Chase?" Cammy was practically shrieking. "Those are the actors? Oh, my gosh, I've got to let my aunts know. And my mother. I'd better call her, too. They watch those sappy romance movies all the time. No offense, Norrie. Oh, my gosh. Priscilla McCoy and Gavin Chase. Right here in this winery."

"Cammy, I—"

Just then, Glenda burst through the doorway. Her usual bluish green hair had morphed into shades of mauve and lavender but her oversize earrings that hung to her shoulders remained as steadfast as ever. "I sense a certain energy in the air. A seasonal shift. I'm getting more crackers. Seasonal shifts make people hungry."

"Then send them to our bistro." Cammy looked back at me. "Can we tell her? Can we tell the crew?"

I shrugged.

"Tell me what?" Glenda asked.

"A film crew, well, actually a movie production company, will be sending a film crew to our winery. It's for one of the screenplays I wrote."

Judging by Glenda's demeanor, I was surprised her feet were still planted on the floor. "I knew it! I felt something in the air. I'm never wrong about these things. When? When should I be prepared for my appearance?"

"They're not filming our winery," I said. "They'll be here to film a love scene in one of our vineyards. With paid actors. Not our tasting room staff, or any of our workers, for that matter. Paid actors."

Glenda looked as if she'd dropped an ice cream cone to the floor. "Won't they need background people? Crowd scenes?"

I shook my head. "Nope. Priscilla McCoy and Gavin Chase are the only people they'll need."

At that point, Glenda grabbed my arm and shook it. "Priscilla McCoy? *The* Priscilla McCoy who allegedly broke Jay Herandez's heart?"

"Yes, her," I muttered.

"Then we have our work cut out for us. We'll definitely need to cast a purifying spell on the winery. My friend Zenora has more than enough sage sticks at her place."

"No spells! No sage sticks!" Heat rose in my cheeks at the thought of spells and sage sticks. So far, I'd been able to dodge Glenda's wacky ideas. "They're not filming in the winery building. They'll be outdoors. If it makes you feel any better, we can ask John Grishner to have someone from his vineyard crew rake the soil or something."

"We'll need more than soil raking," Glenda said. "I sense Two Witches will be on unsteady ground until the summer solstice."

Chapter 2

With that, Glenda grabbed two boxes of crackers and headed back to the tasting room.

"What the heck was that all about?" I asked Cammy.

"You know how she is. Spirits, séances, heaven knows. If you ask me, she must have consumed lots of those magic brownies back in the sixties."

We both laughed but not until making sure Glenda was out of earshot.

"Listen," Cammy said, "I'm not telling you what to do, but you may want to let the rest of the tasting room crew know about the film company. I don't think the winemakers are going to be all that fazed. But the vineyard guys will pitch a fit if the vines are destroyed."

"Right. Might as well get this over with."

"I've got to unload the dishwasher and then I'll be back in the tasting room. By the way, do you have a preference for our cheese dish? We narrowed it down to Cheesy Mushroom Pancetta Bread Pudding or Southwest Baked Mac and Cheese with jalapeños and creole seasonings."

"Go for the mac and cheese. Anytime I hear the word *pancetta*, I think it's going to involve more work. Besides, who doesn't love mac and cheese?"

"Mac and cheese it is. I already checked with the other wineries in our little group, and none of them are serving that. Rosalee Marbleton from across the road at Terrace Wineries is doing quesadillas. I ran into her at Wegmans this weekend along with Catherine Trobert from Lake View. They're doing Georgian Cheese Bread. Gee, I guess you'd better notify them about the film crew, huh?"

"Oh, good grief! Once Stephanie Ipswich gets word of it, there'll be no stopping her. And once Gavin Chase gets a look at her, there'll be no stopping him! With her long honey-blond hair and that figure of hers, no man is safe around here."

"She's married, isn't she? With twins."

"That doesn't stop her from flirting. The woman has mastered the hair flip like nobody's business. Oh, it doesn't matter. By the time word gets out, every hair-flipping woman from Geneva to Watkins Glen will be here. And every college guy in the Finger Lakes will be stalking Priscilla McCoy. Darn it. Why couldn't we have brutal weather like they do in the Niagara corridor?"

"Get a grip. It'll be fine. Then again, once my mother and my aunts find out, who knows what they'll do? And don't tell me to keep it a secret or I'll never hear the end of it."

I let out a long sigh. "Tell them. Tell everyone. Send a tweet. If nothing else, it'll drum up business."

I walked back into the tasting room and perused the tables. The handful of customers that I'd noticed a few minutes ago had swelled. Glenda, Sam, and Roger all had full tables. Typical for a Friday morning this time of year. I skirted past the tables and waved, keeping an ear out for the conversation. Usually it was about wine, wine pairings, and local attractions, but sometimes, in Roger's case, it was about the French and Indian War. It was a passion of his and, in the blink of an eye, customers found themselves listening to Roger recount how General Edward Braddock was killed and his army ambushed by the French when the last thing they remembered asking was "Does this wine go well with fish?"

Thankfully, the only murmurings I heard had to do with wine. Lizzie, our bookkeeper/cashier, was stationed at the small counter by the entrance. With her wire-rimmed glasses perched midway down her nose and her short, tightly curled gray hair, she reminded me of those early-eighteenth-century renderings of Mother Goose. As I approached her counter, she looked up from the computer screen.

"Good morning, Norrie. I said good morning earlier but you raced into the kitchen. I wasn't sure you heard me."

"Oh, I'm sorry. I had to catch Cammy before things got hectic around here."

"Just wait until the Wine and Cheese Festival. It'll give hectic a whole new meaning. I've been keeping track of the tickets the wine trail sold, and so far we're up to two hundred and ten. That's a record for so early in the year."

"Wow. At least it's just one weekend and not two like the holiday events."

"True. And unlike the fall, I doubt many tourists will want to pose in our vineyards for those self-photos that seem to be so popular. The ground will be snowy and muddy. Not exactly a postcard scene."

"Um, about that, we may have tourists in our vineyards because the movie production company that handles my screenplays plans to film a scene in the vineyards that weekend. I got a call last night from my producer."

"Oh, dear." Lizzie shoved her eyeglasses farther up the bridge of her nose and widened her eyes. "Couldn't they pick another weekend?"

"Don't I wish. And it's not just the weekend. It may be all week. Seven people in all, including the production crew and the actors. Priscilla McCoy and Gavin Chase."

"Never heard of them. Then again, I'm not much of a movie buff."

Just then, Sam darted over to the counter, his red hair flying all over his forehead. "Priscilla McCoy? Did I hear you say Priscilla McCoy is going to be here?"

"Uh-huh. You heard right. Along with Gavin Chase."

"Did you guys hear that?" he announced to the group of wine tasters that had just finished up at his table. "Priscilla McCoy."

"Hope your winery has lots of fire extinguishers because she's smoking hot!" one of men exclaimed. The red-haired woman standing next to him jabbed him in the arm.

At that moment, Glenda's group, along with Roger's, vacated their tables and were now scoping out the wines and gift items.

"I'm telling you, Norrie," Glenda said. "You need to cleanse the winery."

"Spray it with Lysol and call it a day." Sam looked directly at me.

"When is she getting here? How long is she staying? I hate to duck out on some of my college classes but holy cow! How often does an opportunity like that come someone's way?"

"It's not an opportunity. She's filming a movie. Actually, one scene. One lousy scene in our vineyard. And she better not be a prima dona. We had enough of those at the Chocolate and Wine Festival."

"Okay, fine," Sam said. "What day? When?"

"I'm not exactly sure but it doesn't matter. They'll be outside and we'll be in here greeting all of our visitors for Wine and Cheese."

He shook his head and laughed. "That's what you think. Face it, the papers will get wind of it, and don't get me started about social media. If it's a done deal, it's probably trending by now somewhere."

The minute he said *trending*, I froze. "Look, would one of you do me a favor and let Fred and Emma in the bistro know? I'd better give Franz the heads-up before he has a conniption. And John, too."

"Are you going over to the barn or the winery lab?" Sam asked.

"Nope. My office. Much easier to call them."

"Chicken."

Glenda pointed to the entrance and started back to her table. "I'll take these customers. Sam can share the impending disaster with our chefs."

"It's not an impending disaster," I replied. "An inconvenience perhaps. Or maybe even a nuisance, but it's not going to be a disaster."

Who the heck am I kidding?

Suddenly, I was the only one standing in the middle of the room. Glenda was back at her table and Sam was off to spread the news to Fred and Emma.

"Lost or meditating?" Cammy asked. I was so engrossed in my own thoughts I hadn't heard her footsteps behind me.

"Huh?"

"Relax, we've been through worse. What can possibly go wrong?"

• • •

I echoed those words to Don and Theo later that night when we met for dinner at Port of Call, a neat lakeside restaurant with a fabulous deck and even better food. We had gotten there by seven and were able to snag a great table by the large gas fireplace that spanned the entire wall in their main dining room.

"Enjoy it now," Theo said. "Once April hits, we'll be jammed into the bar like sardines waiting for a table to vacate. Ugh. Tourists."

Don centered the votive candle on our table and smiled. "Tourists who keep us in business. It's a double-edged sword. And speaking of swords, what makes Glenda so uneasy about the filming?"

I rubbed my temples. "Glenda's uneasy about everything. The moon's orbit, the seasonal shifts, red tides somewhere in the world, who knows? And those are just the earthly things. She really gets freaked out about restless spirits who aren't able to move on."

Don shuddered. "Yeesh. At least the movie production will take place in the real world. Say, you never mentioned who's going to be in that scene. Did they tell you?"

"Uh-huh. Priscilla McCoy and Gavin Chase."

"Gavin Chase? Why didn't you tell us sooner? How long were you going to wait? Gavin Chase! Right here in the Finger Lakes. When? When is he getting here? Where's he staying? Did they tell you?"

"Get a grip, big boy." Theo grabbed Don by the wrist and held on. "He's a seasoned actor and you're an adult. Pull yourself together."

Don sat up straight and ran his hand under his chin. "I need to lose ten pounds before the Wine and Cheese event."

Theo rolled his eyes and laughed. "Have you looked at tonight's specials?"

Don picked up the menu and bit his lower lip. "I'll look into that keto diet tomorrow."

"Good grief. Everyone's getting worked up about those two actors. If I'm not careful, Sam will be crouched down in a vineyard somewhere stalking Priscilla. And from what Cammy told me, her aunts might not be any better as far as Gavin Chase is concerned. And these are the people we know. I can't even imagine how the public will deal with it."

"Forget the public," Theo said. "How did John take the news?"

"Horribly. He's positive we'll be overrun by curiosity seekers and movie star fans who'll think nothing of trampling our vineyards to get a better look. Or worse yet, selfies. The last time our vineyard was besieged like that was when those poor vineyard guys found a body in the Riesling section. Apparently yellow crime scene tape doesn't mean much."

"What do you intend to do?"

"John and his crew will rope off the area once we know exactly what part of the vineyard the movie company plans to use. They'll also post signs."

"Rope and signs aren't going to hold a crowd back. Too bad you can't hire some barroom bouncers," Theo said.

"Oh, my gosh. I can. Well, not exactly barroom bouncers, but Cammy's two college nephews, Marc and Enzo. They're tall, muscular, and pretty sure of themselves. They go on spring break in three weeks. And I'll insist the movie company pay their wages. Knowing those two kids, they'll chomp at the bit to be part of 'the protection detail.'"

Don winced. "They're not bodyguards."

"No," I said. "They'll be providing protection for the vines, not the actors."

At that moment, the waiter arrived to take our orders. Firecracker egg rolls and shrimp chowder for me and the appetizer medley for Don and Theo, until they could make up their minds what they wanted for an entrée.

Don took a cheesy breadstick from the basket on the table and bit the tip. "Maybe we're all overreacting and word of the production won't leak out on social media or the news."

I shook my head. "The tourists will notice something when they see a film crew at our winery."

"Tell them you're filming a documentary about winemaking. Nothing bores customers more than hearing the words *film* and *documentary* in the same sentence."

Just then, my phone vibrated and I checked the screen. It was a text from Cammy and it read, "Brace yourself. Two Witches is on the news."

Chapter 3

I tapped my news app and froze. "Channel 13 WHAM out of Rochester just announced that actors Priscilla McCoy and Gavin Chase will be filming at Two Witches Winery in Penn Yan, commencing in three weeks. It says 'sources at their hotel in Geneva shared the news today.'"

"Nice of them not to mention the name of the hotel," Don said. "Maybe we should notify Channel 13 of that little tidbit."

Luckily the waiter arrived and placed a steaming hot bowl of chowder in front of me. For an instant I forgot how ticked off I was. My news from Renee wasn't even twenty-four hours old and now everyone in hell's creation knew about it.

"How much do you want to bet there'll be three phone calls waiting for me when I get home? Stephanie, Madeline, and Catherine from our WOW group."

"Not Rosalee?" Don asked.

Theo chuckled and grabbed a cheesy breadstick. "Rosalee's probably asleep by now. Besides, she doesn't give a hoot about Priscilla or Gavin. I doubt she even knows who they are. Now, if it was someone from back in her day, say William Holden or Clark Gable, she might bat an eyelash. Still, I wouldn't bet on it."

I spooned a large shrimp from my chowder and devoured it. "This whole thing has nightmare written all over it and we're three weeks away."

The waiter returned with the appetizer medley and my firecracker egg rolls. For the next few minutes none of us said a word.

Finally, Theo broke the silence. "What do you say we order another appetizer medley and the three of us can share it?"

"Works for me," I said. "I can't believe I'm still hungry. Must be nerves."

He hailed the waiter back to our table and placed the order.

"Prosciutto parmesan palmiers," Don said once the waiter left.

I widened my eyes. "You're ordering that, too? I didn't see it on the menu."

"No, it's what we're serving for the Wine and Cheese event. It's a recipe I've been meaning to try for a while. It should pair nicely with our Riesling."

"Mac and cheese for us," I replied. "I'd pair it with grape juice but they'd throw me off the wine trail."

"Hmm, speaking of grape juice, is John planning on adding more vineyards for the Concord grapes?"

I shrugged. "I'm not sure. The only reason we grow those grapes is to sell the juice to distributors. Oh, and to give Francine something else she can use to make jellies and jam other than strawberries or raspberries. It's not like we make Concord wine. Not much of a demand except for the kosher wines and most of them are produced on the other side of the lake."

"Clearing off more unused land for vineyards makes sense because that demand may grow," Don said. "With the new Empire State Business Incentive, more companies are starting up in the region. I read recently that one of them is a huge candy manufacturing company that plans to pull out of Mexico and relocate to the Finger Lakes. In fact, they were scoping out that old industrial park in Geneva. They'll have to buy their grape juice from somewhere."

My napkin slid from my lap and I grabbed it before it landed on the floor. "But that means less product for the local grape juice producers."

Don nodded. "I know. It could cause a real divide for wineries. True, it may drive up the price, but it will create a rift. I mean, who do we sell to and how much?"

At that moment, the second appetizer tray arrived and we wasted no time selecting our favorites.

"The candy company is a ways off," Theo said. "But remember, it takes years for the root stock to grow. No harm in starting early. We already ordered Concord root stock last fall. It'll be delivered in a few weeks. Just in time for spring planting."

"Hmm. Guess I'd better double-check with John."

• • •

However, worrying about selling grape juice was the last thing on John's mind. He was as nervous as hell about visitors wreaking havoc in our vineyards. This time of year, his crew was pressed for time making sure they completed the pruning before budbreak. Once the leaves came out on the canes, it was difficult to prune due to the risk of knocking off the emerging buds.

And pruning wasn't all. The vineyard workers needed to remove the mounds of soil that they'd plowed over the vine grafts in the fall to protect them in winter. And then there was the cleanup. I was sure there was a professional word for it, but essentially the vineyard guys gathered the pruned canes from the ground, bundled them up, and dragged them out of the rows to be picked up and discarded.

The thought of having a film crew in the midst of the tight spring schedule gave John a pit in his stomach that "won't be gone until they are." His words.

• • •

I kept out of John's way for the next two and a half weeks. Mainly because I didn't want to aggravate him any further. Same deal with Franz in the winery lab. Franz took the news better than John. He ordered giant signs that read *Verboten* to replace the smaller ones that said *Employees Only.* He figured the word *Verboten* would scare people off.

A new and larger sign was placed on the gate to Alvin's pen, adjacent to the tasting room. It read *Please do not feed the goat. We will not be responsible if he upchucks on you.* Yes, a goat. A Nigerian dwarf goat to be exact. Apparently my sister and brother-in-law thought it would be a nice addition to the family-friendly winery. And while Alvin seemed to enjoy the attention and head pats from children, the same couldn't be said about his reaction whenever I approached his pen. Usually he spat at me. Needless to say, I tried not to visit with him.

With the film crew slated to arrive on the Friday before Wine and Cheese, everyone in the tasting room seemed to be on high alert. Sam started shaving and even broke down and bought new jeans. Glenda told us she started a new ritual—meditation bowls. And even Cammy's hair boasted new highlights. The only ones who seemed to be oblivious were Roger and Lizzie.

As for Fred and Emma, I wasn't sure, but that changed on the Tuesday prior to the arrival of our guests. I got an early-morning phone call from Renee telling me she was sending one of the camera operators along with the film director's assistant a few days early so they could check out the logistics. It was less than a five-hour drive from Toronto, and the weather was mild for April. The men would check into the hotel late at night and check out Two Witches the following day.

• • •

What she didn't tell me was what a pain in the neck they would be. Beginning with their demands for Fred and Emma. The first thing Stefan Olinguard, the director's assistant, did when he and cameraman Skylar Randall walked into the tasting room on Wednesday was to hand Fred and Emma a detailed list of the director's dietary needs. Gluten-free, plant-based, and organic. "Devora's extremely particular about what goes into her body," Stefan said. I had just walked him to the bistro and introduced him to our chefs.

Fred perused the list and folded it. "I'm sure she'll be fine with our menu." He went on to explain about our omelets, paninis, and salads but got cut off by Stefan, who expounded on Devora Dobrowski's demands. "There must be stores that specialize in organic and gluten-free foods in Penn Yan."

I all but choked. "Penn Yan specializes in bacon, sausage, pancakes, eggs, and chicken-fried steak. Oh, and submarine sandwiches, too."

Stefan froze.

"We're not Toronto," I continued, "but I'm sure Fred and Emma can see what Wegmans in Geneva has so Ms. Dobrowski won't wither away. For your information, Wegmans is more than a supermarket. It's a culinary experience."

Thanks for the heads-up, Renee. I didn't know we had to feed them while they're filming.

Stefan brushed some strands of his wispy blond hair from his forehead and nodded. "I suppose that will do."

Emma, who hadn't said a word up until that moment, smiled at Stefan. "And do you have any special dietary requirements?"

"I prefer whole grains and I avoid sugar, but that's about it. I have a naturally thin frame and I intend to keep it that way."

"And you?" she asked the cameraman.

Skylar, who looked as if he bench-pressed weights for fun, replied, "Pizza, meatballs, spaghetti, burgers, and nachos."

I did a mental eye roll, thanked Fred and Emma, and ushered the two film crew members out of there and into the tasting room. "Listen, we'll try to accommodate you as best we can but we're running a business here and that's our priority. So, I suppose you want to check out the vineyards and select a location spot. Correct?"

"Yep, that's exactly what we need to do."

"Fine. Give me a minute to grab a jacket from my office and I'll show you around."

I was familiar with Devora Dobrowski's reputation as a film director but had never met her. After hearing her dietary requirements, I wasn't sure I wanted to. Then, when Stefan mentioned the need to shop for Egyptian cotton sheets, preferably from Giza, because the Ramada Inn couldn't verify where theirs were from, I was positive I didn't want to meet her. Unfortunately, avoiding her wouldn't be an option.

"The vineyard is sectioned off by variety. Some grapes do better closer to the lake while others are fine farther up the slope," I said as we neared the Merlot grapevines. "This time of year, it's impossible to tell which grape is which because the vines haven't come into bloom. Of course, the vineyard is just going to be a backdrop for the characters so it really doesn't matter."

"Uh-huh." Skylar looked around as if he planned on purchasing the property, not filming it. "We'll need the view of the lake. We can do a panoramic sweep and then focus on the paths in between the vines where Priscilla and Gavin walk."

"As long as you make sure no equipment winds up anywhere but on those paths." I don't know why, but I got edgy. I was probably being silly and overreacting in terms of protecting our vineyard, but I had an off feeling about the project and I couldn't quite explain it.

Not wanting to make Stefan and Skylar think I was babysitting them, I pointed out our property lines and told them they were free to wander about in order to select the spot they needed for filming. I told them they needed to let us know ASAP so we could cordon the area off. *And plant Marc and Enzo next to it.*

"Remember," I said, "the barn and the winery lab are completely off-limits, but if, for some reason, Devora wants to shoot a scene in the tasting room, let us know."

Of course, that would mean a rewrite on my part, but I was used to that sort of thing.

"Sounds good," Stefan said. "We'll be back in the afternoon to see what the lighting is like at that time of day. Then early-early tomorrow." I had no idea what "early-early" meant, but as long as they didn't pound on my door before nine, I was good with it.

According to Robbie Jensen and Travis O'Neil, our vineyard

workers, who got stuck feeding Alvin and adding fresh hay to his pen, Stefan and Skylar spent lots of time scoping out our vineyard in the two days that followed. They drove in and out, parking their car in the far corner of our lot and traipsing about the vineyard like future proprietors.

"At least they steered clear of our workers. But boy, can their voices carry," Travis said.

I noticed he had gotten a haircut and the day-old stubble around his face was gone. Same deal with Robbie. I figured the two twenty-something guys, as well as Sam, were counting on meeting Priscilla McCoy. Meanwhile, I was counting the hours until doomsday was over.

Chapter 4

"That Devora lady must be a real pain in the butt," Robbie added. "One of the guys said he'd like to shove a cantaloupe down her throat the next time she opens her mouth, and the other one said he'd like to see her facedown somewhere with no means to get up."

I was flabbergasted. The last thing we needed was a temperamental diva directing a scene in our vineyard.

"Did they say anything else about her?"

The guys shook their heads. "Not directly," Travis said, "only that one of them told the other he shouldn't be putting up with all her crap."

Nope. We'll be the ones putting up with it.

I shared my frustrations with Bradley Jamison, the hunky lawyer I was dating, when we had dinner the Friday night prior to the Wine and Cheese Festival. I'd met Bradley a few months ago via Rosalee Marbleton when one of her workers was accused of murder.

"I'll try to get over to your winery sometime tomorrow," he said, "that is, if Marvin doesn't bury me in paperwork. He's been a bear the past few weeks."

Marvin Souza was a fixture in the Finger Lakes, a seasoned attorney with more connections to people and institutions than most senators. I always thought he resembled Hal Holbrook but with bushier eyebrows. Their firm specialized in family law from wills and codicils to divorces and alimony.

"Please don't tell me you plan on ogling Priscilla McCoy because you'll have to take a number."

Bradley leaned across the table and grasped my wrists. His cobalt blue eyes were eye to eye with mine. "Nah, the only one I want to ogle is you." Then he winked and let go of my wrists.

• • •

I awoke at five the next morning with a nervous energy surging through my body. I'd come out of a dead sleep more wide awake than I could ever remember. Charlie bounded off the bed and charged downstairs. Since it wasn't hunting season, his doggie door was open and I was pretty sure he raced out to do his business.

I washed, threw on a sweatshirt and jeans and made my way to the kitchen. He was already staring at his empty dog dish when I got there. I remedied that with a mound of kibble. Twenty minutes later, with a full cup of coffee and a bowl of Cheerios in my system, I took a shower and dressed for the day.

The Wine and Cheese event had a start time of ten but I had no idea what time the film crew would arrive. I prayed they'd inconspicuously park at the far end of our lot and disappear somewhere on the hill. So much for wishful thinking.

When I got downstairs and looked out the front window, I was stunned. The parking lot looked like Costco before Christmas and people were all over the road/driveway. Only Fred and Emma would be in the building, and if they were smart, they'd barricade themselves.

My hands shook as I ran for the landline and called John Grishner. Before he could utter a word, I shouted, "People are all over the road. Everywhere. How fast can you get here? Wake up your crew. Can we get anyone else's crew to help? My God, John, they're like locusts in a cornfield."

"Whoa. Slow down, Norrie. I was on my way out the door when you called. We always arrive between six and seven. I'll call over to Terrace and Gable Hill and stop by the Grey Egret. See if any of those guys can give us a hand. This time of year is impossible but we'll give it a try. What about off-duty EMTs? I've got Penn Yan's number if you need it."

"It's right here on the wall. Francine wrote everyone's number. I'll call them."

My next call was to Cammy since Marc and Enzo had already agreed to do guard duty. She promised she'd "wake up those two buggers and get them over here pronto." She also said she'd hurry over as well and notify the tasting room crew.

Ralphie at the EMT dispatch said he'd make a few calls and see what he could do. I promised him the men and women would be compensated for their time. I also promised to make a donation. *Get out your checkbook, Renee.*

Not wanting Charlie to risk getting run over by a crazed fan in a fast-moving car, I closed off the doggie door and left him in the house. Then I bolted for the winery building. I must have set a record for speed walking.

Sure enough, I spotted a black van with a Canadian license plate. It was parked on the side of our lot, close to the road. As I approached, I saw the film company's logo. From that vantage point, it was impossible to tell where in the vineyards they could be shooting the scene. The only thing I remembered were the words *panoramic sweep*. They had to be uphill yet I didn't notice anyone on my way down.

Figuring they may have pounded on the winery door and been let inside the building by Fred or Emma, I did the same. Only I had a key.

"Fred! Emma!" I yelled when I got inside. "Have you seen the film crew?"

"Hell, yes!" It was Fred's voice and it was louder than usual.

I rushed to the bistro and was almost out of breath. "Where are they? Where'd they go?"

Emma, who was cracking eggs in a bowl, stopped for a minute. "Stefan was in here about a half hour ago with a different cameraman. He asked if we had Perrier water and when I told him we only had Fiji, he all but had a panic attack. Said something about Devora not wanting Fiji. The cameraman laughed and suggested tap water but Stefan wasn't amused. We sent him to Wegmans."

"What about the rest of their crew? Did they indicate where they'd be filming?"

"It was only the camera guys and Stefan. Devora and the actors won't be here for another hour. The camera crew needed to lay up the shots. Or something like that."

"Dear God." I tried to take slow, deep breaths. "Did you see that crowd out there?"

Emma shook her head. "We got here at four thirty. Even Alvin was asleep in his little house. We've got to get the cheese dish ready as well as the regular bistro stuff."

"Hmm, if Stefan went to Wegmans and the rest of the crew won't be here for an hour, then whose van is parked in our lot?" I asked.

"It's the equipment van," Fred said. "They took three cars. According to the cameraman, the video engineer, who also handles the sound, is in that van getting things set up."

I sighed. "Okay, I'm going outside to play crowd control until backup arrives. Don't let anyone in unless you know who it is."

"Yes, Mom." Fred laughed.

The next three hours gave new meaning to the words *frantic* and *frenetic.* In addition to help from the Grey Egret and the handful of vineyard guys from Rosalee's and Stephanie's wineries that John managed to rope in, Ralphie from the Penn Yan EMTs said he'd make it as soon as his shift was over. He was also able to commandeer four thirty-something men and one woman who was close to my mother's age. I had them positioned up and down the road, along with Marc and Enzo, with the directive, "Don't let them step foot in the vineyards."

Bravo for that. When our doors opened at nine, the ticket holders for Wine and Cheese were more interested in Priscilla McCoy and Gavin Chase than our Southwestern Mac and Cheese paired with Chardonnay. We were flooded with questions.

"Is Miss McCoy in this room? Where?"

"Does the movie need any extras?"

"Will Priscilla and Gavin be signing autographs?"

Then, the unspeakable happened. Devora Dobrowski made her entrance into the Two Witches tasting room like Cruella de Vil. The only thing missing was a cigarette holder. She was tall with an angular face and layered black hair with one white streak that framed the left side of her face. Her complexion was pale and in the back of my mind all I could think of was, "Nothing a Big Mac couldn't cure." Her tortoiseshell wingtip glasses, complete with jeweled rims, completed the look.

I was standing by the counter chatting with Lizzie when Devora approached us and announced, "The noise level in the vineyards is interfering with our filming. My actors can't concentrate. You'll need to dispense with this crowd. Direct me to the person in charge."

"Um, that would be me. Norrie Ellington. I'm also the screen-writer."

She eyeballed me as if she was about to pick lint from my sweater. "That would explain a great deal. Now then, when can I expect the crowd to dissipate?"

"At five. That's when the event officially ends for the day. Of course, the winery will remain open until five thirty. Same deal tomorrow. It's a two-day event."

Devora lifted her head and sniffed the air. "I smell cheese. Cheese is horrible for the body. It causes mucus."

I felt my face get warm. "It happens to pair nicely with wines, and for your information, these events are what help us stay in business."

"Well, you won't be staying in business as a screenwriter if you don't do something about this unwieldy mob."

I gulped. "Please don't tell me you're threatening me."

She narrowed her eyes. "Threatening you? Of course not. Only your place in the industry."

"That's unconscionable." I didn't realize it at the time, but I was apparently yelling. So loud, in fact, that a small crowd gathered around us. "If anything, you're the one who needs to worry."

With that, I stormed off, went into my office and slammed the door. My heart was beating a mile a minute and I worried that I'd really screwed up. I counted to twenty-five, took a breath, and sat at my desk.

"You're the one who needs to worry." I didn't even know what I was saying.

At that moment, I heard a knock on my door.

"Are you all right, dear?"

I recognized the voice. It was Lizzie. She was impeccably dressed in a long mauve skirt with a white frilly top that matched her grayish white hair.

"I'm fine. Annoyed, but fine." I opened the door and looked around. "Did the she-demon leave?" I asked.

"If you're referring to the lady with the strange hair and unpleasant disposition, the answer is yes."

"That was Devora Dobrowski, the director for the movie they're filming."

"No wonder all those Hollywood stars get divorced. They have such volatile temperaments."

"I suppose I should try to smooth things over later today," I said. Then I took a breath. "Much later."

With that, I grabbed my jacket and stepped outside. The road crowd had diminished by quite a bit thanks to the cavalry I'd called in. I really owed them. When I stepped back inside the tasting room, I asked Fred to make sandwiches for everyone. Sam, who was dying to get a glimpse of Priscilla, offered to bring them to the workers, insisting Glenda could cover his tasting room table as well. I agreed and had him take sodas to the workers as well.

Four hours later, with the Wine and Cheese event in full force, we were privy to another grand entrance from someone in the movie production. This time it was none other than Priscilla McCoy herself.

With a sea of fans surrounding her, she flew into the tasting room and all but hyperventilated. Her ash-blond hair flowed past her neck, draping her shoulders in perfect curls. She had cinched the belt of her tan winter coat, showing off her tiny waist and accentuating the rest of her body. No wonder Sam was so enamored. "I hate that witch!" she cried. “I absolutely hate, abhor, and despise her. I wish she’d drop dead.”

At that moment, the glass Glenda was holding slipped out of her hands and fell to the floor. She looked down and then straight at me. “Let me call Zenora. We need to do a sage stick smudging of the winery tonight. There’s far too much negative energy.”

I bent down, grabbed a towel from her table, and helped her pick up the large shards of glass. “The negative energy will be back in Toronto by midweek.”

“Don’t be too sure of that, Norrie,” she said. “A negative aura, like the one we all witnessed, can manifest itself in many ways.”

Yep, leave it to Glenda to hit the nail on the head.

Chapter 5

By now, Priscilla was engulfed in a crowd of fans. I motioned for Glenda to get back to her table and then rushed over to Priscilla. "Step aside, please," I announced to the crowd. "Winery business." Then I took her elbow and ushered her into my office. "I'm Norrie. The owner. Well, part owner. Hurry up before there's a stampede."

"I guess I don't need an introduction," Priscilla said, "just a reprieve from Devora. That woman's impossible. 'Take slower steps. Not that slow. Move with urgency and reflection.' Tell me, how can someone move slow and fast at the same time? When I asked her what she meant, she called me a 'moronic piece of fluff.' That's when I stormed off and came here."

Priscilla dusted off her coat, even though it was spotless, and reached into one of the pockets, pulling out a perfectly folded pink tissue. "Damn it. I never had any problem working with Gordon Wable. But Devora? I don't think I can last another day. The filming has been horrendous. And you have no idea what that woman can do to ruin an actor's career. Just ask Lori Lynnwood or Bailey Wagner. Lucky for them they were able to recoup. "

Just then I heard shrieking and yelling from the tasting room. My first thought was that Alvin had managed to break through his pen and had come inside. He did that once and the cleanup from broken bottles was extensive. Not to mention the cost.

"Um, stay here for a minute, will you? There's bottled water on the small table by the window. Help yourself."

Without waiting for a response, I opened the door slowly and peered into the room. No Alvin, but throngs of women pushing, shoving, and shouting as they charged to the door. It took me a few seconds to realize what was going on and when I did, it was accompanied by stomach pangs.

Gavin Chase had made *his* grand entrance as well. I remembered my mother telling me about how my grandmother and some of her friends went to New York City to see the Beatles in 1964 and how they had stormed the Plaza Hotel. Now, in my own winery, I watched another version, only instead of John, Paul, George, and Ringo, it was Gavin Chase in all his masculine glory.

Broad-shouldered and tall, with light brown hair and a cleft chin, Gavin looked every bit the part of a movie star hero. No wonder the women were going berserk. I took a deep breath, steadied myself, and wove my way into the crowd. Gavin stood a few feet from Lizzie at the counter and it appeared as if he was trying to speak with her.

I stood on my tiptoes and shouted, “This way! This way to the office!” I motioned for him to get through the crowd but no one was going anywhere anytime soon. The tasting room resembled a football field and Gavin was in the middle of a huddle. At that instant, I seriously thought of bringing Alvin inside.

Then I heard Ralphie’s voice from the entranceway. “Make room! Make room!” He and another burly EMT elbowed through the crowd, outstretched their huge, muscular arms, and honestly, like Moses parting the Red Sea, made a clear path for Gavin to hightail it into my office.

“Boy, do I owe you one,” I said to Ralphie as he opened my office door and all but shoved Gavin inside.

“No problem. You should’ve seen the crowd last year when a couple of NASCAR drivers who were racing in Watkins Glen stopped in to one of the bars in Penn Yan. We’re used to this. I’ll stay right here in case those two need to be escorted back to the vineyard. Guess there was quite a brouhaha up there according to Chad, one of my EMTs. He was only a few yards away and could hear everything.”

“Brouhaha?”

“Yep. That’s what Chad said. He heard Gavin tell that prissy director that this would be the last film he ever made with her. And that’s not all. Chad heard him say he’d see to it that it was the last film she ever directed.”

I gulped. It better not be the last screenplay Renee wants from me.

"Thanks, Ralphie. Help yourself to our mac and cheese, and yeah, stick around with Chad."

As things turned out, Priscilla and Gavin had no intention of returning to the vineyard to complete the filming.

"We'll pick it up tomorrow," Gavin said. "Devora can just deal with it."

Priscilla sniffled a bit and kept dabbing her eyes. "I'll force myself to get through it. It doesn't say much for me as a professional if I walk off the film. Maybe someone can get word to Stefan and he can drive us back to the hotel. Devora can hitch a ride back with one of the cameramen, or maybe our video guy, Rikesh, can stick her in the back of the van. I don't care. She can walk, fly, or swim as far as I'm concerned."

It was tricky but somehow we managed to get Priscilla and Gavin out of Two Witches without another crowd scene. Ralphie, along with a few EMTs, as well as Marc and Enzo, escorted the actors out of there like a seasoned security detail.

About a half hour from closing time, Bradley sent me a text. He apologized profusely for not stopping by but Marvin had given him enough paperwork "to last until the next century." He also said he'd call me later tonight.

With the exception of Sam, who was in a world of his own having met and chatted with Priscilla when he delivered the sandwiches, the rest of our crew looked as if they had walked off a battlefield. Even Cammy, who usually has an abundance of energy, was worn out.

"So help me," she said. "If one of those bartenders calls in sick tonight, my aunts will have to find someone else to work at Rosinetti's. I'm way too pooped."

"Tomorrow should be a much easier day," Lizzie said as we finished clearing the tasting room tables and stacking the dishes in the washer. "The first day of an event is always the hardest. Why, I all but guarantee tomorrow will be a walk in the park."

Uh-huh. That's what she said. "A walk in the park." Good thing for her she was a bookkeeper and not a fortune-teller or she'd be out of business.

• • •

Bradley kept his word and called me at a little past eight. We agreed to grab a pizza during the week because there was no way he could make it to the winery tomorrow. Then I got another call, this one from Godfrey Klein at the Experiment Station in Geneva. Like my brother-in-law, Godfrey was an entomologist whose passion for insects was downright disturbing. Godfrey kept tabs on Francine and Jason via a satellite phone in Costa Rica and he shared information with me as best he could. We'd also shared a kiss a few months ago and haven't said a word about it since.

"Hey, Norrie, thought you'd like to know, Jason has spotted the Mansonia titillans in its resting place. And, are you ready for this? He was able to document a number of blood-engorged females. Do you know what that means?"

"Uh-huh. Stay the hell out of Costa Rica. They're still coming back in June, aren't they? Please tell me they're coming back in June."

"Uh, as far as I know. The grant only runs for a year. Of course, grants get extended all the time, especially when—"

"Don't say it. Don't even think it. I don't care if he discovers an insect that can speak seven languages fluently. They need to get back to Two Witches."

For the next five minutes, I went on and on about my producer and how I got duped into letting her send a self-serving narcissist to our winery in order to direct a scene in our vineyard.

"Wow. Sounds like you've got real issues with this one," Godfrey said. "If you want, we can meet over coffee and you can spew out all the details. I promised Jason I'd be there if you needed anything. I suppose having someone to vent to meets that criteria."

"Great. I'll take you up on the offer and I'll call you back this week."

At that point, I was totally wiped out. Too tired to even nuke an egg, I ate pretzel rods dipped in cream cheese and slices of apples dipped in Hershey syrup. Then I collapsed in bed and didn't wake up until the following morning. I was so tired I forgot to close up Charlie's doggie door and paid the price the next morning.

• • •

That annoying Plott hound bounced on my bed at sunrise, shaking water and mud all over me. If that wasn't disgusting enough, he dropped a slippery, slimy cattail on my chest. His wake-up call worked better than an alarm clock. I tossed the blanket to the side of the bed and got up.

"What am I going to do to keep you out of the Gable Hill's irrigation pond?"

He looked at me with those deep, loving brown eyes and I bent down to pet his head. Then I reached over to the bed to grab the cattail and throw it out. That's when I noticed something shiny wrapped up around it, and when I took a closer look, my heart started to pound.

It was a five-cent Canadian coin necklace on a double-wound silver chain. A necklace I'd seen the day before, and it wasn't entwined on a waterweed then. It hung gracefully from the wearer's neck.

"Holy crap, Charlie," I said. "This better not mean what I think it does."

Not knowing what to do first, I left the cattail and the necklace on the floor by my bed. I was so freaked out by his latest find that I washed quickly and threw on some clothes. I didn't even stop to brush my teeth. In a series of quick motions, I emptied some kibble from the bag, grabbed my coat, stuffed my cell phone in my jeans pocket and put on my L.L. Bean Wellies. Where I was headed, I needed something that was meant for tromping in mud and gunk as well as wet snow.

"You're staying in the house," I told the dog. Then I secured his doggie door and charged across the field that separates our property from Stephanie Ipswich's. The sun hadn't yet broken over the horizon but the sky had lightened and it was easy for me to see where I was going.

"Please tell me I'm wrong," I muttered to myself as I made my way over to the pond that Charlie had taken a liking to. Like most vineyard ponds, it wasn't huge but it was deep, at least eight or nine feet. Clumps of cattails framed part of the pond with smaller weeds around the remainder of the circumference.

Careful not to slip on the wet snow and mud, I walked slowly to the edge and stared at the surface. At first I didn't notice anything unusual but the water was murky. Then I caught sight of what appeared to be a large branch that surfaced and then slipped beneath the water. I held still for a moment, refusing to even take a breath. That's when the branch reappeared. Only it wasn't a branch. It was someone's arm.

At that moment my body felt as if it had been zapped with a Taser. I jumped back and forced myself to take slow, deep breaths. Then I pulled out my cell phone and called Stephanie. The second she answered I said, "There's a dead body in your pond and I think I know who it is."

Chapter 6

"Did you hear me, Stephanie?" I asked. "It's Norrie and I'm standing in front of your irrigation pond."

"I know it's you, Norrie. It's the rest of what you said that I didn't hear correctly. The boys are making too much noise with their model train set. They've been up for hours. On a school day I can't wake them, but on Sunday, they get up with the roosters."

"Forget the roosters and the train. I'm telling you, there's a dead body in your pond. Maybe you should call the sheriff. Maybe I should. Holy crap. This is a nightmare."

"A dead body? In our pond? Are you sure?"

"Unless the arm I saw is floating on its own, I'm sure."

"Oh, my God! Don't do anything. Don't call anyone yet until Derek and I get there. Thank goodness my mother-in-law is here for Wine and Cheese weekend to watch the boys. Give me a few minutes, I'll wake Derek up and we'll both head to the pond. Stay where you are."

I eyeballed the rutted dirt road that used to be a footpath that bordered their property. Finally, after what seemed like hours, I recognized their dark green pickup truck. Derek stepped out and thundered over to where I stood. His dark hair was unkempt, and coupled with the day-old stubble on his face, he looked as if he'd spent the night in the Bowery and not a comfortable bed.

"There had better be a dead body floating around, Norrie, because I lost a good two hours of sleep."

"There is. And I lost sleep, too." Of course, I was probably responsible for the dead body in an offhanded way, but still . . .

"Holy hell!" Stephanie shrieked from the truck. "Is there really a body in there? Can you see it? I'm not getting out of the truck if there is."

Derek turned to her and shouted, "Give me a second, will you?"

Then he walked back to the pickup, grabbed a hoe from the bed of the truck and returned to the pond. "I don't see anything," he said.

I crossed my arms in front of my chest and sighed. "Wait a second and watch the surface of the water."

The two of us stood there without saying a word. Finally, the arm surfaced again and Derek rushed over with the hoe. One lift and we knew it wasn't a branch. Branches don't have nail polish or cuff bracelets.

"What the hell," Derek said. Then he shot me a look. "On the way over here, Stephanie told me you might know who this is. What's going on?"

"Well, as you may or may not know, because everyone seems to know at this point, a movie is being filmed in our vineyard. A scene, actually. One scene." Then I sort of got a bit incoherent. "One long scene that I wrote and the Niagara corridor can't be used for the filming because of the snow and ice so the producer—"

"Give me the short version, huh?"

"I think it's Priscilla McCoy, the lead actress. Charlie came back from your pond with a necklace wrapped around a cattail. I saw Priscilla wearing that necklace yesterday when she took off her coat at the winery. She kind of had a meltdown because the director, Devora Dobrowski, is a she-witch."

Derek clasped his hands and let out a breath. "Guess I'll need to phone the sheriff."

"I'm the last person Deputy Hickman's going to want to see. Maybe you could speak with him first while I go home to brush my teeth and wash up."

"Norrie, Gary Hickman will want to know how I happened upon a dead body in our irrigation pond at the crack of dawn. What am I supposed to tell him? That I got up and said, 'Gee, maybe there's a body in our pond. I'll go take a look.' Damn it. Why couldn't they have dropped the body off at the other side of our hill by that bed-and-breakfast?"

"Okay, okay. You call him while I run home to get changed. I'll be back in a jiff. Besides, it'll take them a few minutes to get here."

Derek glanced at the truck where Stephanie was sitting. "Look, I'll drive my wife back to our house and make the call from there. Then I'll meet you back here. All right?"

"Yeah. Fine."

I waved to Stephanie and shot out of there as fast as I could considering the ground was damp and muddy and Wellies weren't exactly running shoes. The minute I got in the door, I raced upstairs, brushed my teeth and jumped into the shower. I figured it would be a horrendous day and who knew when I'd get the chance to wash. Minutes later, I was in clean jeans and a Two Witches sweatshirt with a cauldron on it that read *Stir Up Some Magic With Our Wine.*

Then I gave Charlie some more kibble and stepped outside to lock the fence that we normally keep open. No sense risking Grizzly Gary's temper if Charlie got out and messed with a crime scene. No sooner had I latched the mechanism than I heard sirens. At least they wouldn't be headed up our road. Unfortunately, something worse was already there.

By the time I put on my coat and locked the door, our driveway had three TV vans lined up near the winery. I recognized them from the last time they covered the "breaking news" at Two Witches.

"Idiots," I mumbled to myself. "The crime scene is next door."

I was positive news of a dead body surfacing at one of the wineries had hit the scanners once Derek called the sheriff. I was also positive those news crews had Two Witches on speed dial, so to speak, and drove directly here. Not wanting them to take up space in our driveway, I hustled over to where they were parked with the intention of directing them to Gable Hill Winery. That's when I found out they had no idea about a dead body.

"Norrie Ellington, right?" the reporter from Channel 13 WHAM asked as soon as I approached his van. "We got word they're shooting a movie in your vineyard with Priscilla McCoy and Gavin Chase. Talk about increasing our ratings. One quick interview and viewers will be glued to the news."

"Um, yeah, about that . . . I don't think the actors can give interviews while they're filming." *Especially since one of them might be dead.*

The guy was undaunted. "Hey, even if we get some good shots, it'll interest viewers. Too bad the competition is right behind us."

I turned and faced the other two vans. Channels 8 and 10. Yep, all the networks were accounted for. "Stay here," I said. "I don't even know if the film crew has arrived."

The guy laughed. "Look in your parking lot. That's the film company's van, isn't it? I can read the logo from here."

"That's the sound and video equipment. I doubt viewers will be mesmerized by it. Stay here. We'll keep you posted."

Terrific. Derek expected me back at the pond but someone had to let Fred and Emma know what was going on. And in less than an hour the rest of the tasting room crew would be there. Not to mention the vineyard workers, who were there seven days a week. Rats! They're probably up in some vineyard removing feeler roots or tying up the canes. I motioned for the reporter to stay put and walked toward the winery building. When I got to the door, I pulled out my cell phone and called John Grishner. He answered immediately.

"John, thank goodness you're there," I said. "We've got a problem."

"Don't tell me the tourists are already there. It's only eight thirty. It's Sunday. The event starts an hour later today, doesn't it? I've got the guys down below in the Chardonnay section and I'm in the barn. What's up?"

"You mean besides the three news vans from Rochester who got wind of the filming?"

Before he could answer, I went on. "That's not why I called you. Priscilla McCoy's dead body is floating around the Ipswiches' irrigation pond. I think she may have drowned. Charlie got out early this morning and came back home with her necklace entwined in a cattail. I raced over to the pond and saw her arm in the water. I'm sure it's her arm."

"Take it easy. Slow down. One thing at a time. Did you call the sheriff?"

"Derek Ipswich did. I'm supposed to go back to the pond. He's waiting for the sheriff. I was there but had to go home to brush my teeth. Didn't you hear the sirens? They must be there already. But right now, the news crews don't know a thing about it."

No sooner had I said that than the Fox News van made a three-point turn in our driveway and flew down to Route 14. Channel 8 followed and seconds later, WHAM 13.

"Um, I think they just found out. The news vans are turning left on Route 14. Toward Gable Hill. They wouldn't do that unless they got word of other, more breaking news. Oh, my gosh. Poor Stephanie."

"Calm down, please. I'll make sure our crew and the EMTs are posted on the driveway like yesterday, but the Gable Hill guys will have enough to worry about at their own place. In fact, Ralphie's EMTs probably got wind of your pond discovery by now. Knowing how fast word spreads, I'll bet a few of them are over there already. Try to keep this thing under wraps. Like a need-to-know kind of thing. See what the sheriff's office does. We'll touch base later, okay?"

A need-to-know kind of thing? Everyone needs to know!

"Okay. Fine." I ended the call and stepped inside the winery building. The aroma of freshly baked bread wafted through the air, and as I got closer to the bistro I could see Fred and Emma rolling out dough.

"Hey, guys," I said. "You didn't happen to see anyone from the film crew here this morning, did you? The van's parked in our lot."

Fred looked up from kneading the dough. "Skylar and Rikesh were in to grab coffees and let us know they'd be on the east side of our property this morning. In case you wanted to know. Said there was a bit of a to-do last night at the hotel. Stefan and Gavin exchanged words at the bar, but according to Skylar it was late and not many people saw them.

"What about Priscilla and Devora? Did anyone see them?"

Fred shook his head. “Skylar didn’t say. But from what I understood, Gavin and Priscilla will be driving themselves to the shoot this morning. Devora and Stefan will most likely hitch a ride with Mickey, the other cameraman.”

“Unless Devora decides to use her broom,” Emma announced from a few feet away. Then she looked directly at me. “Is everything all right? You look kind of spooked.”

“Listen, I probably shouldn’t say anything, not until the sheriff releases the information, but I found a dead body in the Ipswiches’ irrigation pond this morning. Charlie brought home a souvenir from there. Wrapped in a cattail. It was the necklace Priscilla wore yesterday.”

Emma clasped her hands together and froze. “Priscilla’s dead?”

I nodded. “Yeah, I think she is.”

Chapter 7

"Promise me," I said, "you won't breathe a word of this to anyone. Not until I've spoken with Cammy."

Fred and Emma shook their heads in unison.

"I've got to get back to the Ipswich property. I'll catch up later."

When I left the bistro, I darted into my office and made two quick calls. The first was to Cammy, who kept saying "Oh, my God, Norrie, not again," and the second was to Don and Theo, who pretty much said what Cammy did only without the histrionics. I was about to trek back up the hill and over to the pond when I made one more call. This time to Godfrey Klein.

"You're absolutely positive it was a body?" he asked.

"Unless branches are now wearing nail polish."

"And you're sure it's Priscilla McCoy?"

"It was the necklace. Who else could it be?"

"All right. Listen. Let the sheriff's office take over. That's what they're trained to do. Let them notify the film company and all the rest. Are you going to be okay today?"

"I'll be fine." *I think.* "You don't suppose I should call my producer? Filming here was Renee's idea."

"Until you know for certain whose body it is, don't call anyone. Let the authorities deal with it. Just answer their questions. That's all."

"I don't know what I can tell them. Heck, I don't know if it was foul play or if Priscilla went storming off in the dark, didn't see the pond and fell in. Maybe she couldn't swim. Maybe she got caught up in weeds. That would explain the necklace."

"No, that would explain your theory. Like I said, let the sheriff handle this."

"I'm a wreck if you haven't noticed. An absolute wreck, and in a few minutes I'll be under Deputy Hickman's microscope as if *I* had something to do with this."

"Take a breath, will you? Look, I'm off work today. I was going to the office to review someone's recent dissertation on the Coquillettidia, whose larva does not live underwater like the Culex species, but I can put it off and get over to Two Witches if you want."

"I'll be all right. Really."

"Are you sure?"

"Uh-huh."

"I'll call you later, Norrie. Maybe we can grab that coffee tonight."

"I'll need something stronger."

"Fine. Expresso."

When I ended the call to Godfrey, I hustled across the parking lot, up the hill past the field that separates Two Witches from Gable Hill and over to the pond. Even from a good thirty yards away I could see the commotion. Red and blue flashers on a Yates County Sheriff's car, a fire truck with *Yates County Fire and Rescue* plastered on the side, and the news vans that had left our property minutes before. The only thing missing was the coroner's van, and I imagined it would be pulling up pretty darn soon.

For the life of me, I couldn't imagine who would want to kill Priscilla McCoy. It didn't appear as if the camera and video guys had any issues with her, and Stefan was so busy catering to Devora's every whim, he'd hardly have had time to bother with Priscilla. Unless there was something going on with Gavin. Had he been one of her ex-lovers? Darn it. I never read the tabloids. As far as Devora was concerned, what possible motive could she have? Unless of course she had another actress lined up in the wings and needed to get Priscilla out of the way. But that would mean an entirely new filming. I shuddered at the thought.

As I got closer to the pond, I saw Derek standing next to Deputy Hickman. The usual five o'clock shadow on the deputy's face was replaced by a stubby grayish brown beard and mustache. I wasn't sure if it was a new look for him or if he'd gotten tired of shaving. Both of the men had their arms crossed and both of them eyeballed the pond. Then Deputy Hickman walked to his car and I hurried over to Derek.

He threw his hands in the air and glared at me. "What on earth took you so long? You said you'd be back in a jiff. What is it with women and their sense of timing?"

"Um, I can't speak for the rest of my gender, but when I left the house there were news vans in our driveway and I had to deal with that."

Derek looked at the vans parked alongside the rutted road that framed his property. "So you sent them here?"

"Don't be ridiculous. They were at Two Witches because they wanted to interview the actors. A few minutes later, while I was on my way into our winery building, because I had to check on things, they left for your place. They must have heard about the body from the scanners."

"Whatever."

"Is she, um, still in the water?"

"Uh-huh. The recovery vehicle arrived a few seconds ago. The divers are suiting up now."

"Divers? I thought they'd use a winch or something."

"It's a person, not a car. Besides, they need to locate the body first before they can extract it. Not with a winch. They use a rescue litter. You've seen them. They look like surf boards with straps."

I heard what sounded like a car driving up. "Turn around. Looks like the coroner finally made it."

"Holy hell. What a circus. How the heck did an actress from your little movie wind up doing the backstroke in our pond?"

Just then Deputy Hickman shouted, "Stay right where you are, Miss Ellington." He slammed the door of his car and marched directly over to me.

"He's all yours," Derek muttered to me. "I've got to get back to the house and let Stephanie know what's going on."

With that, he left and Deputy Hickman arrived. The next thing I knew I was staring into Gary Hickman's furled brow. "I should have known you'd be involved somehow in this recent situation, for lack of a better word at this time."

"Er, well, I—"

The deputy took a step back and let out a slow breath. "Mr. Ipswich informed me that you may know who the unfortunate victim is. I'm impressed, Miss Ellington. Not many people have the skills to identify a corpse when they spot an arm under murky water."

"It wasn't the arm. I mean, yeah, it's a woman's arm. Her fingernails had nail polish on them."

"And from that you were able to ascertain her identity?"

"Not exactly. My dog was in that pond this morning and came home with a cattail that had a necklace tangled in it. I saw that necklace yesterday on Priscilla McCoy's neck when she took off her coat at our winery."

"Is that someone you're acquainted with?"

"I met her, if that's what you mean. She's a, I mean, *was* a well-known Canadian actress who appears in lots of romance movies."

"I see. And she was visiting your winery?"

"She was filming a scene in our vineyard along with another actor and a small crew. Only the director, her assistant, a video technician and two cameramen. They're staying at the Ramada Inn in Geneva."

"I'll need those names along with the necklace. You still have it, don't you?"

I tried not to roll my eyes. "It's at home. On the floor of my bedroom." *With a dripping wet cattail.*

Deputy Hickman sighed. "It's probably too late, but try not to get your fingerprints on it. Put it in a plastic bag for now until I can pick it up. I'll also need a statement from you. Once the Yates County Fire and Rescue Team extracts the body and it's taken to the morgue for a positive identification and not a speculation, I'll head over to your winery. I'll need to question everyone who's been in contact with the woman. Should it turn out the body doesn't belong to this Priscilla McCoy actress, I will be sure to inform you."

"Oh, it's her all right. I'm pretty certain. Does this mean I can go back to our winery? The Wine and Cheese event is today, and as far as the film crew knows, they're still shooting a scene in the vineyard. Did you want me to tell them—?"

"Good heavens, Miss Ellington. You are *not* the town crier. Do not tell anyone anything! Am I clear? As I said a few minutes ago, I will stop by Two Witches once the body is taken to the morgue. Understood?"

I nodded. "Yes. Absolutely."

Priscilla McCoy was a stunning woman and I wanted to remember her that way, not see her bloated puffy corpse hoisted onto a board with a tarp thrown over her. I didn't waste another second. I traipsed back to our property the way I had come and headed straight for our tasting room.

Like yesterday at this time, our parking lot was full. Same deal with the driveway. The only discernible difference being that there were fewer EMTs and vineyard workers to manage the crowd of fans and wine tasters. Too bad that crowd was about to get one hell of a shock.

When I stepped inside our tasting room, everything appeared to be in order. No one would ever suspect our staff knew about Priscilla's unfortunate demise. The tasting tables were packed and the mood was jovial. Only Glenda caught my eye and motioned me over.

"Psst! It's not too late, Norrie," she whispered. "Zenora knows a powerful cleansing chant."

Wonderful. She can sing it in the shower.

"Uh-huh. We'll talk later."

I scurried off to check the mac and cheese setup and began to relax. Nothing out of the ordinary. Emma and a few part-time college kids who worked events for us were serving the Southwest Mac and Cheese. Fred was at the bistro, and from the look of things doing a brisk business. The only one I didn't spot was Cammy, and that changed in the blink of an eye.

She came out of the kitchen and made a beeline to where I stood. "Is it public knowledge yet?" she asked.

I shook my head vehemently. “No! Deputy Hickman will lock me up for interfering with an investigation if I were to open my mouth and blab it to everyone.”

“No worries. I told our staff that if they dared say a word, they’d be working at the Orange Julius juice bar and not here.”

“Whew. At least everything seems to be running smoothly. I’m surprised no one from the film crew came in to ask if we’ve seen Priscilla.”

“Actually,” Cammy said, “Stefan was in a few minutes before we opened. He wanted to get Devora’s coffee so it would be on the vineyard set when she arrived. He said he drove over with Mickey.”

“Hmm, that’s interesting. I spotted the equipment van in our parking lot, so that means Skylar and Rikesh got here early to set up. I’ll bet Gavin and Devora are back at the Ramada waiting for Priscilla, only they don’t know she’s dead. Unless, of course, she was murdered and one of them is the killer.”

“Yeesh.”

“I know. Right? Deputy Hickman said he’d be in here as soon as Priscilla was taken to the morgue. Unless he goes to the Ramada Inn first. I told him that’s where the crew was staying.”

Cammy winced. “I hope I can keep a poker face if Skylar or Stefan walk in here looking for the actors. Or the director, for that matter.”

“I doubt that will happen. Most likely they’ll phone Devora at the Ramada and ask what’s keeping them. Nothing else we can do at this time except wait for Grizzly Gary to show up. Meanwhile, I haven’t even had my morning coffee and my stomach’s grumbling. I hope Emma made croissants this morning. Heck, I’ll settle for saltines at this point.”

Cammy chuckled and I headed for the bistro. Behind me I could hear the laughter and animated conversations emanating from our tasting tables and the serving line for our cheese dish. When I reached the bistro, only one person was ahead of me, and I heard Fred say, “Your panini will be ready any minute.” Then, out of the blue, Skylar rushed in.

"Do you mind?" he asked. "I got an urgent request for a ham and cheese sandwich on sourdough bread."

I shook my head. Poor guy had no idea about Priscilla. "Don't tell me Devora changed her diet to include whole grains."

He rolled his eyes. "That'll be the day. Nah, it's for Priscilla. She didn't eat breakfast this morning."

"Priscilla? Priscilla McCoy?" I must have sounded like a moron. If that wasn't her in the Ipswiches' pond, and the crew was in the vineyard filming, then who the heck was in that pond with her necklace? A crazed fan?

I couldn't very well tell Stefan what was going on at the winery next door, so I bobbed my head and said, "I'm not in a hurry. Fred can make your order first."

"Good," he said. "Because we're running a technical shoot first and that takes a while."

"A technical shoot?"

"Yeah. Lots of lighting and sound adjustments. The actors run their lines but the director doesn't need to do anything. Or even be there, for that matter, unless they're real controlling like Devora. But even she steps back and lets us get on with it. Once everything's copasetic, we can do a regular shoot."

With that, Fred handed Stefan the sandwich and watched as he raced toward the door.

"What's the matter, Norrie?" Fred asked. "You look as if you've seen a ghost."

"That wasn't Priscilla's body in the pond. The sandwich you made was for her. Stefan acted as if everything was hunky-dory. This is a terrible thing to say, but I'm so relieved the dead woman had nothing to do with the film crew. Hallelujah. Geez, I shouldn't say Hallelujah. That's terrible. Some unfortunate person wound up in the Ipswiches' pond. Although it still doesn't explain the necklace. Unless the necklace had nothing to do with the dead woman."

"Uh, did you want to order anything?" Fred asked.

"Oh, yeah. A ham, cheese, and tomato panini. It's odd, isn't it?"

"Tomato on the panini?"

"No, the necklace. Unless someone threw it in there."

Fred shrugged. "I'm sure the sheriff's office will sort it out."

The sheriff's office. Oh, my gosh. Deputy Hickman thinks the body belongs to Priscilla thanks to me.

The minute Fred handed me my panini, I sat down, gulped it in a few bites and washed it down with a Coke. Then I called the Yates County Public Safety Building, hoping to reach their star deputy.

Chapter 8

Gladys Pipp, the civil service secretary, answered immediately. She was the only friendly person in that facility, and thanks to Francine's homemade jams, forged a friendship of sorts with me. Her voice, like her appearance, complete with bouffant hairdo and bedazzled glasses, was unmistakable. "You have reached the Yates County Public Safety Building. If this is an emergency, hang up and dial nine-one-one. Gladys Pipp speaking. How may I direct your call?"

"Gladys, hi! It's Norrie Ellington."

"Goodness, Norrie. It's always something at those wineries. How awful for your neighbors. Imagine finding a dead body in your pond. Is that why you called?"

"Uh-huh. I need to speak with Deputy Hickman. I saw him this morning and told him I knew who the victim was. Only it wasn't. I mean, the person that I thought it was isn't the body that was in the pond. I need to let him know."

"He's in his car right now, en route to your winery as a matter of fact. Is that where you're calling from?"

"Yes."

"Then sit tight. He should be there momentarily. Oh, and Norrie, he hasn't had his breakfast yet, so if he was in an unpleasant mood earlier, it's bound to be worse."

"Thanks for the heads-up."

"Anytime, dear. By the way, I do hope your Wine and Cheese event goes well. Too bad I have to work weekends a few times a month."

I thanked her, too, and then charged over to the bistro. "Quick, Fred! Can you make some toast and pour a cup of coffee for Deputy Hickman? He's on his way. I'll be in my office."

In the three or four minutes that followed, I told Cammy about my faux pas and asked her to discreetly inform the staff that Priscilla McCoy was alive, and as far as I knew chomping down on a ham and cheese sandwich. Then I went into my office and left a similar message for John Grishner on his cell phone.

Since I hadn't bothered to say anything to the winemakers, I left things as is. I debated whether or not to give Godfrey an update, but at that moment Deputy Hickman pounded on the doorjamb and stepped inside my office. He had a clipboard in his hand and looked frazzled.

"The body is on its way to the morgue and a forensics team is working the scene. I trust you'll keep that Plott hound of yours tied up at the very least. Or better yet, kenneled until they've concluded their investigation."

"I will. And for your information, if it wasn't for Charlie, no one would have discovered her until it was time to irrigate or spray. It's not like that's a recreational pond or anything."

"Right now it's a possible crime scene. We won't know anything until a positive identification is made and the coroner completes an autopsy on the body."

"Um, uh, yeah, about the body. It's not Priscilla McCoy. I guess I jumped to the wrong conclusion when I saw her necklace."

Deputy Hickman moved a chair close to my desk and sat. "Really? You jumped to the wrong conclusion?"

"You don't have to rub it in. It was a logical conclusion."

"Nonetheless, that's why we have trained investigators in the sheriff's office."

Another knock on my doorjamb, only this time it was Fred with a hot cup of coffee and a plate of toast and jam. "Thanks, Fred," I said.

He placed the coffee and toast on the edge of the desk, directly in front of the deputy. "Compliments of Two Witches," he said and then took off.

"That was nice of you, Miss Ellington, and I appreciate it."

He took a few sips of coffee and a quick bite of the toast before he spoke. "As you know, we'll need a statement from you regarding the discovery of the body. The form's on the clipboard. Next year we expect to have everything on iPads, but for now it's old-school."

"Old-school's fine," I replied.

"Be sure to include the approximate time you left your house and the time you arrived at the pond. Include any pertinent details."

It was a short statement—drippy wet cattail entwined with a necklace belonging to Priscilla McCoy, trek to her pond, branch that turned out to be an arm, phone call to Stephanie Ipswich. When I finished, I slid the clipboard back to the deputy and asked, "Did anyone have any idea who she was? I mean, our film crew is all accounted for as far as I know and so are my employees. Unless it was a tourist who over-imbibed and somehow wound up at the pond and fell in. But that doesn't explain the necklace, huh? Oh, my gosh. Maybe you should talk with Priscilla McCoy. It was her necklace, after all."

"Again, Miss Ellington, we cannot presume the necklace was hers. We cannot make assumptions willy-nilly. For all I know, those things could have been mass-produced in Canada and are hanging on more women's necks than we'd care to count. And yes, we are following procedure. We will need to interview everyone on that film crew as well as your employees."

He slid the clipboard back to me. "Page two is for a list of names."

I groaned and filled it out while he devoured the rest of his toast and finished his coffee. Then he spoke. "Would you please arrange a time this week for me to speak privately with your staff? Maybe one of them saw or heard something. Naturally, I will be doing the same thing with the staff at Gable Hill, considering the body was found on their property."

"Sure." *This isn't my first rodeo. And if I'm not mistaken, I still have the schedule from the last time. All it needs is some tweaking.*

With that, Deputy Hickman stood, grabbed his clipboard and walked to the door. "Good coffee. Jam's not bad either. Thanks."

"Anytime."

I waited a few minutes to make sure he left the building. When I looked outside, the place was still packed. Lots of oglers in the driveway who were most likely hoping to see one of the actors, and of course the festivalgoers, who were more interested in food and wine.

For the life of me, I couldn't imagine how that necklace wound up in a pond with a dead body, but I was relieved the body wasn't Priscilla's. Deputy Hickman refused to reveal the details, so I had no idea if it belonged to someone who was eighteen or eighty. I doubted the nightly news would have an answer either. It was much too soon.

I sent a quick text message to Don and Theo that read, "Forget earlier conversation. The body is not Priscilla's. Talk later." Then I left the same message on Godfrey's cell but I added, "Tim Hortons for coffee around eight? Text me." I figured he was totally engrossed in that non-water larva dissertation and didn't expect to hear from him until late afternoon.

With a packed tasting room and a huge serving line for the mac and cheese, I decided to help out as best I could. Not wanting to get stuck in any particular place, I offered my services as a runner if anyone needed anything. In retrospect, I should have planted myself at a tasting table or on the serving line. For the next two hours, I literally hoofed it back and forth from the kitchen to the tasting room. It seemed as if everyone needed something—more napkins, more water, more crackers. The worst was the wineglasses. I found myself loading and unloading the dishwasher more times than I could imagine.

Then, out of nowhere, Stefan walked into the kitchen. "The older lady at the cash register said I'd find you in here."

I pushed the Start button for the dishwasher and wiped my hands on a towel. "What's up?"

"Devora. That's what's up. Her morning coffee's beyond cold. So much for me trying to anticipate her every move. I tried calling her on her cell and at the Ramada but she's not picking up. I thought maybe she arranged for a ride from the Ramada and stopped in here like she did yesterday."

"You mean you haven't seen her today?"

"Nope. But that's not unusual. I've worked with her before.

Actually, it's better if she's not around when we do a technical shoot, but the guys wanted to go over some footage with her before they continued."

"What did Gavin and Priscilla say?"

Stefan shrugged. "Not much. They thought Devora would be driving in with me. Heck, she probably decided to book herself a nice spa treatment this morning and didn't bother to say a word to any of us."

Unless that spa treatment was in the Ipswiches' irrigation pond.

"Leave your cell number with Lizzie at the cash register. If she shows up, I'll call you right away."

"Thanks. The crew still has quite a bit to do so, you know where to find us. I'm going to get a coffee for myself and trek back to that vineyard. If nothing else, I'm getting my exercise."

The only sound in the kitchen was the hum of the dishwasher as the water began to fill. The worst thought of all entered my mind and I couldn't shake it—Priscilla must have gotten into a fight with Devora and strangled her with that necklace before shoving the body into the Ipswiches' pond. But what were they doing all the way up there when the vineyard scene was on the other side of our property?

Without wasting a second, my hand reached into my pocket for my cell phone. I called Gladys Pipp again and spoke before she could give the "call 911" spiel.

"It's Norrie. Everything's fine but I have urgent information for Deputy Hickman," I said. "Is he in the office?"

"Hold on. I'll get him."

Everything's fine? Am I nuts?

"Ms. Pipp said you were on the line. What is it, Miss Ellington?"

"Okay, okay. So maybe I jumped to the wrong conclusion before about the dead body. But this time I'm sure. It's Devora Dobrowski, the film director."

"Devora Dobrowski. And who will it be next time? The secretary of state? As I indicated earlier, our coroner and our forensic team will make a positive identification."

"You were there when they removed her body from the pond. You must have seen something. Just tell me. Was it a middle-aged woman with layered black hair and one white streak?"

"Miss Ellington, I am not at liberty to tell you anything at this juncture in time."

"Fine. I thought maybe you'd like a head start on the investigation."

"What I would like, other than you staying out of it, is to have a conclusive determination by our trained professionals so that we can proceed with a proper investigation that does not waste anyone's time."

"But, but—"

"Good day, Miss Ellington."

The call ended and I groaned, just as Cammy walked in with another tray of wineglasses.

"What's the matter, Norrie? Don't tell me the dishwasher is acting up?"

"No, Deputy Hickman is."

I proceeded to tell her about Stefan's visit a few minutes earlier and the fact that Devora seemed to be missing.

"That body in the pond was hers," I said. "It *has* to be. That's what I told Grizzly Gary but he pretty much blew me off."

Cammy leaned against the counter and rubbed the back of her neck. "I hate to say it, but maybe you should wait until it's definitive. Maybe Devora *is* having a spa treatment. I overheard Stefan by the doorway. She does that kind of thing."

"Only one way to find out. Hold on."

I pulled out my cell phone, called the Ramada and asked if Devora Dobrowski had booked a spa, or any other treatment, with them today. I explained that we could not reach her in her room or on her phone.

"We don't have an appointment listed for her," the receptionist said. "However, walk-ins are welcome."

"Then could you please call them and see if she's there?"

"Give me a moment and I'll put you on hold."

Barry Manilow's "Mandy" was the next thing I heard.

"I'm on hold," I said to Cammy.

She nodded. "I figured."

Seconds later, the receptionist returned. "I'm sorry but no one by the name of Devora Dobrowski has been or is currently in our spa treatment area."

I was about to thank her and hang up when I got another idea. "Wait. This is important. Can you please call Housekeeping and see if she's in her room. I'll hold as long as it takes."

"I'm afraid we can't tie up our phone lines that long."

"Fine. Fine. Then will you check and call me back? It's really, really important."

The receptionist agreed and I gave her my cell number.

"And what if she's not in the room?" Cammy asked when I pocketed my phone.

"Then I'll find out from Housekeeping if she slept in her bed last night."

Chapter 9

The kitchen door flung open and Lizzie announced, "Bradley Jamison is on the winery phone for you, Norrie. Said his calls kept going to voicemail. I've got to hurry back to the cash register. Sam's keeping an eye on it for me."

The last time I spoke with Bradley was last night. Last night! What the heck was wrong with me? I was dating the guy, after all. Shouldn't I have at least called him about the body in the pond? It was a good thing he couldn't see the look on my face when I picked up the phone. There was only one word to describe it—sheepish.

I tried to sound nonchalant. "Bradley, hi!"

He sounded as if he was out of breath but it could have been the connection. "Sorry to bother you during a wine event," he said, "but I thought you should know something. Marvin called me from his sister's house. His nephew is an EMT in Yates County and he was supposed to have a family luncheon with them today, only he got called over to your neighbor's property for a search and recover. Gable Hill Winery. I don't know the details but thought you should be aware. I hope it doesn't have anything to do with the wine event."

At that moment I felt like the biggest heel in dating history. I should have at least phoned him. I took a breath, cleared my throat and said, "Charlie found the evidence leading up to finding a body in their irrigation pond this morning. It's been a circus ever since. I was going to call you but Deputy Hickman showed up at the winery and things sort of spiraled from there."

"Hey, don't beat yourself up over it. I understand. Is there anything I can do?"

Not unless you can wave a magic wand and make all of this go away.

"Not really. The sheriff's office hasn't made an official identification of the body but I'll tell you who I think it is. It's the film director for *Windswept Love.* Devora Dobrowski. The she-witch from

Toronto. Oh, my gosh. I shouldn't speak ill of the dead."

Then, for the next five minutes, while dodging Lizzie's looks since the phone was right behind her counter, I went on to tell Bradley everything about Devora and the rest of the crew.

"Yeah," he said. "You mentioned what a tyrant she was but you never told me her name. Devora Dobrowski, right? Could it possibly be the same woman from that infamous Dobrowski divorce case in Canada that wound up in law school classes everywhere? Not the divorce itself, mind you. The property division and all the tentacles that went with it. Including a multitude of legal briefs, but that's not all. Are you ready for this? It's still going on. Not only that, but since Canadian divorce laws are akin to ours, there are law classes that deal solely with that divorce."

"You've got to be kidding? I thought Canada was a no-fault country as far as divorce goes."

"It is. They operate under the premise of a marriage breakdown. But we're not talking divorce per se, we're talking settlement."

"And you think it could be the same woman? The director?"

"I know the husband is Gerard Dobrowski, the CEO of Brouse Candies, a multinational company, but I'm not sure about the wife. Look, how about if I do a little digging and let you know?"

"That would be fantastic. If it *is* her, then maybe her estranged husband had something to do with her death. And notice I'm saying *death* and not murder because, according to Deputy Hickman, 'the situation is under investigation.'"

"That means the body, too, Norrie. As a lawyer as well as the guy you're dating, please take my advice and don't say anything to anyone until the sheriff makes a positive ID. Okay?"

Define "anyone."

"No problem."

"How about I pick you up on Wednesday and we chow down at Uncle Joe's, or maybe even Stonecutter's Tavern?"

"You've got a deal. See you then."

I kept my word as far as not telling anyone else about my recent revelation regarding the body in the pond. At least until four fifteen. That's when Stefan came back into the winery looking for me. I was helping Emma dole out the last of the mac and cheese since the part-time workers were on break.

Stefan spotted me and hurried over. "Skylar, Rikesh, and Mickey are done for the day. At least in the vineyard. Gavin and Priscilla left for the Ramada about an hour ago. They would've left sooner but Priscilla went nuts because her necklace was missing. Pain in the butt for us, too, since that necklace appeared in prior footage. I told her to get her rear end over to Walmart or Target and buy something that looked similar. You can't believe how berserk viewers get when all of a sudden something a character was wearing isn't there anymore. Especially in the same scene."

"Won't they notice a different necklace?"

"Nah. We'll make sure not to zoom in on the necklace." Then he sighed. "What a day. If looking for the necklace wasn't enough, Priscilla wound up posing for selfies with a few fans and two of your guys who looked like college kids."

Marc and Enzo, no doubt.

I started to say something but Stefan kept talking. "Listen, if Devora shows up, tell her we went back to the hotel. Skylar and Rikesh need to review the footage with her. With my dumb luck, we'll probably pass her on the road and not know it."

It was all I could do not to blurt out, "Your director is dead," but I bit my lower lip and mumbled, "Uh, sure thing."

"Great," he said. "We'll be back tomorrow morning. Should be a tad easier, eh? Without that wine and cheese thing going on."

Easier was the last word I'd use to describe the situation but I bobbed my head and smiled. Either Priscilla was a better actress than I thought and pretended to have lost the necklace when in fact she used it to commit a murder, or she really did lose it and someone else found the perfect weapon.

• • •

A half hour later, the Wine and Cheese event officially concluded. Of course, the winery stayed open until five thirty since it was a special event, so the last of our customers didn't leave until almost six. No one wanted to rush them as they made their wine and gift purchases.

Then the cleanup began. Glasses that needed to be washed, tables that had to be wiped down, food trays from the mac and cheese that had to be scoured, and ugh, bathrooms that had to be sanitized.

Fortunately, Cammy arranged for a local cleaning service to handle the really dirty work and their crew arrived at six thirty. Two men and a woman. They had worked for us before and knew the routine but Cammy still went over it with them.

"Did you catch the five o'clock news?" the heavyset woman asked. "They found a body at the winery next to yours. It was a woman."

I all but tackled her. "Did they give a name? Did they say who she was?"

The cleaning woman shook her head. "Nope. The news anchors on Channel 8 said it was still under investigation and a positive identification hadn't been made."

"What else did they say?"

"I don't know. I had to turn off the TV to drive over here from Waterloo."

Drat. The next news wouldn't hit the TV until seven. That meant sweating it out for the next half hour because I seriously doubted my news app would have more to offer up. Cammy must have sensed my impatience because she said, "We'll be fine, Norrie. You might as well get out of here while you can." Then she pulled me aside and whispered, "Call me if you find out anything."

"Thanks, everyone!" I shouted. I was out the door before anyone could say anything. Especially Glenda. The last thing I needed was to hear about restless spirits, or worse yet, the stinky and unsavory herbs needed to rid ourselves of them.

As promised to Deputy Hickman, Godfrey, and Bradley, I didn't say a word to Stefan, but I wondered how long it would take them to notice Devora's absence, catch the nightly news, and put two and two together.

Charlie rolled his kibble dish into the living room as soon as I opened the door. In all honesty, I couldn't remember if I'd fed him this morning or not. I immediately poured a heap of his grain-free kibble and then took off my jacket. At least I knew Alvin would be well-fed. The last thing those vineyard guys needed was to have that goat knock down his fence in an attempt to locate some grub.

I turned on the TV but still had fifteen minutes until the news came on. True, I had given my word to keep mum about the pond incident, as I began to call it, but I felt as if I owed it to Renee to keep her informed. That's when I devised a way to ease her into the situation.

Thanks to speed dial, the connection was instant. Renee picked up after two rings and sounded as chipper as ever. "Hey, Norrie, how's the filming going? I got a report yesterday afternoon from Devora. She said things were moving slowly due to 'an overabundance of intoxicated wine drinkers who clogged up the area.' I reassured her that the event would be over today and she'd have a peaceful week to finish up."

"Uh, yeah. It'll be peaceful for her, all right."

"Good. Good. Did she need you to make many script changes?"

"No, but I didn't see her today. In fact, neither did her crew. Skylar said they were doing a technical shoot so it wasn't too unusual for the director to be absent."

"I know. Lots of adjustments for lighting and sound. At least the weather in your neck of the woods is decent. Wet snow on the ground but no storms. Much better than what we've got going on here."

Don't bet on it.

"Oh, we've had our share of issues here, too. A body was found in the irrigation pond at the winery next door."

"Oh, dear. That's horrible. An intoxicated tourist maybe?"

"Oh, hard to say. Um, anyway, I just wanted to check in, that's all."

"All right, then. And thanks, Norrie, for being such a sport. We'll be out of there in no time."

When I ended the call, I had five minutes to go before the news came on. If nothing else, I had laid the groundwork for what would become a really nasty surprise for Renee. At least I could always say I kept her apprised of things. Then I plunked myself on the couch, flipped on the TV and read my texts. Godfrey said he'd meet me at Tim Hortons at eight. I immediately called him rather than send a text.

"Hey, Godfrey. Can we change the meeting place to the Ramada Inn?"

"Please don't tell me you plan to snoop around?"

"Not exactly, but I plan to look for evidence."

He sounded exasperated. "What evidence? The sheriff's office hasn't even identified the body."

"The five o'clock news on Channel 8 said it was a woman. I'm really positive it's Devora and I'm pretty sure Priscilla may have had something to do with it. Stefan, Devora's assistant, told me Priscilla lost her necklace. She probably said that to throw everyone off."

"Even if what you say is true, what do you expect to find at the Ramada?"

I spoke slowly and enunciated every word. "Evidence on Priscilla's hands."

"You've lost me."

"Look, if Priscilla used that necklace to strangle Devora, chances are her fingernails are chipped, or at the very least there are small cuts on her hands. Devora must have fought back. When Priscilla was in our winery yesterday, I observed a perfect manicure. I need to see if that's the case."

"What do you plan to do? Knock on her door and demand a hand inspection? She's not in the army."

"Don't be silly. We'll hang out at the bar and buzz her room to invite her for drinks along with the rest of the film crew."

"And if she declines your offer?"

"I'll think of something else. In fact, I'll have a plan B in the works."

"Heaven help us."

"Then you'll meet me at the Ramada?"

"I have to. I'm afraid to leave you alone."

Chapter 10

The seven o'clock news came on and it wasn't any different from what the cleaning woman had told me. I flipped from Channel 8 to Channel 10 and finally landed on Channel 13, where Cara and Kenneth did their nightly shtick.

Cara looked at Kenneth and then straight at the camera. Her tight blond curls were perfect and her red sleeveless dress accentuated her every curve. "No news yet on the grim discovery of a woman's body at Gable Hill Winery in Penn Yan. Sources close to the investigation believe she may have been out walking following the annual Wine and Cheese event and may have accidently fallen into the winery's irrigation pond."

Oh, yeah. That's exactly my thought as well. And what sources? At this point, Alvin knows as much as the next guy.

"Indeed," Kenneth added. "It's a very sad situation. Official cause of death is still unknown. Please stay tuned to our station for any late-breaking updates. The minute *we* know, *you'll* know. And be sure to tune into Channel 13's *News at Noon.* Remember, viewers, don't just think *nutrition* when you have lunch, think *information* as well."

I wanted to gag. I turned off the TV and went upstairs to freshen up before meeting Godfrey. No sooner had I slipped my sweatshirt off than the landline rang and I grabbed it.

"Norrie, it's me, Stephanie. Have you heard anything? Derek had to give that deputy a list of our employees for questioning by the sheriff's office. My husband's furious and thinks this will hurt our business."

"Tell him to relax. If anything, it'll bring in more customers. Lots of curiosity seekers. I should know. Same thing happened over here and at the Grey Egret."

"I suppose. But what a dreadful way to attract visitors. By the way, did you say anything to our WOW group?"

Sharing intel with the gossipy women from Wineries of the West was the last thing on my mind. “Uh, no. Only Don and Theo. I haven’t really had the chance.”

Stephanie groaned. “I’ll let Catherine at Lake View know what’s going on and I’ll ask her to tell Madeline and Rosalee. By Thursday’s meeting the rumor mill will be in full force.”

“We have a meeting Thursday?”

“Don’t you read your emails? We need to talk about that candy company. I heard it was a done deal. Good thing we ordered Concord root stock a few months ago.”

“Um, yeah. Don and Theo mentioned the same thing now that I think of it. But what’ll happen if we wind up with lots of grape juice and no outlets to sell it?”

“There are always outlets for grape juice, and a few wineries are starting to make Kosher style wine.”

“Kosher style?” I asked.

“You’d never know the difference to taste it, but Kosher wines must meet a specific criteria for the grape, the machinery, and the processing. And the process must be overseen by a rabbi. Kosher style can be made by non-observant Jews but Kosher wines cannot. In any case, our wineries won’t lose money if a candy manufacturing company doesn’t pan out, but if it does, we stand to make a decent profit.”

“Root stock, huh? I’d better say something to our vineyard manager.”

“Trust me, he already knows.”

“Stephanie, if that candy company is built, and they require lots of juice, won’t that create a major division for us in terms of who we sell to and at what price? We’ve always supported the local juice companies.”

“That’s why we need to talk on Thursday. Call me if you hear anything about the woman in our pond. I don’t care if you wake me up.”

“Derek might care.”

"He won't. The guy sleeps like a rock."

As soon as the call ended, I washed up and put on a fresh shirt and clean jeans. Then I poured kibble in Charlie's bowl, changed his water, and took off for the Ramada Inn.

The Ramada was located in downtown Geneva and hugged Seneca Lake. With panoramic views that faced the east, the Ramada had become a popular hotel for tourists and business people alike.

Its Tuscan-themed bar opened into the dining area, allowing for light as well as privacy, depending upon where guests sat. From bar and bistro seating to comfy lounge chairs, the designers thought of everything.

Godfrey was already at a table in the back and waved me over. "Okay, Sherlock, now what?"

"I'll use the house phone to call Stefan and invite the crew to join us. If I call Priscilla first, it may look too obvious."

"The house phone's in the corridor. Want me to order you something while you make the call?"

"Thanks. Tonic water and lime. Oh, and ask them for some of those mixed nuts they serve at the bar."

The house phone was in a small alcove opposite the reception counter and the elevators. I picked up the receiver and directed the operator to connect me with Stefan Olinguard's room. As the phone started to ring, two Geneva police officers approached the counter. It didn't faze me at first, but when the next person made his way over there, I froze. It was Deputy Hickman, and next thing I knew, the three of them left the counter and walked to the elevator.

No one had noticed me and I intended to keep it that way. Just then, Stefan answered the phone.

"Hello. This is Stefan Olinguard."

"Stefan, it's Norrie. I'm downstairs at the bar. I called to ask if you and your crew wanted to join me and a friend of mine for drinks, but you may be getting a few visitors."

"You mean the police? I phoned them a little while ago. Devora's missing. They told me we had to wait forty-eight hours to report a missing person. Maybe they changed their minds and sent someone over for a report."

"Uh, yeah. About that, have you turned on the local news?"

"No. All we need is the weather report and we get that from our phone apps. Why?"

"Because a woman's body was found in the winery's pond next door and—"

"It might be Devora's? That's preposterous. Unimaginable really."

Two seconds later, I heard a knock on Stefan's door. "I'll let you answer that," I said. "Meet me in the bar when you get done with them. Bring your crew. We need to talk."

"Sure thing. I could use a drink after today. We all could."

I hurried back to the bar and picked up my tonic and lime. "I saw Deputy Hickman and two Geneva policemen get into the elevator. How much you want to bet they're on their way to question the film crew?"

Godfrey widened his eyes. "Did they see you?"

"No. I spoke with Stefan and he's in denial. They knocked on his door while we were on the phone. At least I'm pretty sure it was them. I mean, why else would a Yates County Sheriff's Deputy be working with the Geneva police?"

For the next forty minutes, Godfrey went on and on about mites and the damage they can cause to grapevines, while I spouted off at least a half dozen theories about who could have killed Devora Dobrowski. Provided, of course, she *was* killed and didn't just fall into the pond as one of the news anchors suggested.

"Desmia funeralis," he said.

"Huh? What? Did you say something about Devora's funeral?"

"What? No. I was talking about the desmia funeralis, a minor grape pest."

"Well, I happened to be talking about who could have killed that witch. I hate to think it was Priscilla but she did have a motive. Devora humiliated her beyond belief. Then, of course, there's Stefan. Talk about a whipping boy. Of course, Gavin might have wanted to protect Priscilla from Devora's wrath and things went a little too far."

"Shh. Take a look behind you. Two men are headed our way. Not the police."

I turned, and sure enough Skylar and Rikesh pulled some chairs over and sat.

"Looks like we've got enough seats for everyone," Skylar said. He reached out his hand and introduced himself and Rikesh to Godfrey.

"Where's the rest of the crew?" I asked.

Skylar took a handful of salted nuts, but instead of eating them he all but crushed them in his hand. "Mickey's reviewing some footage and said he'd be down in a while. Stefan and Gavin went with a deputy from Yates County to their morgue at the hospital in Penn Yan. They need to identify a body that may be Devora's. This is a nightmare. A freaking nightmare."

I bit my lower lip. "And Priscilla?"

"That's another story altogether. Hell. She got unglued having to go over to Target this afternoon to get a replacement necklace. And get this. She never left the car. Had Gavin do it."

Rikesh rubbed his temples and stood. "I need a drink. Anyone else?"

"Get me whatever they have on tap," Skylar said. "What about you guys?"

"We're fine," Godfrey replied. "Better, I suppose, than your crew. Norrie told me all about Devora's absence. Still, just because a body was found at Gable Hill doesn't mean it's hers."

Skylar opened his palm and downed the salted nuts. "If it's not her, then where else could she be? Devora may be obnoxious as hell but she's a professional. It isn't like her to go missing without telling one of us."

"Did the deputy give you any indication of when Stefan and Gavin would be back?"

Skylar shook his head. "No. He wanted Priscilla to go with them but she literally had a nuclear reaction. Said she'd vomit, faint, or have heart palpitations."

I did a mental eye roll. "Is she prone to that sort of thing?"

Skylar gave a quick laugh. "She's an actress. Need I say more?"

"So she's upstairs in her room?"

"I doubt it. She said something about going to the sauna and making an appointment at the reception desk for a manicure tomorrow morning. I told her that if Devora is alive and well, we need to be on the set, in your vineyard, no later than seven thirty. A manicure, for crying out loud! Our director's missing, the authorities think she may be the drowning victim, and we've got to film the final scene of *Windswept Love* by week's end. And where's our lead actress? Scheduling a damn manicure!"

Rikesh, who had just returned with drinks from the bar, whispered, "Maybe she's in shock."

This time it was Skylar who rolled his eyes. "Fat chance."

"What now?" I asked. "Did anyone call Renee?" *Other than me.*

Skylar and Rikesh looked at each other before Skylar responded. "We were told by the deputy not to say anything to anyone until an official identification of the body can be made."

"And if it's not Devora?"

Again, the men looked at each other and again Skylar spoke. "Then the missing person's report goes into effect and your authorities take it from there. Either way, Renee will be notified by one of us by tomorrow. In the meantime, I intend to make myself quite comfy right here."

With Skylar and Rikesh planted at our table, I couldn't very well tell Godfrey what I intended to do. I only hoped it wouldn't take too long.

I stood and backed away from the table. "If you'll excuse me," I said, "I need to make a call. I forgot to tell my tasting room manager something and won't see her until tomorrow." Then, while Skylar and Rikesh weren't looking, I mouthed the words "plan B" to Godfrey and shot out of there.

Chapter 11

Having been to the Ramada Inn a few times for winery events and dinners, I knew where the pool and spa were. If Skylar was right about Priscilla going to the sauna, I could see for myself if her nails were chipped or if she had tiny cuts on her hand. Unfortunately, the spa was keyed entry only and that posed a slight problem. But it wasn't so much of a problem that my own acting skills wouldn't come in handy.

The pool was visible from the hallway and I watched the handful of guests who were making use of it, mainly families with older kids. I stepped up to one of the glass panels and rapped on it. Within seconds, a middle-aged man opened the door and I spoke. "Oh, thank goodness. This saves me a trip to the front desk. I was here earlier and I think I left my makeup bag in the locker room. Do you mind?"

The man motioned me through. "No problem. My wife is always losing things."

I thanked him and darted into the locker room that led to the sauna and steam room. Not wanting to take a chance getting my phone wet, I stashed it in the closest locker to the door. Thankfully, the pool lockers came with their own numbered keys on small blue bracelets. I slipped mine over my wrist and thanked the Ramada Inn under my breath for taking the security of personal property seriously.

Poor Skylar and Rikesh. I wondered how long they could hold out listening to Godfrey pontificate about blood-sucking, vine-eating, larva-producing insects while I tried to catch a glimpse of Priscilla McCoy's hands without having her see me. Then again, I could always come up with plan C if I messed up plan B.

The sauna was adjacent to the bank of lockers, while the steam room was down a short corridor. I figured I'd start with the sauna. I held my breath and opened the door slowly. The thing weighed a ton, and hanging on to the knob while trying to allow in only a sliver of light was a feat of its own.

I pressed my face to the opening but it was too narrow, so I pulled the knob closer to me and tried again. The intense heat made my eyes water and I blinked. In the next second or two, I tried to see if Priscilla was in there. No luck. Empty benches and hot coals. It had to have been a while since someone was in the sauna since every bit of steam from adding water to the coals had dissipated.

The steam room was another story altogether. When I tried the same tactic, a burst of moist hot air flew into my face and I was positive it removed every bit of eyeliner I had on. Then I pressed an ear to the opening and stood absolutely still. Not a single sound. If Priscilla was in there, she had to be alone. Most people strike up conversations, and someone as high-profile as Priscilla McCoy was bound to be recognized by TV viewers.

It was now or never to make my move. I fished out a hairbrush from my bag, opened the door a bit wider, and tossed the brush on the floor of the steam room. Then I covered my mouth, leaned in and said, "I must have dropped my hairbrush while I was in there. I'm dressed and don't want to get wet. Can you slip it to me through the door?"

Not a sound from the steam room. Maybe Priscilla wasn't in there after all. And ew! No way was I going to use that hairbrush again. I waited for another few seconds, when all of a sudden I felt a whack on the back of my head and heard a raspy woman's voice. "Voyeur! Peeping Tom!" Then I heard her yell, "Don't just stand there, Teresa, go get your uncle Milton and tell him to call the management."

Wonderful. The last thing I needed.

I spun around, gave the woman a shove and noticed a beach bag on the floor. Probably the thing she used to whack me over the head. I must have set the world record for opening a locker and getting the hell out of a place before winding up in the back of a police car.

By the time I got back to the bar, I was panting.

"What did you do?" Godfrey asked. "Run all the way?"

By now, Mickey had joined the group and moved over to let me sit. I took the last sip of my tonic water and tried to compose myself.

"Didn't want to keep everyone waiting," I said. "That's all. Um, any word from Priscilla?"

Mickey shook his head. "Last I knew she was in the sauna."

"Good place for her," Skylar added. "At least we'll be spared the crocodile tears if the body turns out to be Devora's."

Two full water glasses were on the table and I reached for one of them. Not the most ladylike move, but I took a giant gulp of the iced water. "Whoa. Doesn't sound like any love lost there."

Skylar propped an elbow on the table and leaned in. "Let's put it this way, Devora doesn't exactly have a big fan club. She's a top-notch director but it goes hand in hand with another less-favorable attribute. I don't need to spell it out."

"We're out of those salted nuts," Rikesh said. "Drinks, too. I'll be right back."

I watched as he walked to the bar, then I turned to Skylar and Mickey. "What do you suppose Devora would have been doing up there by the Ipswiches' pond? She didn't strike me as someone who enjoyed nature walks."

Mickey groaned. "She's a cameraman's worst terror. Just when you think the scene is done, she decides she wants to try it at another location. It wouldn't surprise me in the least if she trekked up the hill, spotted your neighbor's pond and decided a love scene would be better with pond water in the background instead of a lake."

Rikesh returned to the table with fresh drinks for all of us. "It's on the company tab," he said and laughed. For the next twenty or thirty minutes, we made small talk. I imagined none of us wanted to presume Devora was dead until we knew for sure. But that changed the moment Stefan and Gavin walked into the bar.

Stefan looked paler than most corpses and Gavin didn't look much better. Skylar hailed them over to us and pulled up another table. "Well?" he asked. "Was it her?"

Both men nodded and sank into their seats. For a minute, no one said a word. Finally, Gavin broke the silence. "It was awful. I hope to

God I never see another drowning victim again. She was bloated, and according to the coroner, there was white foam around her mouth, which meant she'd been in the water for hours or a day maybe."

"Did the coroner think it was accidental?"

Gavin shook his head. "Not with the small ligature marks around her neck. He said they were consistent with a necklace that was presumed to be found at the scene. My God! If that necklace turns out to be the one Priscilla lost, they'll book her for murder. None of you can say a word to her. Not until they're certain it was hers."

"It's circumstantial," I said. "Even if the necklace belongs to Priscilla, it could have fallen from her neck and someone could have seized an opportunity to commit murder."

Stefan stared straight ahead, not making eye contact with anyone. "I need to call Renee. She's got to be informed."

It was almost eleven and I couldn't believe three hours had passed. "Devora's going to be just as dead tomorrow as she is right now." The minute those words came out of my mouth, I realized how insensitive they sounded. "Um, sorry for being so blunt but there's no sense ruining Renee's sleep. She won't be able to do anything tonight anyway."

"Norrie's right," Rikesh said. "I vote to wait until morning." Then he looked at Gavin. "Did the deputy tell you anything else once you and Stefan identified her?"

"Yeah. Don't leave town."

Skylar pushed himself back from table and stood. "We'll hang around here tomorrow until we speak with Renee. No sense trying to second-guess things."

If I knew Deputy Hickman, he'd be at the Ramada first thing in the morning to question everyone. And when that was done, Gable Hill and Two Witches would be next on his list.

Gavin and the film crew guys said good night and left the bar.

"I suppose that's our hint," I said to Godfrey.

"What a night." He stood and shoved his chair into the table. "I kind of figured it was Devora. I mean, given the circumstances with her missing and all. By the way, what took you so long? Did you find Priscilla?"

"No, but I nearly got nabbed for voyeurism. I'll tell you about it once we get out of here. Talk about a long night."

"I'll say. Do you have any idea how boring it was for me to listen to Skylar and Rikesh go on and on about manipulating digital images and mixing audio? My eyes glazed over. I thought they'd never stop."

I took one look at Godfrey and nearly burst out laughing. "Sometimes people get really passionate about their work." *And at least theirs don't come with an "ick" factor.*

• • •

It was eleven fifty when I finally crawled into bed, and it felt like seconds later when the landline rang. I reached across my nightstand and picked up the receiver. Still groggy from a late night, I barely mumbled a hello.

"Norrie, it's Stephanie. They identified the body. It was on Channel 8's *News at Dawn.* It's probably on every other station, too."

Who in their right mind watches *The News at Dawn*?

I sat upright and rubbed my temple. "Did they give a cause of death? Did they say it was a homicide?"

"They might as well have. They said the drowning was suspicious and that the victim was film director Devora Dobrowski from Toronto who was in the area for a movie production."

"They said 'in the area'? That's nebulous enough."

"That was for starters. They said the body was found at Gable Hill Winery in Penn Yan but that the movie was being filmed at Two Witches next door."

"Oh, hell, no."

By this point I had flung my legs over the side of the bed and reached for my jeans and the T-shirt I had thrown on the floor. "What else did they say?"

"Only to stay tuned to their network."

"Network! Those networks all have sister stations in Canada and heaven knows where else. Crap! My producer's probably getting up right now and turning on Toronto's news. That'll get her adrenaline going before she can even make herself a cup of coffee. I've got to phone the Ramada. Talk to you later."

Poor Stephanie. I didn't even give her a chance to respond. My cell phone was still in my jeans pocket and I fumbled for it. Thirty seconds later, thanks to Safari, I dialed the number and asked for Stefan Olinguard's room.

Stefan must have been expecting someone to call because he answered on the first ring. "Hello? That was quick."

"Huh? It's Norrie Ellington."

He sounded disappointed. "Oh, Norrie. I thought it was Renee. Skylar woke me at some obscene hour. Devora's death is all over the news. Not the specifics. Not yet. I called Renee immediately and she was too stunned to continue the conversation. Said she'd call me back."

"How long ago was that?"

"Ten, fifteen minutes maybe."

I wondered how long it took the human brain to process news of an unexpected death, let alone one that might be a homicide. A half hour? A few hours? A few days? I didn't have that long.

"Stefan, listen. I need to speak with her. I'll wait a few minutes and call her. In any case, call me back in an hour. You've got my cell number."

Stefan agreed and we ended the call. I threw on my clothes, washed up and went downstairs to open Charlie's doggie door and fill his food dish. Then I made myself a cup of coffee and sat at the kitchen table. I didn't realize my hands were shaking until I moved the coffee cup to my lips.

Now what? Knowing Deputy Hickman, there was no way he was about to let that film crew drive back to Toronto. Especially since one of them could be a cold-blooded killer. But who?

I grabbed a pad and pencil from the small table by the phone and jotted down the seven names, pausing to draw a line through Devora's. Other than the usual tabloid stuff about Priscilla and Gavin, everyone else was an enigma. And frankly, so were the two actors. I took another sip of coffee and all but jumped when my cell phone rang.

"It's Renee. It's incomprehensible. I'm still trying to wrap my head around it. Devora? Drowned under suspicious circumstances? Stefan gave me the news as well as the name of the investigating deputy in your county. I'm going to let our company solicitor deal with it. I'm sure I'll be questioned by the New York authorities since I'm the producer for the film. Oh, goodness, listen to me ramble on. I can't even think straight. When we spoke yesterday, I never imagined those two unrelated events were connected."

"I know. It's a shock at this end, too. I'm very sorry for your loss."

More like "I'm sorry you have to deal with all of this."

"I'm calling an emergency production team meeting and will keep you posted. I told Stefan to remain in New York until he hears from me."

"Um, yeah. That's probably a good idea considering the authorities will most likely want to question the film crew regarding the, um, unfortunate death."

"You can say it, Norrie. Murder. Devora had to have been murdered. There's no other explanation. I've got to go. I've got a million calls to make. We'll be in touch."

She ended the call before I could say goodbye. And while Renee wasn't familiar with the routine, I sure as heck was. Deputy Hickman would begin questioning the film crew at the Ramada, in cooperation with the Geneva Police Department. From there, he'd notify Gable Hill about his intentions and then do the same at Two Witches. The man was so stubborn and obstinate, he'd insist on conducting all the interviews himself. Given the timing, I estimated we'd be off the hook until tomorrow.

Good thing I wasn't taking a math exam, because I was way off with my estimation. When I arrived at our tasting room at nine twenty-five, his car was parked out front and he was standing by the cash register.

Chapter 12

"I need to have a moment of your time, Miss Ellington," he said. "Since the wineries open for business at ten, I presumed you'd be here already."

What do you plan to do? Give me detention for being tardy?

"Hi! We have a tasting room manager. She's here by nine."

He didn't say a word and I motioned for him to follow me into my office. "How can I help you?"

Deputy Hickman sat in the nearest chair and took out a pad. "I've already spoken with the management at Gable Hill and they're arranging interview times for their staff. I'll need you to do the same. *All* staff. You can fax the list to Gladys Pipp at the Public Safety Building. I can interview your staff on the premises or they can drive to my office."

"I can't afford to have them waste, er, I mean, *take* so much time away from their work, especially the winemakers and the vineyard crew. We're in planting season now."

"Miss Ellington, I don't care if you're in holiday season, this is a murder investigation. I'd like those interviews to take place Wednesday."

"Fine. You can use the small banquet room off the kitchen. It's private."

"Very well. I'll see you Wednesday morning at nine."

He stood and faced the door.

"Wait a minute," I said. "What about the film crew? Did you want to interview them here as well?"

Deputy Hickman spun around and sighed. "No, those interviews will take place today at the Ramada. I've already notified the director's assistant, Stefan Olinguard. In addition, the crew's passports are under lock and key at the Ramada and will not be returned until the preliminary investigation is completed."

Ka-ching. Ka-ching. Ka-ching. This is going to cost the production company beaucoup bucks.

"I know about the ligature marks. I was at the Ramada when Stefan and Gavin returned from the morgue last night."

He eyed me and ran his fingers through his hair. "You just *happened* to be at the Ramada?"

"Yes, I was having drinks with a friend when they walked into the bar."

"They should have kept that information confidential. The autopsy results haven't been released and toxicology results won't be in for at least two weeks. I trust, Miss Ellington, you won't share that knowledge with anyone else at this juncture in time."

I nodded but felt like I did in seventh grade with my fingers crossed behind my back. "Ligature marks mean strangulation, don't they? And that necklace from the pond was pretty substantial. It wasn't one of those flimsy ones that would break apart. It was one of those designer double chains. And the last time I saw it was on Priscilla McCoy's neck. Is she under suspicion for murder?"

"Right now everyone is under suspicion. My department *investigates*, it doesn't *speculate.* Be sure to send that fax to Gladys this morning. Good day, Miss Ellington."

He walked out of my office and I heard a loud thud as the front door to the winery closed behind him. There was no way I could keep that information from Don, Theo, Bradley and Godfrey, not to mention Cammy.

The words *town crier* came to mind and I cringed. Taking a breath, I picked up the phone and called the Grey Egret. Don answered on the second ring. "Hey, Norrie. We caught the news this morning on Channel 10 after the farm report. Theo was going to give you a call but we had to get ready to open the winery."

"Sure thing. I just wanted you to know that Deputy Hickman was over here. He'll be questioning our staff and the staff at Gable Hill. The film crew had their passports locked up and will be questioned today."

"How are you doing?"

"Better than Stephanie Ipswich. She's a basket case."

"Yeah, well, no wonder. The body was found in her pond."

"I know, but if it wasn't for my screenplay, none of this would have happened."

"If it wasn't for your screenplay, you wouldn't have a job. Listen, I've got to get going. Let's catch up later, okay? Maybe grab a quick bite after work."

"Sounds good. Talk to you later."

I caught Bradley between clients but we only had a few minutes to chat. He, too, had heard the news on one of Syracuse's stations.

"It's not surprising that their passports have been locked up. That's protocol for a murder investigation when suspects live outside the United States. By the way, I started doing some digging on Gerard Dobrowski. The wife named in the case-study documents is Devora Aileene Dobrowski. Check with your producer and see if it's her."

"Uh, right now my producer is one step away from posttraumatic stress syndrome but I'll try. This may sound like a funny question, but if the divorce isn't final, then how is it the law schools are teaching about it?"

"It started with the separation agreement. That *was* finalized and recorded. It was so compelling that the Dobrowski solicitors approached their clients for permission to share the divorce documents with law journals and schools since it offered an entirely new insight into the legal divorce proceedings and could have an impact on future similar situations."

"I see."

"Anyway, we can talk more about it the day after tomorrow. I'll pick you up at seven. Does that work for you?"

"It's fine."

"Miss you. Hang in there."

Yep, "Miss you" was about as good a catchphrase as anything since we were dating but not really involved. Both of us knew I'd be returning to Manhattan in a few months and long-distance relationships usually don't have great track records. Still, I was attracted to him like crazy, and given his reaction, he felt the same way. We could barely keep our hands to ourselves on the ski lift at Greek Peak this winter, and half the time when we watched movies we missed the critical parts.

I took a deep breath and pulled out the scrap paper from my pocket with the seven names I had written on it this morning. Then I left my office in search of Cammy.

"She's grabbing some more T-shirts from the storage area," Lizzie said when I approached the cash register. "Glenda and Roger are at their tasting tables, and as you know, Sam has his college classes at the beginning of the week."

I remembered Sam telling me he was able to finagle his schedule this semester so that he'd be available to work for us during the busier days—Thursday through Sunday. I thanked Lizzie and was about to walk to the storage room when she asked, "Will that dreadful deputy who hastened out of here a few minutes ago be interviewing us like last time? I saw the news this morning on Channel 13 WHAM during their *Wake Up in the Morning* show."

Channel 13. Yep, that completed all of them. Not to mention the Syracuse stations. I looked at Lizzie and shrugged. "I'm afraid so. It's standard procedure. I mean, after all, the film crew was shooting the scene over here."

Lizzie straightened her back and looked directly at me. "Nancy Drew will tell you that every killer requires a motive, a means, and an opportunity. None of us would have had a motive to kill that woman, nor would we have had an opportunity. We were all working here at the Wine and Cheese event. I know you've read the *Nancy Drew Handbook*. Maybe you need to pass it along to the Yates County Sheriff's Office."

Oh, yeah. That's bound to endear me even more with Grizzly Gary.

"Um, I'm pretty sure they know what they're doing." *Even if Nancy doesn't concur.* I had to tread lightly because Lizzie was a diehard Nancy Drew fan, and as far as Lizzie was concerned, Carolyn Keene's fictional sleuth was as alive and breathing as I was.

Just then, Cammy returned with an armload of T-shirts and shouted, "Good morning, Norrie!" That was all I needed to thank Lizzie and get away from the cash register.

"I'll help you put those on the shelves," I said to Cammy. "Give me a batch."

She handed me the bright green ones and a few of the fuchsia-colored shirts. "The doors open in five minutes. I wanted to get these shelved."

We moved to the clothing and gift section of the tasting room, where Cammy lined up the bright orange shirts in their bin. "I heard Deputy Hickman's voice as he was leaving. Let me guess. Another go-round of interviews?"

"And then some."

Cammy shrugged. "I figured as much. It was on the early-morning news."

"Don't tell me you got up at the crack of dawn to watch one of the networks?"

"Are you kidding? I try to get as much shut-eye as I can. My mother woke me up screaming about putting Marc and Enzo in harm's way. I told her they were surrounded by off-duty EMTs and a slew of vineyard workers, but she still wasn't convinced. She and her sisters think a deranged killer is stalking the vineyards in search of victims. I told her to quit watching *Criminal Minds*."

"I don't know what's worse—a deranged killer or someone from that film crew."

"True. It *is* kind of creepy to think that someone working on the film set for your screenplay is also a murderer."

"That's why we need to act fast. Deputy Hickman's going to interview everyone here on Wednesday. He'll be doing the same at Gable Hill. Today he'll be at the Ramada to grill the cast and crew of *Windswept Love.* That'll take forever. Not to mention the autopsy and the toxicology report. That's where we come in."

Cammy furrowed her brow and straightened a few of the T-shirts. *"We?* What exactly did you have in mind?"

"Face it. There's no one on our payroll or Stephanie's who would have had any motive to murder Devora Dobrowski. Heck, half the employees didn't have a clue who she was. However, as far as her own crew was concerned, she was Captain Bligh. Now we just have to figure out who was Fletcher Christian."

"How do you propose to do that?" She stepped away from the T-shirts and widened her eyes.

"We need to get every last piece of dirt we possibly can on the three film crew guys plus Stefan, Gavin, and Priscilla. Oh, and let's not forget Devora. Something in her past or present is bound to be lurking on the internet." *And if Bradley is right about her identity, she'll be lurking all right.* "Face it, they all must have social media pages, especially the actors, so that's a good start. We'll have to look for little clues that might point to a more substantial motive other than 'the woman was a witch on wheels so I did her in.'"

"Do you have any idea how much work that is? Facebook could take you all day. Not to mention Instagram, Twitter, Tumblr, Pinterest, and probably some new ones I haven't heard of."

"Don't worry. We'll divide and conquer. I know Theo and Don will help out and I'm positive Stephanie will as well. She's pretty adroit with computer searches."

"Were you thinking of divvying up the names?" she asked. "If so, I get dibs on Gavin Chase."

"You may have to fight Don for him, but sure, he's all yours. I'm going to pay Stephanie a little visit today and see if she'll pick up two of the crew members. I want to sink my teeth into Priscilla and Devora. No love lost there as far as Devora is concerned."

"Fair enough. I'll scrounge around on social media tonight and see what I can come up with, but I don't think we're going to get too far."

I straightened my back and stretched my arms. "Social media is only step one. Online background checks and criminal reports are next on my to-do list. They run from fifteen to twenty dollars a person. At the high end, it would cost a hundred and forty dollars. I'll get Stephanie to split the bill with me. Heck, she spends more on lattes during the week."

"Whatever you do, don't mention this to Glenda. She'll want to cast a purifying spell on the place, or worse yet, try to contact Devora's restless spirit. Next thing you know, we'll all be up at the Ipswiches' pond chanting something none of us understands."

"Um, that may be step three."

Chapter 13

Gable Hill Winery was situated at the bottom part of Gable Hill Road, the next road over from Two Witches. Both our wineries faced Route 14 and Seneca Lake. And both of our wineries had been in operation for a number of years before we became the current proprietors.

Unlike Two Witches, the original owners of Gable Hill converted their farmhouse into the winery building, adding on a modern production lab and tasting room. When Stephanie and her husband purchased the place, they didn't want to live at another location so they built their house on the hill as well.

The original owners must have been enamored with *Anne of Green Gables*, because the winery building looked exactly like Anne's house on Prince Edward Island in all the photos I'd seen: A white wood-framed house with steep dark green gables, a wraparound porch, and a pristine picket fence.

The sign in front read *Welcome to Gable Hill Winery, Stephanie and Derek Ipswich, Owners.* I stepped inside their tasting room, where the Green Gables theme continued throughout the interior: farm-style tasting tables, a large vintage cooking stove that was more decorative than functional, framed paintings of country scenes, and pastel painted walls. The aroma of freshly baked cinnamon cookies permeated the room.

Like Two Witches, they also had their cash register/computer situated by the front door, and Stephanie was the one seated behind it.

The minute she saw me, she looked around as if something was about to jump out at her. "Hi, Norrie. Oh, no. You're here in person. Does this mean bad news? I've been twitchy and skittish all day. Thank goodness the boys are at school and my tasting room staff can function on their own."

I shook my head. "Relax. Other than Grizzly Gary stopping by to tell me we're going to be questioned regarding Devora's drowning, there's no other news."

Stephanie brushed a strand of her honey-colored hair from her brow. "Same here. I didn't sleep at all last night and I must look atrocious."

If atrocious could be described as knock-down gorgeous, then she certainly fit the bill.

"You look fine. The reason I'm here is to ask for your help. We all know that none of our staff members would have a motive to kill Devora Dobrowski, but that film crew sure did. They despised her. She chastised Priscilla no end, barked at her assistant constantly, and, according to the video and sound guys, plagued them constantly."

"I'm not sure how I can help. Isn't the sheriff's office investigating?"

"Come on, Stephanie, they couldn't find a cow in the pasture if you marked a big X on it."

"Don't say that out loud."

"Okay, so maybe I'm exaggerating, but they move so slow that it will be weeks until they make any progress. The film crew's passports have been locked up and they're stuck in Geneva until an arrest is made. Meanwhile, our wineries are going to get a black eye over it. You know how rumors fly around here."

"They've already flown. We've had curiosity seekers traipsing up the hill all morning. The crime scene tape around the pond doesn't help matters, either. Derek had to put *No Trespassing* signs on vineyard rows, and he wasn't a happy camper about it."

"That's why we need to do something."

"What did you have in mind?"

"Nothing prevents us from prying into that film crew. You know, social media, background checks, the usual."

"I'm not a detective. I don't know the usual."

"We watch enough TV shows to figure it out. There's got to be something one of them is hiding regarding their relationship with Devora. I mean, we've all had bosses we've hated, but we don't go strangling them and shoving them into irrigation ponds. It has to be something more."

"Social media? What am I supposed to find out on Facebook? That they like cats?"

"Don't be ridiculous. We need to find out their other relationships and all the nuances that go with it. Then we can move on to background checks. I figured at most it would cost us each seventy bucks."

Stephanie moistened her lips and sighed. "If all it takes is seventy dollars to move this thing along, then I'm game."

"Great. Cammy's going to look up anything she can on Gavin Chase and I can get Don and Theo to take Stefan and two of the video and sound guys. That leaves one other guy."

"What about Priscilla and Devora?"

"I figured I'd do Devora and we can split Priscilla, so you'd actually be taking a person and a half. We can figure the logistics later."

Stephanie twirled a long strand of hair around a finger. "Give me the best-looking of the crew."

"You're not picking a date for the prom, and besides, that's a terrible criteria."

"Yeah, but it makes it more fun."

"They're all thirtyish and decent-looking. Skylar is tall and muscular with that Brad Pitt stubble thing going for him, Rikesh is adorable with average height, darker skin, deep brown eyes and dark wavy hair. Mickey is also average height with lighter hair, broad shoulders and a cute smile."

I can't believe I'm actually telling her this.

"Oh, I don't know. I'll take the first name."

"Fine, you can have Skylar—"

"What? What's the matter?"

"I just realized I don't know all their last names, only Stefan's and Skylar's. Never mind. I'll find out today from my producer and call you. Anyway, I need to get going."

"Keep me posted if you hear anything. See you Thursday at our WOW meeting."

"Yep. Another opportunity for Catherine Trobert to mention her son and how much she wants us to connect. I could retch."

"At least you've managed to dodge him so far."

"That's because he lives in Maine, but one of these days he's going to show up to visit his parents. I can only hope I'll be back in Manhattan by then."

Stephanie laughed and I headed out the door.

I went home, completed the interview schedule for Deputy Hickman and faxed it to Gladys. I emailed it to everyone on our staff and even called the tasting room, the winery lab, and the barn to make sure they'd check their emails. Only Franz responded, indicating it was "a preposterous waste of time," but nevertheless he'd be most cooperative.

The rest of the day was tedious as I had to edit one of my screenplays, but it did give me the perfect excuse to call Renee for advice and then ask her for the film crew's last names, "Just in case we needed to share them with the authorities."

Renee was more focused than she was during our earlier call but not her usual upbeat self. I couldn't blame her, considering the circumstances. To add to the strain, Stefan had informed her that the passports were under lock and key and the crew was essentially under "house arrest" in New York.

"The loss of production time and the overall expenditure will undoubtedly put a dent in our profits," she told me. "Our production team is hashing this out at the moment and we should render a decision shortly regarding the direction we need to take. I'll keep you posted, Norrie."

As soon as the call ended, I made up my mind to never, under any circumstances, write another screenplay with a vineyard in it.

• • •

Don, Theo, and I agreed to meet at Tim Hortons for that "quick bite" after work since the soup of the day on Mondays was chili and

Theo had a hankering for it. The restaurant was on Hamilton Street in Geneva and close to Wegmans, so I figured I could pick up a few things after I ate. With the weather being "unseasonably cold" for this time of year, according to the news, I added a scarf around my neck and put on warm boots instead of my usual sneakers.

Don and Theo must have gotten the same memo because both of them showed up with long scarves and higher boots.

"As soon as we think winter is over," Don said as he took a seat next to me, "we get a lousy forecast and boom! Back to heavier clothes."

"Huh? Are we supposed to get snow?"

He nodded. "Not for a few days but a spring storm is on its way. It's that heavy wet crap that doesn't even look good."

"I guess it won't matter as far as the filming goes because there's no director and the actors are stuck at the Ramada along with the crew."

"Any word from your producer?"

"She's reviewing her options or something like that. Anyway, there's no reason whatsoever we have to put up with Deputy Hickman's glacial investigations when we can get a head start ourselves."

Don looked at me as if I'd suggested we take a cold plunge in the lake, but before he could say a word, Theo leaned toward me. "What did you have in mind?"

"Nothing at all like the last time. Honest. This would be more of an armchair investigation rather than—"

"Your usual show-up-where-you're-not-wanted ones?" Don asked.

"Hilarious. What I had in mind was a simple, painless internet search of the film crew and the actors. People spill out all sorts of things on social media without even realizing it. Cammy and Stephanie already agreed to help out."

Don made a sound that was halfway between a chuckle and a chortle. "That's because Cammy works for you and Stephanie's in as deep as you are."

I must have registered a pained look or something because the next thing I knew, Don said, "Relax. I'm sure you've got some sort of plan brewing in that head of yours. Spit it out."

Five minutes later, Don and Theo agreed to dig the dirt on Stefan Olinguard, Rikesh DeSai and Mickey Permutter. Don was somewhat disappointed that Cammy had beat him to Gavin Chase but he said he'd get over it. We agreed to get started as soon as possible and share notes after the WOW meeting.

Since Don and Theo had already "taken out a second mortgage" to shop at Wegmans a few days ago, they headed home after we ate. I, on the other hand, had my heart set on their homemade chocolate chip cookies and one of their giant roasted chickens. I figured that thing would be my meal staple for at least three days.

I made a mental note to always shop at Wegmans on Monday nights since the parking lot wasn't packed with cars and I was able to snag a spot close to the door. I grabbed a shopping cart and immediately began to fill it with necessities—freshly baked bread, double chocolate chip muffins, assorted trail mixes, flavored butters, and natural dog biscuits for Charlie.

Remembering I was out of Band-Aids, I made my way to the health and beauty aisles, trying not to make eye contact with anything in between. No sooner had I tossed a box of assorted-size bandages into my cart than I noticed Skylar a few feet in front of me. His shopping cart was directly behind him.

He held a tube of Neosporin in his hand and then flicked it into the cart. It bounced off the six-pack of Molson Canadian and landed on top of a large bag of pretzels.

As he turned toward the cart, our eyes met.

"Norrie. Hi. Guess this is the local hotspot, huh?"

I peered into his cart and smiled. "Sadly, you're right. Did you get cut? I couldn't help but notice the Neosporin."

"Not me. Priscilla. She asked me to pick up an antibiotic cream for her as well as something for rough hands. I figured this was as good as anything. She said her hands got scraped when she backed up against some grapevines the other day. She didn't want to make a big deal of it but said the scratches were bothering her. Both hands, too. She must not have been paying attention."

I looked down at the orange box with its brightly colored label.

"What's wrong?" Skylar asked. "Should I pick out a different antibiotic cream? I have no idea about this stuff."

"Um, no. Neosporin's the best. I was just thinking about how uncomfortable those scratches must be."

"Yeah, well, next time Priscilla will be more careful about where she positions herself when we film outdoors."

I'll say. And too late for Devora.

Chapter 14

"Any word from Renee?" I asked.

"She sent Stefan a text. Said she was working on something. If we have to quit now and reshoot later, we'll lose all the continuity from the scene. Especially if the weather changes drastically. You can't have wet snow during the first part of a dialogue and practically nothing on the ground by the time someone finishes a sentence."

"Oh, I think you'll have snow all right, but maybe more than you bargained for."

"All of this is more than what we bargained for. Our director found dead under a haze of suspicion and not very pleasant interviews with your local deputy today. In fact, I think I'll swing by the beer section and grab another six-pack."

"Tell Priscilla I hope her hands feel better. Scratches can be nasty."

I had a hard time keeping myself from jumping up and down shouting that I knew it. I knew Priscilla got scratched up fighting with Devora. I only prayed Deputy Hickman had the same revelation.

Skylar turned toward the beer aisle when I suddenly remembered something. "Hold on a second. Did Deputy Hickman mention anything about the timeline for Devora's death?"

"What do you mean? How long she'd been underwater?"

"*That*, and who saw her last."

"According to the coroner's report, Devora had been dead for at least fourteen hours, possibly sixteen. That means she wound up in that pond late Saturday afternoon. As for who saw her last, it was anyone's guess. All of us thought she was driving back with someone else. The only thing anyone could agree on was that Devora asked Rikesh to stash her purse in the van sometime during the shoot, which he did."

"Once Priscilla stormed off the set," Skylar continued, "Gavin followed. Rikesh went in the van to check the sound feed and I joined him a few minutes later. Mickey was still toying around with the cameras when Stefan said something about calling it quits for the day.

Frankly, I wasn't paying attention to Devora's whereabouts. I thought maybe Stefan drove her back but apparently that wasn't the case. He thought she went to the winery to have it out with Priscilla and Gavin, but by then I was already in the van with Rikesh."

"What do you think happened?"

"I think Devora intended to go to the winery building but changed her mind and trekked up the hill instead. She wasn't all that thrilled with the location we selected so maybe she thought she'd find a better spot. Anyway, that's what I told the deputy."

"What about at night? When you all went back to the hotel?"

"No one saw her and she wasn't bunking with Priscilla anymore. Priscilla told us she didn't have to put up with Devora Saturday night because another room opened up."

"Thanks, Skylar. I was curious. That's all. Have a good evening."

"You, too."

I watched as he made a beeline for the chilled six-packs and then headed for the checkout counter. It seemed odd that Devora slipped out of sight without anyone noticing. Then again, I'd been so engrossed in work from time to time that I hadn't noticed what was going on around me either. Still, it didn't add up.

With enough snack staples to get me through the next few days, I drove home, changed into comfy sweats and sacked out on the couch. Charlie took his usual spot at my feet and proceeded to scratch himself. And when he wasn't doing that, he was biting himself. Exhausted from the craziness of the past few days, I sat mindlessly before booting up my laptop and scoping out Priscilla's social media spots. Other than cutesy staged photos on Facebook and an endorsement for a skin product, there was nothing. Not on Instagram, Twitter, Tumblr or Pinterest. Finally, the news came on at nine and I listened half-heartedly as I munched on Cheetos, pausing occasionally to give some to Charlie. The bag was almost empty and I debated whether or not I wanted to open another one when I heard a familiar voice on Channel 13. It was TV anchor Cara Oakland and she had just announced Devora's preliminary cause of death. I grabbed the remote, turned up the volume and listened.

"Authorities are still waiting on the toxicology report but the coroner has determined the victim, movie director Devora Dobrowski, died of strangulation. The ligature marks were consistent with small yet substantial chains like the ones found on necklaces."

Then Cara went on to tell viewers about Devora and the movies she had directed. If that wasn't enough, she reiterated the fact Devora was at Two Witches filming a scene for a romance. Wonderful. The woman managed to name our winery, but not the movie title. The entire segment was probably less than a minute but it felt like thirty. When she finally moved on to the growing concern over potholes on city streets, I muted the volume and called the one person with whom I hadn't shared my recent plan of action.

Godfrey answered after a few rings. "Is everything okay?"

"I suppose. Thanks to the news media the whole world knows Devora was strangled. Not only that, but Cara Oakland on Channel 13 reminded viewers where the movie was being filmed, so if they didn't get to trample on our property over the weekend, they could make another attempt."

"Catch a breath. I doubt any filming will be going on without a director. Essentially, that crew is in stasis, so to speak, while the investigation continues."

"Oh, they're in stasis all right. Deputy Hickman confiscated their passports. Well, not confiscated, but he had the Ramada lock them up until further notice."

"You mean until they have a viable suspect?"

"Until they have the murderer."

"That could take weeks. Longer maybe."

The words *cold case* came to mind and I froze. "I know. That's why I came up with a plan."

"Not another plan. You got walloped with a beach bag in a locker room as a result of your last plan."

"This is different. It involves internet searches. And maybe some background checks."

I explained how I divided up the film crew so that Cammy, Stephanie, Don, Theo, and I could dig up information that might be useful in terms of ferreting out the killer.

"I suppose I should be relieved you didn't hand me a name," he said.

"Oh, I thought of it but I knew you'd be too busy reading all those boring dissertations and doing whatever it is you do with those insects."

"Right now I'm looking into insect-borne diseases as they impact the agriculture in our area."

"See? I knew you'd be too busy."

Godfrey groaned and I continued to explain. "Devora was strangled with a small but heavy-duty chain, like the one Charlie dredged up on that cattail. And exactly like the one Priscilla said she lost. I give it two, three days max and Deputy Hickman will have her charged and arrested for murder."

"Maybe she did it. We don't know what goes on in people's heads. She could have snapped from the pressure. As I recall, you wanted to examine her hands for scratch marks that would indicate signs of a struggle."

"Uh, yeah. About that, she's got them all right. I ran into Skylar at Wegmans this evening and he was buying Neosporin for her. She told him she backed up into some grapevines while they were filming and her hands got cut up."

"Norrie, I hate to say it, but the evidence is pointing right at her."

"Or maybe she's telling the truth. That's why we need to figure out who else could have a motive, other than Priscilla. Maybe Devora was blackmailing one of them and they got sick of it. Or, maybe it was her estranged husband who did her in. Did I mention Bradley cited a famous Canadian divorce case with one Devora Aileene Dobrowski? Long story short, if it *is*, I mean *was* her, the husband may have had good reason to knock her off. Greed and money are strong motivators."

"I suppose you've already tracked down the husband?"

"Only by name. And reputation. It's Gerard Dobrowski, the CEO of Brouse Candies. Bradley told me all about it."

"Hmm, I seem to remember hearing that name while I was skimming through some department news from the agriculture and food sciences division. Usually I gloss over that stuff but this one caught my eye. It mentioned the possibility of a major candy manufacturing company moving one of its Mexican factories to the area. That means food consultants as well as entomology consultants."

"Ew. Why would you be consulting on something like that?"

"Remember the overwintering pests from the convent? That was nothing. Think food pests. Flies, weevils, roaches. Not to mention the sawtooth grain beetle. And if we're talking sugary confections, think ants. No candy manufacturing company wants to use heavy-duty pesticides, so we work together to find other, safer deterrents. The agricultural experiment station is a vital resource for area industries. It's not only the wineries who call on us."

And he complained about Skylar and Rikesh discussing digital imaging.

"Well, if the name turns out to be Gerard Dobrowski, it very well could be the husband. Which begs the question—Was he in the area during the time of her murder? Can you find out by going through those agricultural department notices?"

"Aargh. Really? You want me to sift through mindless memos and department tidbits to see if there's any mention of the Brouse Candies CEO having a sojourn in Geneva?"

"Uh-huh."

"Boy, will you owe me. And I'm not talking coffee at Dunkin'."

"Fine. We can share a pizza at Uncle Joe's. So you'll do it?"

"Anything to get you to stop nagging."

I thanked him profusely and turned my attention back to the TV. It was either late-night comedy, the weather station, HGTV, or some old Turner Classic movie. I opted to head upstairs and call it a night. Charlie apparently made that decision while I was on the phone. He was already sprawled on my bed when I turned on the bedroom light. Minutes later I joined him, and for once I didn't toss or turn all night.

• • •

John Grishner's phone call woke me the next morning, but surprisingly I wasn't my usual early-morning comatose self.

"Hope I didn't wake you, Norrie, but I wanted you to know your film crew is back in the vineyard. I thought things were on hold."

"Uh, yeah. So did I."

"It doesn't matter. We'll work around them. Listen, while I've got you on the phone, I wanted to talk to you about developing those three acres on the east side for Concord. I meant to tell you this before but got blindsided with the filming. I purchased enough Concord root stock in December to get us started. Seems I was the last holdout. The other wineries made their purchases in October and November. I wanted to be sure the candy company was a done deal and not local scuttlebutt. My sources are pretty accurate so I'm confident it was the right move. That candy manufacturing company will want Concord grape juice for their sucking candies. They'll either process it themselves or buy the extract from an existing juice company. Either way, it translates into a higher demand than we already have. Even if the deal doesn't come to fruition, we'll still wind up making a profit. Concord is one of the easiest, heartiest grapes to grow. It was here before we were."

"I suppose you're right. In fact, our little WOW group plans on discussing it Thursday, if we can get past the local gossip."

John laughed. "The timing should work for us if we start now. It takes vines at least three years to produce consumable grapes. I figure it's going to take that company at least a year to get the needed permits and licenses. Then, the actual construction process for their plant. Factor in hiring and training and we'll be neck and neck with them."

"Have you mentioned this to Franz and his crew?"

"Actually, he was the one who mentioned it to me. Since it only involves harvesting and crushing the grapes, he has no problem with it."

"Good to know. I'd better go see what's going on with the film crew. Like you, I thought everything was stalled."

"If we get a crowd of lookie-loos I'll let you know. We may have to provide some security."

"Thanks, John."

I had no idea why the film crew would be back in our vineyard, so after feeding Charlie I washed up, threw on a pair of well-worn jeans and a sweatshirt, and trekked over to the east side of our property.

Chapter 15

"Didn't Renee tell you?" Skylar asked. He stepped away from the camera setup and took a step toward me. "She had no problem waking me up while it was still pitch-black outside. I thought she was going to tell me the production would be shelved indefinitely."

"No, she didn't call. Um, then again, she might have but I was on the phone. Maybe she left me a voicemail on my cell. Drat! It's on the table in the house. What's going on?"

"More like *who.* She was able to twist Gordon Wable's arm and he agreed to catch a direct flight out of Vancouver later today so we can finish the shooting this week. Talk about timing. He just wrapped up one of the Lanna Linn mysteries a few days ago."

Gordon Wable. That's the director Priscilla enjoys working with. Or at least the one that doesn't send her off the set in tears.

"Wow. That was sudden."

"Expedient would be more like it. Renee made that perfectly clear this morning. She said, 'None of you have been arrested so far but we can't afford to waste time. Gordon Wable's flying in. I booked a room for him at the Ramada. And have Stefan call me. He's not answering his phone.' Some wake-up call, huh?"

Must be the morning for it.

I glanced at the camera setup and then back to Skylar. "Uh, since the director won't get here until tonight, why are you guys here?"

"It's just Mickey and me and we're taking footage of the vineyard in the early-morning light so Gordon can review it when he gets here. We'll be doing the same thing at midmorning, afternoon, and dusk. He may have a totally different take than Devora did regarding the ambience he wants that scene to convey."

"It's the final reconciliation for the characters. Forgiveness and all that."

"Hey, all I need to know is whether he wants the sun to come up, go down, or do something in between."

"It's the Finger Lakes. Good thing you can see the sun at all. But don't hold your breath. That spring storm is supposed to make its way in a couple of days."

Skylar pulled up the collar on the heavy cable sweater he was wearing. "Gordon will work fast. I'm not so sure about that deputy you've got."

"None of us are. Good thing Priscilla made a fuss about losing that necklace of hers, otherwise she'd be behind bars. If those news guys are right, the necklace was the murder weapon. The thing is, who the heck got their hands on it?"

"You mean 'Who had a motive?'" Skylar gave the sweater's collar another tug. "None of us liked working with Devora but I wouldn't go so far as to say it was a motive for murder. Heck, half the films produced would never hit the screen. There's so much backstage squabbling, backstabbing, and downright orneriness that it would blow anyone's mind. And I'm just talking the crew. Throw in the actors and a miserable situation can become toxic real quick. Good thing we're all professionals. Or at least, I like to think we are."

"Yeah, me too. Let me know if there's anything you need. Although I'm sure Stefan will be the first one to do that."

"When he wakes up and returns my call, I'll tell him."

"Is it like Stefan to sleep in? He didn't strike me as one of those laid-back types."

"He's not," Skylar said. "He's about as OCD as they come, but he probably zonked out from all the tension. Frankly, our collective stress level hit the roof once Devora's body was found."

"Yeah, it didn't help the wineries' reputations much either." I turned in the direction of Gable Hill and then back to Skylar. "I'm headed to our bistro for a cup of Fred's coffee. Much shorter than hoofing it back to the house. Um, maybe I could meet the new director tomorrow. I'm sure you'll be plenty busy tonight catching him up."

"Sounds like a plan to me."

• • •

Fred and Emma were the only ones in the building since we didn't open for another two hours. The aroma of chicory coffee and freshly baked hot cross buns got stronger the closer I moved to the bistro.

"Hey, guys, the film crew's back in the vineyard, otherwise I'd still be sleeping. Any chance I can get some coffee?"

Fred poured me a cup and handed me a toasted hot cross bun. The white icing was still warm and melted in my mouth.

"I thought everything was on hold," he said.

"The producer got ahold of another director. A guy by the name of Gordon Wable who's flying in tonight from Vancouver. Priscilla's worked with him before and likes him. That should save us some money on Kleenex."

Emma removed more hot cross buns from the oven and walked over to where I was seated. "I thought the crew would have to remain under house arrest or something like that until the investigation was completed."

"Nah," I said. "They just can't leave the state. I think Deputy Hickman may call them in for more questioning. Skylar told me he had a very unpleasant experience with Grizzly Gary when I ran into him last night at Wegmans. Guess our Canadian friends are becoming well acquainted with our supermarkets."

Fred looked up from the cutting board, where assorted lettuces were being prepared for sandwiches. "Is that all he told you?"

I nodded. "Uh-huh. Why? Do you think there's more?"

Fred pushed the romaine off to the side. "I bet he was told to keep mum. Some people actually listen when they're given those directives from the deputies." Then he smiled and gave me a wink.

"Very funny. If *I* didn't share information, no one would know what was going on. It's called communication. Which reminds me, don't forget about tomorrow when Two Witches gets the third degree in our banquet room."

"I'll be sure to keep Grizzly Gary's coffee warm and have an extra pastry on hand. Seriously, Norrie, I doubt it will take him that long. None of us had a reason to murder someone we didn't know."

I nodded. "True, but someone might have seen or noticed something."

Fred grimaced. "With the Wine and Cheese event going on? All I noticed was the crowd."

"Ditto," Emma said, "and the noise."

"Hmm, maybe that's why the killer chose that particular time. Smack dab during a festival when no one would be paying attention to anything more than eating and drinking."

"Does this mean you believe her murder was planned out as opposed to an act of passion or anger?" she asked.

"I don't know what I believe, but unlike Deputy Hickman, my list of suspects is more of a tight-knit group than a sports arena packed with spectators."

"Uh-oh," Fred said. "Does this mean what I think it does?"

"Only on paper. Honest. Internet searches and all that. Last thing I need is to be trapped somewhere with a killer stalking me."

"Good," Emma said. "Keep it that way."

I thanked them for my breakfast and went home to check my phone messages and my emails, making a mental note to carry my cell phone with me at all times.

Charlie was sacked out on the couch when I walked into the house. His food dish was empty and his water bowl half filled.

"I know I fed you this morning, dog, but I'll refill your water."

As soon as I placed the metal bowl in its usual kitchen corner, I checked my voicemails. Yep. Two of them from Renee and essentially the same message—the production team wants to wrap this up before any more unforeseen situations arise. *Like an arrest?* She went on to mention Gordon Wable and told me to call her.

Then I checked my emails. No surprise there but Renee put her voicemail message in print. I picked up my cell phone, tapped the number and waited for her to pick up.

No "Hello." No "How are you?" Renee went right to the point.

"Our crew's passports may be under lock and key but they're essentially free to work. I need to act fast. I promised Gordon Wable his pick of the movies we produce next year if he'd step in and finish that scene. You know who Gordon is, don't you? He's directed a number of movies for us. Anyway, he's arriving in Rochester tonight on United Airlines. Believe it or not, it was cheaper to rent him a car than order up a shuttle to your neck of the woods."

"I know. I talked to Skylar a few minutes ago. He and Mickey are in the vineyard preparing image shots for Gordon."

"Good. No sense wasting time. Gordon will know exactly when the daytime lighting works best for that scene."

It was almost as if Renee had blocked out the real situation, although producing a major film was, I suppose, her real situation.

Then, as if she'd read my mind, she added, "I had our solicitor reach out to some contacts he has in New York. In case we need to hire a criminal attorney. Of course no one's been arrested but our company needs to be prepared. I can't imagine any of our people doing such a heinous thing but I need to think objectively about this."

"About Devora, have you gotten any word what's going to happen with her body? I mean, who the next of kin are and what they plan to do with it?"

"According to the company's solicitor, who's been in contact with your local authorities, the autopsy was completed and her body will be shipped to a funeral home in Toronto. The cost is astronomical. They have to conceal her remains in metal. That's apparently the law when bodies are shipped out of the country."

"Who's paying?" The words sort of jumped right out of my mouth and it was too late to be diplomatic.

"Her estranged husband is taking care of the arrangements but if, for some reason, our company is found culpable in any way, then we may be obligated for some of the debt. Aargh. This is too much to deal with. Right now I need to concentrate on getting *Windswept Love* finalized. Then I can think about burial costs."

"Do you mind telling me who her estranged husband is?"

"It's not a secret. It's Gerard Dobrowski of Brouse Candies. Devora downplayed the legal battle that was going on between them but I'm sure once the press puts two and two together, it'll be all over the tabloid news. All I can hope for at this point is that the film crew is exonerated in all of this and they can get back here. I've got them booked up for the next three months. Worse yet, Priscilla has another obligation for a major motion picture. Not a television romance. If she can't meet that obligation, the understudy takes over and Priscilla's chance for international stardom will have to wait."

Renee may have moved on to Priscilla but I was still stuck on her prior statement—*It's not a secret. It's Gerard Dobrowski.*

"Norrie, are you still on the line?"

"What? Sorry. I was just thinking. Um, what about Gavin? Does he have any obligations after *Windswept Love*?"

"He signed on to film a cozy mystery right here in Toronto. We can be more flexible with his schedule. By the way, if you run into Stefan, tell him to call me. He hasn't returned my calls or my texts. I even had the hotel ring his room but no go. That's not like him at all. Then again, he might have decided to sleep in or use the hotel's fitness facilities. Anyway, be sure to tell him to reach me when you see him."

"Uh, sure thing."

"I've got to run, Norrie. We'll be in touch."

I said goodbye but she ended the call at *good.*

I've been zonked out before too, but not to the point where I don't hear the phone. And as for the fitness facilities, Stefan struck me as one of those guys who wouldn't know an elliptical machine from a treadmill. Maybe Renee and Skylar thought Stefan was snoozing but I had another, more troubling thought.

Chapter 16

Like Renee, I called the Ramada and asked to be connected with Stefan Olinguard's room. When there was no answer, I changed into a pair of jeans that didn't look as if they'd been eaten by a colony of moths and selected a decent sweater to replace my old Penn Yan Academy sweatshirt. Then I drove there. Horrific thoughts of Stefan's bludgeoned body concealed under a designer comforter refused to leave my head. And when they did, they were immediately replaced with even more terrifying thoughts of him facedown in his bathtub.

I was practically a basket case when I approached the front desk. I pleaded for the receptionist to call Housekeeping to open his room.

"The man is subject to going into insulin shock," I lied. "Someone needs to check on him immediately."

The girl behind the desk, who looked like she was still in middle school, picked up the phone and placed the call. "Should I call nine-one-one, too?" she asked me.

"Um, only if he's in trouble. Your housekeeper will notify you."

With that, I got the room number and thundered up the stairs. It's been my experience that elevators can be unpredictable, especially when there's an emergency. Or, worse yet, when there are people inside whom I'm trying to avoid. In this case, Deputy Hickman, who always seemed to catch me at the most inopportune times and places.

The housekeeper was already at Stefan's door when I arrived. Her cart was filled with fresh linen and the usual bathroom amenities.

"Hi! I'm the person who requested you check this room. My friend might be inside with a medical problem."

The middle-aged woman knocked on the door and then used her passkey to open it. She stepped back and waited for me to enter, refusing to budge from the doorway.

"Stefan!" I shouted. "Are you in here?"

The bed was unmade and rumpled. No bludgeoned body occupying it. No sign of blood, either. And no personal items on the nightstand or the dresser. The curtains were open and I got a quick glimpse of the lake before I pulled the closet door open to see assorted trousers and button-down shirts on hangers. My next stop was the bathroom and I took a deep breath.

By now, the housekeeper had entered the room but stood frozen by the side of the bed. The door to the bathroom was partially ajar and I kicked it open, careful not to get my fingerprints on anything in case Devora's didn't turn out to be the only body from the *Windswept Love* production.

My jaw felt as if it was locked in place as I peered into the room. The shower curtain had been pushed to the side and a few wet towels were on the floor. The soaker tub was empty and dry, with a decorative towel tossed over its edge and a cutesy rubber duck resting on top of the soft cotton material.

I walked to the shower and took a closer look. The walls were wet. That meant Stefan had used it recently.

"Is everything okay, miss?" the housekeeper asked. "No one is here. I can clean the room now. Okay?"

"Um, sure. Okay. Thanks for checking. My friend must have gotten up early and didn't bother to tell me. Sorry for your trouble." I reached in my pocket and handed her a five-dollar bill that I had in my wallet. "I'll let the front desk know everything is fine."

With that, I scurried down the staircase and back to the receptionist. "Everything's fine," I said. "When someone has a medical condition, it can be concerning."

She nodded. "I understand. My father has a heart condition, and even though he has a pacemaker, we worry."

I thanked her and walked straight out the door to the parking lot. No sooner had I started up my car than I noticed a black Mercedes pulling up in front of the Ramada and dropping someone off. *Must be nice to have money.* At first, all I could see was the back of the passenger as he or she got out of the vehicle. Tall, thin, with wispy blond hair. Then, the passenger turned and leaned into the car.

It was a *he* and no doubt about it, it was Stefan Olinguard. I skooched below the steering wheel on the off chance he might notice me but I didn't take my eyes off of him. The conversation between Stefan and the driver lasted a second or two and then Stefan headed directly into the hotel.

With only a horizontal view of the Mercedes, it was impossible to see the license plate, but not impossible to follow the driver once Stefan was no longer in sight. There was a rear exit from the parking lot that intersected with the main Ramada driveway. Without wasting a second, I hit the gas, got to the exit and waited until the Mercedes passed by. Then I followed it—close enough to read the six light blue letters against the white background. And close enough to read the word, *Ontario* above the letters. Ontario. I'd seen dozens of license plates like that. It was Canadian for sure, but whose was it and why was Stefan in the vehicle?

It certainly wasn't one of the film company cars and it couldn't possibly belong to Gordon Wable because he was flying in from Vancouver and renting a car. Then whose car was it? The easy fix would have been to confront Stefan, but if he was Devora's killer and the Mercedes belonged to someone working in tandem with him, I didn't need to rattle that cage. I had reached the point where I no longer trusted anyone on that film crew, especially the guy who had been virtually emasculated by Devora.

I rationalized Stefan wouldn't tell me the truth anyway and would concoct some story so I saved both of us the bother and decided instead to see how I could find out who held the registration for the black Mercedes.

By now, the Mercedes was headed north on Route 14 and I continued to follow it, although I let another car pass in front of me. When the vehicles reached the New York State Thruway, I, too, picked up a ticket and followed the Mercedes west. I imagined the driver was headed to Buffalo or Niagara Falls and from there straight into Canada's Ontario province.

Not wanting to make my donation to New York State's highway department higher than needed, I got off one exit down in Manchester and took Route 5 and 20 back home.

My sister and brother-in-law had a number of friends in the area, but none of them were in law enforcement and I certainly couldn't beg a favor from Deputy Hickman in order to track down that license. I doubted Bradley could help, and besides, I didn't want to do anything that would become an issue with his boss. Marvin Souza was a terrific lawyer, but he was also a terrific stickler for playing by the rules. And when it came to tracking down license plate numbers, even I knew that only law enforcement could do that legally.

Instead, I headed back to the tasting room in hopes that someone on our staff would have a friend or relative willing and able to help. Unfortunately, my sister had managed to hire employees whose friends and relatives ran the gamut from educators to welders, chiropractors to stenographers, and physicians to bartenders—not a single person remotely related to law enforcement.

"Sorry, Norrie," Cammy said when I explained what had happened. "No cops in my family. We're a bunch of restaurateurs and a few firefighters. Oh, yeah, and my cousin Sofina who's a seamstress in Cleveland."

Glenda, Roger, Lizzie, and Sam all echoed Cammy's words. Not so much the restaurateurs and firefighters but the fact that there were no relatives in law enforcement.

"I've got an uncle who's a security guard for one of the banks in Canandaigua," Sam said, "but I suppose that doesn't count."

I pinched the blades of my back so far they nearly touched. "You're right. It doesn't."

"What about Fred and Emma?" Lizzie asked. "Did you speak with them?"

"Next on my list."

With that, I rushed over to the bistro, only to be met with the same answer—zilch.

"Never mind," I told Fred. "I'll settle for a ham and Swiss panini while I try to figure something out."'

A few seconds later, while I rested my elbows on one of the bistro tables, Glenda came over. Her hair was now a combination of deep purple and reds but it was shorter than it had been yesterday.

"It's impossible to showcase my earrings with long hair," she said. "I had to make some adjustments."

The silver and gold earrings resembled two or three sea monsters wrapped around each other and I was at a loss for words.

"A friend of mine made these," she said. "He's with an artisan group in New Paltz. It's called Scylla and Charybdis from Greek mythology."

"They're so, so . . ."

"Compelling. I know. Of course, they never got near each other in the myth, but on my ears, they're choking the daylights out of each other."

At that moment, Fred placed the panini in front of me and I immediately took a bite.

"Anyway," Glenda went on, "I didn't stop by here to interrupt your lunch about my earrings. I wanted to let you know about some biblical oils my friend Zenora came across during her recent trip to the Holy Land."

The last time I had seen Glenda's friend Zenora, it was in our tasting room and it resulted in such chaos that I'm still trying to get it out of my mind. I put down the panini and looked at Glenda. "I didn't know Zenora was in the Holy Land."

"It was rather sudden. One minute she was reading her tarot cards and the next she was booking a flight to Jerusalem."

At least Jerusalem is an actual city and not one of her fabrications.

Glenda went on as I took another bite of my lunch. "Zenora brought back some biblical oils that can help you."

"I'm not sure I understand."

"Norrie, you're fraught with tension and that tension translates into negative energy. Tomorrow I'm going to bring you a small vial of biblical oil. Put it on your wrists and behind your ears and knees. The odor usually dissipates in a few hours. Trust me, you need this."

Yep, like spreading Alvin's goat manure on my elbows.

"Thanks, Glenda. I'm very appreciative."

She drifted back to her tasting room table and I gobbled the rest of my panini before picking up my phone and calling Don and Theo at the Grey Egret. Maybe they knew someone in law enforcement.

"The closest we came to law enforcement was when Theo played Officer Krupke in his high school's production of *West Side Story*," Don said when I told him about Stefan's peculiar disappearance and the black Mercedes that dropped him off before going west on the New York State Thruway.

"Have you thought about calling your producer?" he asked. "Maybe it was a company vehicle that they lease or own."

"I doubt it. The crew drove here with two Buicks and a Dodge van. Nothing ostentatious. Plus, I'd really hate to upset Renee. She's working on overdrive and freaked out as it is."

"You could always ask the film crew what vehicles the company uses. Slip it into a conversation without being overt."

"Thanks, Don. I'll figure something out. Will you and Theo be ready to compare notes on Thursday after our WOW meeting? So far, I haven't been able to pull up much on Priscilla or Devora but I'm working on it."

"Same here. Excluding food, parties, and hockey, Mickey and Rikesh's social media pages aren't yielding a whole lot of info. And Stefan's is . . . well, rather odd. Mostly posts about poets, some commentary about certain Canadian politicians, and recipes with whole grains. But Theo came up with an interesting idea."

"What?"

"See who their friends are. That could be quite revealing."

"Hmm, Theo may be on to something. Anyway, let's meet back here after WOW and sift through it. I'll let Stephanie know."

I had every intention of working on my screenplays when I got off the phone with Don, but that was before Emma waved me over.

"Psst!" she whispered. "Cammy just buzzed us. One of the vineyard guys came in to use the restroom and said Deputy Hickman's car is coming up the driveway."

"Oh, geez, no. Now what?"

"Maybe they have a suspect. Or a decent lead."

I wasn't as optimistic as Emma. "He probably wants to remind me to have everyone at the ready tomorrow for those interviews. I don't think the guy trusts me."

Emma laughed. "I don't think he trusts anyone."

I grabbed a bottle of cranberry juice before leaving the bistro and went straight to my office. No sooner had I set the bottle on my desk than there was a rap on the door and Deputy Hickman let himself in.

"Good afternoon, Miss Ellington. Our office received a call from someone who attended your wine and cheese event on Saturday. They witnessed a verbal exchange that you had with the victim, Devora Dobrowski, and once the news of her death became public, they felt they needed to share that unsettling exchange with my office."

"Who? Who needed to share that conversation?"

"I'm sorry but that information is confidential."

"Is that what you came here to tell me?"

"In so many words, Miss Ellington, you are now a person of interest in the death of Devora Dobrowski."

Chapter 17

"Person of interest? That's insane. Who would ever think I'd murder that woman?"

"Apparently, one of the guests attending the event thought so. That's all I can divulge at this juncture in time."

"So are you telling me I need to hire an attorney?" *Because I'm dating one.* Although family law isn't criminal law. And the only thing criminal was that person's ridiculous accusation.

"You're not under arrest, Miss Ellington. Hiring an attorney is entirely up to you. I will need you to tell me where you were between the hours of five p.m. and five a.m. on the night in question. Better yet, write it down and fax it to my office. Mark it confidential."

My face felt warm and it was all I could do to keep myself from making a flippant remark or, worse yet, a gesture I'd regret. Then he would have an excuse to arrest me on the spot.

"I can't believe you're taking that call seriously."

Deputy Hickman, who was leaning against a file cabinet up until now, walked to the door and pushed it closed. He pulled a chair up to my desk and sat down. "Miss Ellington, you had motive, means, and opportunity. The three major criteria for committing a crime."

By now, the heat in my face had reached a new level and I pressed the cold cranberry juice bottle against my cheek. "Huh?"

Grizzly Gary crossed his arms and leaned forward. "Let's begin with motive. Our witness said that when Ms. Dobrowski allegedly threatened your place in the filmmaking industry, you told her in no uncertain terms that . . ." He paused for a moment and pulled out his notepad. He looked down and then continued his thought. ". . . she was 'the one who needs to worry.' In my business, that's known as a veiled threat."

"Well, in my business we call it a retort."

"Now then. Means. Ms. Dobrowski was strangled with a chain consistent with the kind found wrapped around that cattail your dog dredged up from the Ipswiches' pond. You told our office you were certain it belonged to one of the actors, Priscilla McCoy, since you had seen it on her neck the day of the wine and cheese event."

"That part's true. I did see it. On her neck." *Oh, crap. I hope I'm not implicating myself.*

"Miss McCoy informed our office that she had lost it during the filming and her crew substantiates that claim. In fact, she had to purchase another such necklace to continue with that scene. Something about continuity, if I'm reading my notes correctly."

"What does that prove?"

"You were in the area where they were filming. And in the winery. Very easy for you to have come across that necklace and used it to strangle Ms. Dobrowski."

"You don't really believe that, do you?"

"What I believe is irrelevant. I follow the evidence and the facts."

And ridiculous phone calls from kooks and nutcases.

"If I did do such a thing, and believe me, *I didn't*, why would I be so stupid as to tell anyone about the necklace? Or hand it over to you?"

"Because you're a clever woman, Miss Ellington. By handing it over, you made the case that you were the innocent party who came across a clue."

"Oh, brother."

He glanced at his notes again and continued. "Opportunity. Who, better than you, had the opportunity to commit a murder? You could easily come and go at your winery and no one would notice. It was a Seneca Lake Wine Trail event, was it not?" He continued talking without waiting for a response. "Those events are notorious for bringing in throngs of visitors. With a packed winery *and* that film production going on at Two Witches, no one would have batted an eyelash if you disappeared out of sight for a while."

"And do what? Go over to where they were filming and ask Devora to take a little hike with me?"

As soon as I said that, I knew I should have kept my mouth shut.

"Is that what you did?"

"Of course not. I was at the winery the entire time, except for when I went back to the house."

Oh, hell, no. How can I prove I was at the house?

"In any case, Miss Ellington, I'll need the exact accounting of your whereabouts faxed to my office today. Understood?"

I nodded.

"Good. We're on the same page. I'll be back tomorrow to interview your employees. And please, no interference."

Again, I nodded. He was out of my office in a nanosecond. The cranberry juice bottle was now room temperature and I finished it in three gulps. Just then, Mickey rapped on my door.

"Hey, uh, sorry to bother you but we ran out of double A batteries. Any chance you've got some we can use? We'll replace them."

I told him yes and directed him to see Lizzie or Cammy. The conversation I'd had with Deputy Hickman put me on edge.

A person of interest? I'd been in predicaments with Grizzly Gary before, but this was the first time I was a suspect. If I couldn't find out who really murdered Devora, meeting Renee's deadline for my next screenplay would be the least of my worries. Then again, maybe they have WI-FI in the county lockup.

I immediately phoned Bradley, who told me not to worry and that the sheriff's office would have one heck of a time proving anything. Still, he told me to detail everything on my timeline sheet.

"He probably wants to put you on notice, Norrie," Bradley said.

"For what? Murder?"

"No, for snooping. Deputy Hickman is well aware by now that you have a tendency to throw yourself into his investigations. He probably thinks this is one way to slow you down."

"Virtually accusing me of murder isn't going to slow me down. If anything, it's going to speed things up. I'm already using social media to see if I can find anything that might link one of the film crew members to Devora's death. The good news is that I've commandeered Stephanie, Cammy, Don, and Theo to help."

"I'll sleep better if I know you're going to limit those searches to a computer and not the usual stalking around that you've been known to do."

He sounds like Godfrey.

"Don't worry. No one's stalking anyone." *Unless a black Mercedes counts.* "Hey, before I forget, Devora Dobrowski is the one from that divorce case. My producer told me that she's the estranged wife of the Brouse Candies CEO. You know, if anyone had a motive for murder, it would be him. Don't you think?"

"If money was the motive, absolutely. Gee, I wish we didn't have to wait until tomorrow for dinner but I'm buried in work here."

"It's busy on my end, too, so don't worry. Talk to you later. And thanks for reassuring me."

"I'll do more than that if Deputy Hickman makes another move. Miss you."

"Me too."

I figured I'd tell him about Stefan and the black Mercedes tomorrow. There was nothing he could do about it anyway. I tossed the juice bottle into my recycling bin and left the office. Cammy was at the front register since Lizzie was on break.

"Our little data-gathering crew is going to meet here after the WOW meeting on Thursday," I told her.

"Great. I was able to round up a really juicy tidbit on Gavin Chase late last night but I didn't have the chance to tell you."

"What tidbit?"

"It wasn't on his Facebook page but it was on another site that deals with celebrity gossip. Devora pretty much blacklisted Gavin a number of years ago, making it difficult for him to get choice roles."

"Blacklisted?"

"Well, maybe bad-mouthed would be a better word. Anyhow, she told other directors and people in the industry that Gavin was difficult to work with. As a result, he could only get commercials and voice-overs until someone hired him for the movie *Waltzing in Winnipeg* two or three years ago."

"Holy cow. If that's not a motive for murder, what is? She could have destroyed his entire career."

"I know. Isn't there some sort of a quote about revenge being best served cold?"

"Uh-huh. But in this case, it was served wet."

Chapter 18

By the time I sauntered into the tasting room the following day, Deputy Hickman had already interrogated Lizzie, Cammy, and Roger. He told Cammy he'd be back later in the day to speak with Fred and Emma since they had to contend with the lunch crowd. Sam and Glenda were off for the day, and Grizzly Gary agreed to speak with them first thing Thursday morning.

The good news was that Gordon Wable had arrived and was already on the east side of our vineyard with the film crew and the actors. We still needed road security, for lack of a better term, and since Marc and Enzo were on spring break, they were more than happy to earn a few extra bucks and ogle Priscilla at the same time.

The large crowds that had engulfed the area during the wine and cheese event were gone, but thanks to the news channels, we had no shortage of visitors who wanted to catch a glimpse of the actors.

"That Gordon Wable is absolutely darling," Cammy said when I walked into the tasting room. "He was in early with Stefan and Skylar. Fred made them coffees as well as to-go cups for the rest of the crew."

"What do you mean by *darling*?" Cammy never described anyone that way. Not even if they were drop-dead gorgeous. I could detect a slight blush on her cheeks but didn't say anything.

"Well, he looks to be in his late forties or early fifties and he's got this neat cuddly factor going for him. I don't know how to explain it, but he reminds me of an old sheepdog one of my uncles had. The kind you want to snuggle up to."

Or not. "I take it he was friendly and not like Devora."

"Polar opposites if you ask me. Stefan seemed much more relaxed around him and so did Skylar."

"Good. Maybe they can finish the filming and move on. Or out of here, as the case may be. They'll still be stuck at the Ramada until Grizzly Gary gives them the okay to go back to Toronto."

"The news media's been pretty quiet about the investigation. I take it there are no new leads."

I groaned and pushed my hair behind my ears. "I should have told you this yesterday but I was too unnerved. *I'm* the lead suspect."

"What?" Cammy dropped the towel she was holding and it landed in a pitcher of water on her tasting table. "What do you mean?"

"Deputy Hickman paid me one of his not-so-pleasant visits yesterday. He informed me that one of our event visitors called their office about the verbal exchange I had with Devora on Saturday. To cut to the chase, he thinks I had motive, means, and opportunity. Anyway, I'm now officially a person of interest."

"That man's a lunatic. An absolute lunatic if he thinks you could have murdered Devora."

"That's why we need to really dig deep on the film crew's scuttlebutt. Someone's holding back something and we need to find out what it is."

"No problem. I'll keep digging."

Just then a group of six or seven middle-aged women walked in and headed toward us. Roger was tied up with three customers at his table and Cammy had no choice but to motion them to her table.

I gave her a nod. "I'd better let you go. We'll catch up later."

"Hang in there."

The only thing I *could* do was hang in there. Well, that and my own little bit of prying. I had to find out what the heck Stefan was doing getting out of that Mercedes and whether it had anything to do with Devora's death. Then there was Gordon Wable. Cuddly or not, it wouldn't be the first time someone in the moviemaking industry used sneaky tactics to reposition themselves on the hierarchy. Although, stepping in at the last minute to direct one scene in a movie could hardly be considered a step up. And murdering someone for one lousy scene didn't make sense at all. Plus, the guy was in Vancouver. Still, I wasn't about to rule him out.

When I left the tasting room, I told Lizzie I'd be back later to grab a late lunch. Then I walked home and phoned Don and Theo. They were as astonished as Cammy when I gave them the grim news about my new status in the community.

"A person of interest?" Theo shrieked. "Has Hickman gone mad?"

Then Don grabbed the phone. "Did you call an attorney?"

"I, um, spoke to Bradley."

"Well, did *he* call a criminal attorney for you?"

"He said it was too soon. He thinks Deputy Hickman said that to keep me away from the investigation."

Don groaned and I could hear him take a deep breath. "Bradley may be right but it wouldn't hurt to have some legal counsel lined up." Then he gave the phone back to Theo, who said, "Holy crap, Norrie. Don't get yourself too worked up over this."

Actually, I wasn't too worked up until I'd spoken with Don and Theo. "I'll tell you more after the WOW meeting. By the way, which one of you is going?"

"I am," Theo said. "I drew the short straw."

In the background I heard Don shout, "I went last time. I had to listen to Catherine's never-ending description of the dress she planned to wear for Easter dinner. You'd think she was going to a coronation."

I laughed. "Okay. See you tomorrow. And keep hunting down info on *our* suspects."

It was after three when I returned to the tasting room. I waved to Cammy and Roger before charging straight to the bistro and ordering my usual panini.

"I like the new director better," Emma said. "He was in here for lunch along with Priscilla. I had to sneak them into the banquet room before anyone noticed. Thankfully, that miserable deputy was already gone by then."

"What about the rest of the crew?"

"They drove to the Penn Yan Diner. Skylar reiterated what you said about their chicken fried steaks and that was all it took according to Gordon."

"Even Mr. Whole Grains and No Sugar went there?"

"Uh-huh. Apparently someone told him the diner had salads on the menu."

"They do. With the heaviest, tastiest dressings imaginable. I suppose Stefan will take his salad sans the dressing."

"By the way," Emma said, "the director left his jacket in the banquet room. He wasn't wearing it when he walked in, he had it draped over a shoulder. He probably doesn't need it right now since it's in the fifties and he was wearing a heavy-looking sweatshirt."

"Is it still in the banquet room?"

"No, I hung it up in the kitchen closet. Maybe someone can take it to him today. We simply haven't had time."

"I'll grab it. I've got a few things to do at the house and then I'll drop it off. Knowing how many film shoots they take, they're bound to be in the vineyard for a while."

"Thanks, Norrie. Gee, I hope I don't get flustered speaking with that deputy."

"You won't. Tell him the truth. What you saw and what you remember about Saturday. Or whatever else he asks you."

"I'll try."

I ate my panini in record time, grabbed Gordon's lightweight jacket from the kitchen closet and started for the door. I definitely needed to be out of there before Deputy Hickman arrived.

"Have a nice afternoon," Lizzie said when I neared the register on my way out. "Oh, and you might want to tune in to the Weather Channel. The entire Finger Lakes are in the path of that spring storm. What did they call it? Oh yes, Neville. That was the name. Seems Neville is a slow-moving storm so he might not reach us until the end of the week."

Wonderful. That's all we need, a heavy glacial storm named Neville that could last for days while it downed power lines and made plowing impossible.

"Uh, thanks, Lizzie. I'll be sure to catch a forecast."

The first thing I did when I got in the house, other than tossing Gordon's jacket over a chair in the kitchen, was to make sure I had enough food for Charlie and enough dry goods to keep me from starving. I really wasn't that worried about the storm but I didn't need the dog to go without his kibble.

Figuring I had more than enough time to meet Gordon and return his jacket, I threw in a load of wash and pulled up my laptop. I had tons of editing to do on a screenplay that needed to be in Renee's hot little hands in two weeks. Two weeks may sound like a long time but not when it comes to editing. It's a boring, miserable process that saps the creative juices right out of me and I have to practically force myself to do it.

With Charlie curled up in his doggie bed and the afternoon lighting just right, I cozied up on the couch and painstakingly scrutinized the first twenty-five pages of my screenplay. This one was set in Wellfleet, Cape Cod, where Francine and I spent weeklong summer vacations when we were little. Then it was back to Two Witches and Seneca Lake.

"At least it's not a vineyard," I muttered to Charlie. "It's a beach romance. That means I have to leave out the weird fishy smell and yucky stuff that gets swept on to the shore." The dog looked up and then closed his eyes. I leaned back and stretched, careful not to jostle the computer. "Hmm, I suppose *you'd* love it. All those fish entrails you could bring home. At least none of them would be a murder weapon."

Just then I realized it was late and that I'd better get that jacket to Gordon Wable while it was still light out. At least my dinner with Bradley wasn't until eight. Plenty of time for him to pick me up. I closed the laptop, reached for the sweatshirt I'd thrown over the couch and put it on. "I'll be back in a jiff," I said. The dog followed me to the kitchen and grabbed something from the floor. If there was one thing I noticed about that Plott hound, he wasn't very particular about what he put in his mouth. But he wasn't territorial either, so my fingers would be safe when I went to extract it.

I immediately pried his mouth open and retrieved a wet, crumpled piece of paper. "This better not be one of the bills I have to pay." I unwadded it and took a look. It was a boarding pass with yesterday's date and Gordon Wable's name on it. The edges were wet and slimy thanks to Charlie, and little bite marks dotted the document. I took a closer look at it and froze. Gordon Wable had flown to Rochester from Toronto, not Vancouver like Renee had told me. Something didn't add up.

The document was as gooey and sticky as could be and there was no way I was about to shove it back in his jacket pocket. Besides, he'd know it had been tampered with. Instead, I put it in a Ziploc bag and tucked it under a stack of books on the counter. Gordon Wable's flight plans were the least of my worries.

I threw on a heavy fleece hoodie since the winds were starting to kick up, grabbed Gordon's jacket and headed for the spot in the vineyard where they were filming. Judging from the sky, we had maybe a half hour left of daylight. No sooner had I ducked into one of the vineyard lanes than Skylar and Rikesh approached. Both of them were carrying tripods and large black metal cases.

"If you're looking for the rest of the crew, they've already left," Skylar said. "It's getting windy and we've had a full day."

"Things working out with the new director?" I asked.

"Hell, yeah. Priscilla's not a basket case and Gavin doesn't look as if he wants to knock someone's teeth out."

"Oh, before I forget, this is Gordon's jacket. Can you get it to him? He left it at the winery. One of our bistro chefs said he and Priscilla had lunch at Two Witches but that the rest of you chowed down at the Penn Yan Diner."

"We chowed down all right," Rikesh said. He took the jacket from me and tucked it under the arm that held one of the metal cases. "I've never been to a diner where four or five eggs were the norm for omelets."

I laughed. "Welcome to Penn Yan. I guess Gordon and Priscilla wanted some lighter fare, huh?"

"Not food," Skylar said. "Conversation. At least that's my take on the deal. She was the one who pulled him aside, whispered something, and next thing we knew, they decided to eat at your bistro. Hey, for all I know, maybe she needed another shoulder to cry on after getting the third degree the other day from your deputy."

"Not *my* deputy. The county's. And that wasn't the third degree. That was the opening act."

Rikesh turned to Skylar. "At least Gordon will be spared. He was in Vancouver at the time."

I wouldn't bet on it.

Chapter 19

Bradley picked me up a little before eight and we drove to the Stonecutter's Tavern at Belhurst Castle, a sunken bar complete with lake view and fabulous pub-style food. No sooner were we seated at a corner table than I glanced toward the lake and spied none other than Priscilla with an arm draped over the "cuddly hunk" Cammy described.

"Shh! Don't be obvious," I whispered to Bradley. "That's Priscilla, and it has to be Gordon Wable right next to her."

"Um, do you think you should walk over and introduce yourself to him?"

"Are you kidding? Take a good look. They're almost . . . almost . . . well, intimate. And that's not all. Something fishy is going on. I didn't get a chance to tell you sooner. He was supposed to fly in from Vancouver, but I found his boarding pass and guess what? The flight was from Toronto. No stopover from Vancouver."

Bradley gave me a strange look and I proceeded to tell him about the jacket and how I found the chewed-up document in Charlie's mouth.

"Tomorrow I intend to ask Gordon how his flight was and see if he squirms. Toronto's only a five-hour drive from here. Six or seven at most if the weather's a bear. Gordon could have easily driven here, committed the crime, and driven back. According to Renee, he was already done with the filming in British Columbia."

"True, but what's his motive? Getting to film the last scene of a TV romance? That's hardly a motive in my book."

"There had to be something else. I'm adding him to my suspect list and I'll do a little internet digging."

Bradley gave my wrist a pat. "I'm sure this is a long shot, but I'll see if there's anything that connects him to the Dobrowski divorce. That nightmare has tentacles everywhere. Makes a great case study, though."

"Ew. You don't suppose he was having an affair with Devora, do you?"

He laughed. "I'll leave the speculating to you."

Just then our waiter arrived and we ordered clam and corn chowders, blue crab in Gorgonzola and cognac fondue, and marinated jumbo tiger shrimp. True, it wasn't Manhattan, but dining in the Finger Lakes certainly had its culinary advantages.

When the waiter left, I glanced at Priscilla and Gordon, who were still gazing into each other's eyes. *This is a screenplay that could write itself.* Then I looked directly at Bradley. "There was a curious incident with Stefan yesterday. I saw him getting out of a black Mercedes. It was in front of the Ramada. I suppose you'll want to know what I was doing there so here's the CliffsNotes—Stefan didn't show up in the morning for filming and Skylar was concerned. Then, when I spoke to Renee, she was really peeved that Stefan hadn't returned her calls. She said it wasn't like him and I had a horrible feeling something had happened to him."

Bradley rubbed his temples, sighed, and leaned back. "Naturally you went to check it out."

"Uh-huh. Got Housekeeping to let me in the room. No sign of him. Or anything incriminating, for that matter. Anyway, when I left and got back in my car, I saw the Mercedes pull up and bingo! Stefan got out, turned back to talk to the driver, and then went straight into the hotel."

"You sure it was him?"

"Positive. But I couldn't see the license because I only had a horizontal angle. So I followed the Mercedes and got the plate number. Canadian. Ontario province. It had to be Toronto. Plus, when I tailed the Mercedes, they were heading west on the thruway. Doesn't take a rocket scientist to figure out they were going back to Canada."

"Geez, Norrie, what if they were dangerous and noticed you following them? Look, I understand you want to find out who killed Devora, but don't take any risky chances. And as far as Stefan is concerned, he could have walked in on you while you were snooping around his room."

"That part would've been easy. I'd have told him the truth—we thought he was in trouble. And he still might be. Who knows what business he had with whoever was in the Mercedes."

"He's not the only one."

"What do you mean?"

Bradley rubbed the back of his neck and stretched. "Don't discount Priscilla in all of this. She could have lied about losing that necklace. You yourself said there was some animosity between her and Devora."

"There was animosity between Devora and everyone."

"But Devora might have had a stranglehold on Priscilla's career. Oops. Sorry about the bad choice of words."

I bit my lower lip and looked directly at Bradley. "If you're thinking Priscilla lured Devora to the pond under one guise or another, that's impossible. According to the cameramen, Priscilla stormed off the location on the day in question and Gavin followed her."

Bradley crinkled his nose. "Maybe those two were in cahoots."

"Now who's speculating?"

The waiter returned with our food and for the next half hour the only sounds we made were oohs and aahs, When the meal ended, Bradley paid the check and we drove back to my house. Once inside, I asked if he wanted anything to drink.

"Coffee will keep me up all night, and as much as I love the Two Witches wines, I need to get back on the road. I've got a full schedule tomorrow. If I settle down on your couch, I may never get up. At least we have the weekend to look forward to. Or am I being too presumptuous?"

"Be as presumptuous as you'd like."

He planted a soft, warm kiss on my lips, which led to more of the same.

"The couch *is* more comfortable," I said.

"I know. That's why I'm headed to the door."

One more kiss and it was good night.

"At least we've got jumbo shrimp if we want a midnight snack," I said to Charlie as I locked the door. "I brought home leftovers." I watched out the living room window as Bradley's car made its way down our road and onto Route 14. Then I remembered something. The weekend might bring another guest. One I didn't want to entertain. If Neville was as thick and slow-moving as the forecasters predicted, he'd be sure to overstay his welcome.

• • •

It wasn't until the next day, Thursday, with the WOW meeting hanging over my head, that I finally got to meet the cuddly and perhaps not-so-honest Gordon Wable. It was barely nine. I was on my way back to my office with a steaming vanilla latte in my hand when he walked through the door and immediately approached me.

"You must be Norrie Ellington, one of our screenwriters and the proprietress of this winery. You look just like your photo."

"My photo? What photo?" *Does Renee have my photo?*

"The one in today's *Finger Lakes Times*. It got delivered to my room at the Ramada."

Shockwaves surged through my body and all I could think of was a giant headline that read, *WINERY OWNER PERSON OF INTEREST IN POND MURDER.*

"What did it say? Not the photo. The text." I tried to sound calm but it was as if I was holding back a volcanic eruption.

"My apologies. I didn't read the article. I merely looked at the photo of your latest event on this wine trail. Very interesting. Good way to encourage business. Whoever took the photo certainly showcased your winery. You're standing behind a tasting table next to a tall dark-haired gentleman with round glasses. From the look of things, he was giving people an explanation about something. Wines, I presume."

Or the French and Indian War.

The tension slowly left my body and I was able to take a breath without shaking. He had just described Roger, and I remembered seeing a few reporters drifting in and out of the tasting room that weekend.

I smiled and held out my hand. "Yes, I'm Norrie. You must be the new director. The one replacing—"

"Devora Dobrowski. Such a shock." Then he shook my hand, not with one of those flimsy handshakes, or worse yet, a limp one, but a firm and strong grip that wasn't crushing. "Gordon Wable."

"Nice to meet you. Renee told me you'd be flying in from Vancouver to finish up the filming."

"I'm always willing to step in if needed."

"Um, uh, I take it you had a good flight. No jet lag."

"None whatsoever. The trick is to stay hydrated."

"I'll keep that in mind. Uh, how long were you in the air?" I opened my eyes wide and smiled, trying to look as if I was making small talk.

"About eight hours, not counting the brief stop in Chicago."

This guy's good. He even did his homework.

"I'll bet you can't wait to get back to Toronto. I know the film crew is anxious."

"True. There's nothing quite like sleeping in one's own bed, eh?"

"Uh-huh. Um, were you aware the crew may be detained during the investigation?"

"Renee kept me apprised of everything. I can't imagine anyone in our production company doing such a heinous thing and I certainly hope the culprit is brought to justice speedily."

His words sounded like something from a TV script and I almost laughed. "Yeah. Me, too. Um, if you need anything, let me know. We'll try our best to accommodate you. By the way, if you decide to have lunch here, I recommend the paninis."

"Already tried one yesterday and you're right."

Just then, Priscilla approached, this time with the replacement necklace around her neck. She immediately took Gordon's arm. "Gordon honey, be a dear and get me one of their large lattes. I need a morning pick-me-up before we film." Then she smiled at me. "Nice to see you again, Norrie."

"Well, I'd better get our drinks," Gordon said. "Time is of the essence. Again, it was good meeting you, Norrie. Oh, and by the way, your security detail is doing a good job. Not bad-looking guys. We might be able to use them as extras if we film here again."

Oh, dear God, bite your tongue. That's all Cammy needs. Marc and Enzo in a movie. Oh, what am I saying? That's the last thing I need—more filming here.

I didn't have any further contact with the film crew the rest of day, and I wished the same could have been said for the folks at our WOW meeting. My mother was right. It was Seneca Lake's version of gossip central and there was nothing I could do about it

Chapter 20

The WOW meeting at Billsburrow Winery was like watching a ball being batted around with no real destination. Madeline Martinez had set out the usual coffee and cookie spread on her enclosed porch, and once everyone had helped themselves to the refreshments, they immediately began to talk about Devora's murder.

"That must have been awful for you, Stephanie," Catherine said. "I can't imagine finding a dead body floating in your pond."

Rosalee Marbleton put her coffee cup on the end table next to her seat and squared her shoulders. "Well, I can. I found one by the lake not too long ago."

"Your dog found it," Madeline said. "And if I'm not mistaken, it wasn't floating, it was just there."

Theo glanced at me and rolled his eyes.

"Like I was saying," Catherine continued, "you must be beside yourself."

Stephanie broke off a tiny corner from her sugar cookie and nodded. "It's been stressful, that's for sure. Our employees were questioned as if they were seasoned criminals. And Derek's really annoyed because the crime tape is still up around the pond. We've got planting to do. What are the vineyard guys supposed to do? They need access to the pond."

Then Madeline looked at me. "What have you heard, Norrie? It was your film crew after all."

I gulped. "Uh, not exactly *mine*, more like the production company that makes movies out of my screenplays."

"A horse by any other name is still a horse," Rosalee muttered. She shifted in her chair, her love handles scraping against the fabric.

"Okay, fine. *My* company. And no, I haven't heard anything either. Our staff was grilled, too, along with the film production crew. They're still camped out at the Ramada since their passports are under lock and key as per Deputy Hickman."

"It *had* to be one of them," Catherine said. "I mean, who else could it be? A word to the wise—all of us need to be vigilant about keeping our doors locked at night and our windows closed."

Theo, who'd been quiet up until that moment, groaned. "Honestly, Catherine, I seriously doubt whoever murdered the movie director will be eyeing any of us."

"You don't know that for sure. We could have a maniacal killer in our midst."

"If the Yates County Sheriff's Office thought for one moment that that was the case, they'd be issuing warnings," he said. "Heck, last year they issued a warning about package pirates stealing deliveries from FedEx and UPS. And the year before that, they issued a warning about bogus door-to-door salespeople. Frankly, whoever killed Devora Dobrowski had a motive. Now, can we please get on with our meeting? All of us need to get back to work."

Madeline immediately reached for the small notebook on her coffee table and opened it. "Fine. We'll begin with the Concord grape matter. It's surprising but usually we hear from Henry Speltmore about things like this."

"His fingers are probably recuperating after the last epic emails he sent regarding the wine and cheese event," Stephanie said. "I've gotten to the point where I just gloss over them."

The next three or four minutes were spent discussing Henry's emails before Madeline got the group back on topic. "Back to the Concord grapes. As you all know, there's been some talk about a major candy manufacturer buying up property in Geneva's industrial park. If that comes to fruition, they'll need grape juice and plenty of it."

"I'm way ahead of you, Madeline," Rosalee said. "Got our root stock ordered in November. I heard it was a done deal. One way or another, we'd be fools to let that opportunity pass. Concord grapes practically grow themselves and none of us will have any problem selling the juice. It won't matter if the candy company buys the juice directly from us or from one of the companies we already do business with. They'll be buying it. That's all that matters."

"And if that candy company deal turns out to be a rumor?" Theo asked.

I grabbed one of Madeline's snickerdoodles and looked around the room. "We can always sell to the juice cooperatives. Look, none of us are talking about taking vineyards away from our current varieties, or actually producing grape wine, we're merely talking about adding additional vineyards to our wineries. Small plots. That's all. And it's completely up to each of us if we want to do it. No one's forcing us to do anything we don't want to do."

In retrospect, I never should have added that last sentence because it was like a boomerang, catapulting Catherine back to Devora's murder.

"Maybe that's what happened," she said. "Maybe the killer tried forcing the poor woman into doing something and when she refused, he strangled her."

"We don't know that it was a *he*," I said. "And if you'd met Devora, you'd realize that if anyone was going to do the forcing, it would be her."

Theo burst out laughing. "Norrie's got a point. Now, if the victim were Priscilla McCoy, I might be inclined to agree with Catherine."

"Are we talking grapes or murder?" Rosalee asked. "Because I've got a busy schedule."

Madeline looked at her notebook and sighed. "We don't really have anything pressing. Let's share our experiences about the wine and cheese event in case we need to do something different next year."

"I suggest we speak to Henry about moving the event to the last week of April, when we can be reasonably certain the weather will be cooperative. Have any of you listened to the forecast? We were lucky spring storm Neville held off until this weekend," Catherine said. "There's always one horrific spring storm in April, just when the crocuses and daffodils are coming up."

Five more minutes relegated to wine and cheese and we were out of there. Stephanie grabbed my arm as I opened the door. "I thought that would never end. I've got to make a quick stop at home and I'll be at your place in a few minutes."

"Good," I whispered. "If we don't come up with something, Catherine's maniacal killer rumor might go viral."

Even though we had just finished munching on sugary cookies with assorted teas and coffee, I had arranged for Fred to put out some finger sandwiches and juice in our banquet room for our little data-sharing meeting. He also gathered five chairs in a cluster for us so we wouldn't have to shout across the room.

Theo and I arrived within seconds of each other, followed by Stephanie a few minutes later. Cammy was finishing up with customers and mouthed, "I'll be right in" when she spotted me.

"Like I said before, I thought that meeting would never end," Stephanie said. She helped herself to some juice and took the smallest turkey and cranberry finger sandwich. "I think Catherine's going off the deep end. Even I'm not that freaked out about the murder."

Theo tossed a finger sandwich in his mouth, and in a second it was gone. "Catherine goes off the deep end if she gets crumbs on her skirt. I should know. I watched her two meetings ago."

All of us burst out laughing just as Cammy walked in. "Sorry. Hope I didn't keep you. What's so funny?"

"The WOW meeting women," he said. "Don't ask."

I plopped myself down in one of the chairs and grabbed a juice. "Okay, I know everyone's pressed for time so we'll try to be brief. I'll start with everything I managed to dig up and we'll go around the room after that. All right?"

Everyone nodded.

"First off, Godfrey Klein saw some sort of correspondence from the agricultural department about Brouse Candies coming to the area. I asked him to find out if their CEO, Gerard Brouse, was in the area during the time of Devora's murder. He's Devora's estranged husband and he would have had a real motive for knocking her off—money. Bradley Jamison said a real nasty divorce case is going on. He found out because it's such a humdinger that law schools are using it as a case study."

"Holy mackerel, Norrie," Stephanie said. "All you need are a few more boyfriends and you'll have the scoop on everything."

"Godfrey's not a boyfriend, and Bradley's, well . . . let's just move on. What have you got, Theo?"

"Don and I had Stefan, Mickey, and Rikesh. Stefan's about as social media–shy as they get so we're still digging. Mickey's on a few sites and one of them linked him to an actress named Bailey Wagner."

"I know that name," I said. "She had a minor role in *A Swim Under the Waterfall.* One of my screenplays. And I think I heard Priscilla mention it. What else did you find out about Mickey?"

Theo shrugged. "The guy recently bought a new motorcycle. Photos were plastered everywhere. Yellow Harley-Davidson Sportster something-or-other. New. Must have cost him plenty. Same deal with his leather riding jacket."

"What about Rikesh?" I asked.

"Guy's a real sci-fi and tech nerd. Into video gaming and *Doctor Who.* When he's not doing those things, he's at Comic Cons."

Stephanie crinkled her nose and turned to Theo. "Comic what?"

"Comic book conventions. But it's more than that. Way more. Anyhow, I didn't find anything that would give him a motive to murder Devora. Same with the other two guys, but like I said, Don and I are still looking."

Cammy reiterated what she knew about Devora blacklisting Gavin, when I suddenly remembered something.

"Oh, my gosh. I can't believe I forgot this. One of Ralphie's EMTs, a guy named Chad, heard Gavin threaten Devora. Ralphie told me. It was on Saturday. According to Chad, Gavin told Devora that 'he'd see to it that it was the last film she ever directed.' Yikes. I must have pushed it to the back of my mind."

"But there's no context with it," Theo said. "Still, a threat's a threat. Maybe this Chad guy should be contacted so he can share that with Deputy Hickman."

I clenched my jaw. "Grizzly Gary interviewed the EMTs who worked here. Same deal with Cammy's nephews. If Chad was going to say anything, he already did."

At that point, we all turned to Stephanie. She brushed a strand of her long honey-blond hair and smiled. "Skylar Randall's one hot little ticket, if you ask me. Good thing I wasn't doing all those internet searches at night or my husband would have wondered why I was so flushed."

"Skylar Randall the cameraman?" I asked her. "Are you sure you looked up the right Skylar Randall?"

She smiled. "Oh, I'm sure all right. He looks exactly like the photo you emailed me after I agreed to do a little background checking. The other guys in that crew aren't bad-looking either, but nothing like Skylar."

Chapter 21

I rubbed my temples. "We're talking possible murderer, Stephanie, not *The Full Monty*. What's the deal with Skylar?"

"Yeah," Cammy said. "What did I miss? Tell us now before Norrie starts blabbing about Devora and Priscilla."

Stephanie gave me a wink and smiled. "I'm glad I picked Skylar. I could look at those pecs and abs all day."

"Pecs and abs? For goodness sake, Stephanie, there's a killer loose. You were supposed to do some background checking, not admire the guy's physique."

"Relax, Norrie," Theo said. "Don would have done the same thing."

Stephanie shot me a look and crinkled that cute little button nose of hers. "See, I'm not the only one. And besides, I did plenty of background checking. Skylar's really into filming with the intent of becoming the director of photography for a major motion picture."

"Isn't that called the cinematographer?" Cammy asked. "I've seen enough Academy Awards."

"I think the camera operator and the director of photography have to be the same person," I said. "But I could be wrong. Renee sends me lots of info but I don't always read it."

Cammy all but burst out laughing. "Gee, just like the Wine Trail news from Henry Speltmore."

I rolled my eyes and turned to Stephanie. "What else did you find out?"

"He graduated with honors from Vancouver Film School, and that's not an easy feat. The guy seems pretty serious about his career. And before you ask, the answer is no. I couldn't find anything about his love life or any other life beyond his work. At least not on social media."

"Fine," I grumbled. "I might as well share what I turned up, or in this case, *didn't*, on Priscilla and Devora. Other than Devora being a temperamental pain in the butt, and the fact that no one on film sets enjoyed working with her, I couldn't find anything in particular that would wave a red flag in my face."

I reached for one of Fred's mini-sandwiches, stuffed it in my mouth, and kept talking between bites. "The only one who'd really gain from her death is the estranged husband, Gerard Dobrowski. Devora's shares from Brouse Candies were massive. And get this—according to Bradley, who did me a favor and looked into a few things, Devora never changed the beneficiary of her will. Gerard gets it all. If that's not motive, I don't know what is."

"It may be motive," Theo said, "but what about means and opportunity?"

"Um, yeah. I'm hoping Godfrey will be able to find out more. Like Gerard's whereabouts during the time of death."

"Me, too, because I'd hate to think Priscilla was the one who committed the crime." I looked at the tray of sandwiches and grabbed another one. "She did have motive, you know. Devora made her life hell on the set. And, after all, it was Priscilla's necklace in that cattail. She could have lied about losing it. And her hands were all scratched up. She could have lied about that, too. Unfortunately, I couldn't find out much about her social life or her connections based on social media."

"So now what?" Cammy asked.

I rubbed my chin and let out a slow breath. "Think of it as an archeological dig. We uncovered the first layer, now we keep going. Go back to the social media pages and look for secondary links."

"I'm not sure I understand you, Norrie," Stephanie said.

"Okay. See who their social media friends are and scope out their pages. See if anything on them links to Devora. Maybe she really ticked off a friend of a friend."

Stephanie widened her eyes and did that hair flip thing of hers. "Honestly, I don't think real detectives put in as much time."

"They don't have Deputy Hickman breathing down their necks. Meanwhile, I plan to have a little chitchat with Stefan. At first I wasn't going to say anything to him but I changed my mind. A few days ago I saw him get out of a black Mercedes in front of the Ramada. Long story. Canadian license plates. Stefan was supposed to be with the film crew in the vineyard."

"What were you doing at the Ramada?" Stephanie asked.

"My producer was in a huff because he didn't return her calls so I thought I'd check it out."

Cammy poured more juice in her glass and sipped. "More like scope it out if you ask me. So what do you think he was doing?"

I shrugged. "Something secretive or he would have told the crew he wasn't going to be on the set. And he would have called Renee, the producer."

"What makes you think he'll tell you?" she asked me.

"I don't. But I think it will unnerve him if he was up to something nefarious. And that's when people make mistakes."

Theo looked directly at me and held his gaze. "Don't you go slipping up. Don't confront him unless other people are around. As far as I'm concerned, anyone in that film crew could be our killer."

"You sound like Bradley. He wasn't all that thrilled when I told him my intentions either."

"With good reason," Theo said.

"Look, I won't barge over and confront Stefan. I'll be cunning and discreet."

The minute I said that, everyone made coughing, choking noises. "Very funny. I can be discreet. So, uh, are we all set for phase two? More digging?"

The three of them nodded and we agreed to catch up in a few days. "By the way, I'm adding the new director, Gordon Wable, to my list. He lied to me about his plane flight from Vancouver. He flew in from Toronto."

"That doesn't mean he murdered Devora," Cammy said. "Maybe he had business in Toronto."

"Then why lie about it?"

Cammy smiled slightly. "Perhaps it was something he didn't want your producer to know about. Or maybe his business in Toronto wasn't exactly on the up-and-up. Like an affair or something."

Suddenly I thought back to how he and Priscilla were practically cozying up to each other in our bistro. "Nah, any affair he's having is right under our noses."

• • •

Between the WOW meeting and swapping notes with Stephanie, Cammy, and Theo, I'd lost some decent screenwriting time. Still, it was an absolute necessity if I was going to escape unscathed from Deputy Hickman's clutches. *Motive, means, and opportunity.* Really? As if I could kill someone. I tried not to dwell on it when I got home and took out my laptop.

Charlie had eaten a full bowl of kibble and was snoring away in his dog bed. I plunked myself on the couch and picked up where I'd left off—in Wellfleet, Cape Cod. The perfect place for a summer romance.

If it wasn't for the fact my stomach began to grumble a few hours later, I would have stayed in Wellfleet. At least in my imagination. Dinner was the last thing I thought of when I got up in the morning, and unfortunately my choices were slim to none. Aside from bags of chips and some condiments in the fridge, I was left with only quinoa or oatmeal. Ugh. I'd neglected to purchase any real food during my last trip to Wegmans. And forget about my sister's health foods in the pantry. I might as well eat twigs and bark.

It was hard to tell if the sun had just set or if the clouds were particularly thick. It didn't matter. In another half hour or so, it would be dark. I looked at Charlie, who had moved from his dog bed to one of the chairs, and I said, "Want to take a ride to Wegmans with me?"

He immediately shot out of the chair and flew to the door. Yep, I'd spoiled Francine and Jason's dog all right. Sometimes I'd take him to

Wegmans, where he sat patiently in the car until I returned with a treat for him. Usually slices of turkey or ham.

I threw on a jacket, made sure to leave the kitchen light on and lock up, before getting into the Toyota. Charlie beat me to the punch by hopping across the driver's-side seat and into the back as soon as I opened the door.

As I headed down the driveway, Skylar, Mickey, and Rikesh cut across the parking lot to their van. I honked and Mickey waved back. He was the only one with a free hand. The thought of dealing with all that video and sound equipment while trekking across wet snow was as unpleasant as could be. I figured the others had already left for the day.

Unlike the slower-paced Monday night shopping, Thursday seemed to bring out all the pre-weekend warriors. I purchased deli meats, premade salads, and frozen chicken tenders along with some pork chops and seasoned bread crumbs. I added a fresh baked baguette to the mix and called it a night. Then I waited on register seven for what seemed like an eternity. Someone had trouble with their credit card, and after a few tries finally realized it was expired. Fortunately, they had another one in their wallet.

By the time Charlie and I got home, I was ready to tear into the deli meat rather than cook the chicken. The kitchen light was the only illumination in the house since I neglected to turn on the porch lights. It didn't matter. I could make my way into the house blindfolded.

Charlie raced to the kitchen door, and even with three plastic bags of groceries dangling from my arm, I unlocked the door and stepped inside. It was strange, but I had the feeling that something was *off*. Not quite right. Charlie must've agreed because he lifted his head up and began to sniff the air as if it was a new place, or, a new scent.

I stood absolutely still for a moment, not knowing quite what to expect, but nothing appeared to be out of the ordinary in the kitchen. Everything was as I'd left it, including my laptop on the kitchen table, exactly where I'd placed it when I got off the couch.

"We're being silly, Charlie," I said. "I mean, *I* don't smell anything different, but maybe it's the air from the heating system." I put the groceries in the refrigerator and shoved the plastic bags in the flowered bag holder that Francine bought at a craft show.

Charlie continued to sniff around the kitchen before doing the same in the living room. Then he darted up the stairs to the bedrooms, and that's when my overworked brain hit the top of the Richter scale.

With no real weapons to speak of, I reached under the sink and nabbed a can of wasp spray. Then I followed the dog upstairs. *Please don't let there be a crazed maniacal killer in the bedroom.*

I walked quietly but that seemed to make things worse. The sound of creaky wooden steps under my feet echoed in the stillness of the house. *Oh, hell. It's too late to do anything else.*

Charlie went from room to room sniffing and I followed him as if he was Rin Tin Tin, but deep down, I knew he was more like that hound dog from *The Beverly Hillbillies* rather than a trained German shepherd poised to attack.

My fingers shook as I held the wasp spray in front of me. Damn it. I should have left the house and called the sheriff.

Chapter 22

Nothing appeared to be out of place and there was no evidence of a break-in. Still, I had this uneasy feeling that someone had been in the house. Or, worse yet, was still there. I tightened my grip on the wasp spray and one by one opened the closets in the upstairs bedrooms. Meanwhile, Charlie continued to sniff around as if this was a new place and not his house.

"I'm checking under the beds," I told the dog. *And so help me, no one better reach out a hand and pull me under. I've read enough Stephen King, Dean Koontz, and Joe Hill.*

Three beds later, the only thing I discovered were dust bunnies. I made a mental note to buy one of those Swiffer mops. Then, off to the bathroom, where I pulled shower curtain aside as if I was about to reveal a prize on *Let's Make a Deal.* Again, nothing.

"We've still got the downstairs closets and the guest bathroom," I said out loud. Charlie followed me down the staircase and into the kitchen. The pantry looked exactly the same as it had when I left the house. Lots of bland health foods and canned goods.

Neither the coat closet nor the guest bathroom was hiding anyone, either. That left only one more place and I was damned if I dared go there alone. I knew it was still early enough for Don and Theo to be up, so I called them. "Hey, I'm really sorry to bother you, but I came back from Wegmans and it felt like someone had been in the house."

Theo's voice was at least two decibels louder than usual. "What do you mean *felt like*? Was anything broken? Moved?"

"No, it was more like a creepy feeling. Charlie sensed it, too. He's been sniffing all over the place."

"Did you call the sheriff's office?"

"And what? Tell Deputy Hickman I had a funny feeling? The door was locked when I got home and all the windows were closed. Without any sign of a break-in, he'd have my head."

"Yeah, sorry. You're right. Don and I are on our way. Look, I don't want to panic you, but someone may still be there. Wait by the kitchen door in case you have to make a run for it."

"Thanks. That's very encouraging. Hurry up. Now I'm even more freaked out."

I stood by the door and watched the driveway for car lights. In the dim porch lighting, I could see wet snow beginning to fall. *Terrific. Another fun night in the Finger Lakes.* Although Don and Theo's house was only about a mile down the driveway, it felt as if they lived on the other side of the lake.

Just then, car lights got closer, and within seconds I heard the doors slam shut.

"We're here!" Don shouted as he marched to the door. "Flashlight and all."

"And we brought ammo," Theo added as he waved a baseball bat in the air.

"Not a single thing was touched in the house," I said, "but something feels wrong. The only place I didn't look was the basement. I didn't want to go down there alone."

"Wait here, Norrie," Don said. "If we're not back in three minutes, call the militia."

I opened the door to the basement, flipped on the light, and stepped back so Don and Theo could have a clear path downstairs.

"So far only wine racks and cobwebs," Don yelled. "Oh, look! Oh, my gosh!"

"What? What?" I shrieked. "What did you find?"

"Elderberry jam. Francine canned elderberry jam. I thought she only did raspberry and strawberry."

Then I heard Theo's voice, "Oh, for goodness sake, forget the jam and keep looking."

I held my breath and waited while I heard what sounded like furniture being moved. Finally, Don spoke. "You may have a few valuable antiques down here but there's no sign of life. Unless, of course, you count the spiders."

"Yuck. I hate spiders," I said. "No matter how many lectures Godfrey gives me about how helpful they are. Listen, grab some elderberry jam while you're down there. It's the least I can do."

Theo leaned the baseball bat against the frame of the basement door and took a seat at the kitchen table. "You can relax. No one's here."

"Make sure the eye-latch on the top of the door is secured or the door will swing open. I've got to get it fixed one of these days. Along with the pantry door next to it. Nothing like an old farmhouse, huh?"

Theo glanced at the door. "It's secure. They're both secure."

"I feel like an idiot," I said. "But honestly, I had a very real feeling someone had been in the house. And Charlie never acts like that. He usually wolfs down his food, passes gas, and finds a place to sleep."

"Gee, just like Don."

"Very funny," Don replied from the other side of the kitchen. He stood by the window and looked out. "That wet snow is really coming down. Too early for Neville. Unless it's the opening act. Listen, we should get going. Tomorrow's Friday and it's usually a busy day, snowstorms or not."

It was true. For some odd reason, whenever the newscasters predicted a snowstorm, people flocked to three places—supermarkets, gas stations, and wineries. If you were going to be cooped up in a house for days on end, they might as well be pleasurable.

I thanked Don and Theo and watched as their rear lights disappeared into the thick wet snow. Then I made myself a turkey and cheese sandwich, making sure to give Charlie his fair share.

Too wired to have another look-see at my screenplay, I turned on the TV and channel surfed until the late news came on. According to one of the anchors on Channel 8, "Investigators are still pouring through evidence in the murder of Canadian film director Devora Dobrowski." Then, as if Two Witches and Gable Hill didn't have enough notoriety, she went on to reiterate all the details and even flashed a map of the Seneca Lake Wine Trail on the screen with arrows pointing to our location. Heck, she might as well have helicoptered in the next wave of curiosity seekers as far as I was concerned.

"I suppose this will make Henry Speltmore happy," I told Charlie. "But he doesn't have to deal with the crazies."

The dog looked up from the edge of the couch and went back to sleep. I flipped channels for another ten minutes before shutting off the TV and ambling up the stairs to bed with Charlie at my heels. When Don and Theo had left, I made sure the door was locked and even shoved a chair against it, even though I knew I was being ridiculous.

The combination of crummy weather and stress had given me a slight head cold, so when I crawled into bed and turned off the lights, I realized I needed a tissue for my nose. I fumbled for the drawer on my nightstand and dug around for the wad of tissues I kept there. No sense turning on the bedside lamp. By now, I knew the drill.

My hand felt the tissue but it also felt something thin and hard. Other than tissues, a roll of Tums, and a tube of hand cream, I didn't have anything else in that drawer. I continued to feel the object against my fingertips but I was positive I was mistaken.

I pulled the small cord to the lamp, sat up and opened the drawer wider. Leaning over, I got a good look at the object and froze. The tips of my fingers began to shake, and next thing I knew the rest of my body followed suit. I told myself to *get a grip* and that there was a logical explanation for everything. Only, in this case, the logical explanation meant that someone had indeed been in my house.

Resting on a bed of wadded up facial tissues was a pair of wingtip tortoiseshell glasses with oval-shaped jeweled rims. The zircon stones (at least I thought they were zircon) flashed brilliantly under the bedside's LED lamplight. If I wasn't so panic-stricken, I might have admired them.

I shoved the drawer shut and took slow, deep breaths. It didn't help. My hands shook and I swore my eye had developed a tic. The last time, and only time, I had seen those tortoiseshell wingtip glasses, they were on Devora Dobrowski's face. It was when she made her grand entrance into Two Witches to complain about the noise.

Now, they were sitting in my nightstand, all but shouting, "Hey, Deputy Hickman, here's some new evidence in the Dobrowski murder."

Chapter 23

The thought that someone had been in my nightstand, let alone in my bedroom, was creepy as hell. The rational part of my brain insisted Devora's killer was trying to frame me for her murder by planting evidence, while the irrational part of my brain conjured up more *Tales from the Darkside* than Glenda could ever come up with. Both scenarios were frightening.

"I can't call Deputy Hickman," I told Charlie. "He'll think I'm making the whole thing up. No evidence of a break-in and yet Devora's glasses wind up in my nightstand. He'll think I concealed evidence and later regretted it so I came up with a ludicrous story to cover my butt."

The dog lifted his head from the pillow on the opposite side of my bed and went back to sleep.

"Wake up, Charlie," I said. "It's time for a house inspection."

This time I wasn't as nervous as I was when I got home from Wegmans. Don, Theo, and I had already been through the place and no one was lurking about. Whoever left me that *present* was long gone. What I needed to find out was how they got into my house in the first place.

"Forget the second floor, dog. Our intruder isn't Spiderman. And forget the basement. No one can fit through those narrow leaded windows. Heck, those windows were here before prohibition. That leaves the downstairs. What do you say we find out how someone got in?"

Had I been in the mood for a YouTube video, I would have filmed the dog as he got off the bed. He moved so slowly, as if to defy gravity.

"Come on, Charlie," I whined. "This should only take a few minutes."

The dog followed me downstairs, and even though I wasn't exactly shaking in my boots, I still flipped on every light switch I passed. The front and kitchen doors weren't tampered with and the dead-bolt locks were undisturbed. That left the windows. There were four of them in the living room and two in the kitchen. All were double hung with more than enough room for anyone in the "big and tall' category to climb through.

None of the windows were opened and nothing around them had been disturbed. Still, someone found a way inside. I took a breath and began in the kitchen. My father had added sash locks to all of the windows when I was little. Apparently, whoever lived here before hadn't felt the need to have locking windows. After finding Devora's glasses, I wanted to replace those sash locks with the kind that are keyed. *This isn't Mayberry anymore.*

Not only were the kitchen windows closed, they were firmly locked. Charlie and I walked into the living room and began our search clockwise from the left. Well, I began our search. Charlie hopped back on the couch and sprawled out.

The first two windows were sealed shut like the ones in the kitchen, but when I walked past the couch to the window facing the woods, the sash wasn't secured in its place. It wasn't obvious from a few feet away so it was no wonder Don, Theo, and I hadn't noticed it at first. I stared at the window for what seemed like ages and then I remembered something. It was insignificant at the time but now, not so much.

It was at least two weeks ago. I was watching TV when Charlie cut loose with an odor that put a sewage processing plant to shame. I remembered getting off the couch and opening the window. What I didn't remember was to lock it once I'd shut it after the odor dissipated. Whoever got into the house didn't break and enter, they simply entered thanks to my carelessness. And Charlie's penchant for passing gas.

To make matters worse, there were no obstructions in front of the window, unlike the others, which were behind small end tables or large ferns. That meant I had made it easier for whoever snuck in. Heck, I might as well have posted a sign that read *Sneak in here.*

I immediately locked the window sash, because whoever got inside had no need to touch the mechanism. Then I stared at the window, not sure of what to do next. Finally, I checked the last window and found it to be locked like the other two in the room.

"It's too dark and too wet to go outside and look for a clue," I said to Charlie. "But that's the first thing I intend to do as soon as I get up."

The dog trotted behind me as I made my way upstairs for the second time that night. There wasn't a doubt in my mind that someone was setting me up. After tossing around in bed for at least an hour, I came to the conclusion that it had to be Devora's killer and that he or she needed someone else to take the blame. Or worse yet, it was someone trying to protect the killer. Someone who was willing to break into a house at all costs. Either way, it was as unsettling as all get-up-and-go and I was stymied as to what my next move should be.

It was no wonder I had a fitful night's sleep. Every little creak in the house, combined with the wind from Neville's precursor, gave me the willies. When I was little, my parents told me it was the house settling. But honestly, how many years does a house need to settle?

• • •

The next morning I called Don and Theo, only to hear Don say, "You need to call Deputy Hickman. Explain about the window sash."

Then Theo got on the phone. "Where are Devora's glasses now?"

"In my nightstand. I may never open that drawer again. Let Francine deal with it when they come back from Costa Rica in June."

"Ignoring something doesn't make it go away."

"Oh, yes, it does. Ask any of my old high school boyfriends."

"Would you feel better if Don and I called him?"

"He'd only tell you it was secondhand information and if I had an issue, I should be the one to call the public safety building."

"He's right," Theo said. "Call him. Someone was in your house planting evidence. Maybe the sheriff's office can send a forensic team to dust for prints."

"Okay, fine. But if Grizzly Gary brushes me off, Devora's glasses stay right where they are."

"He's not going to give you the brush-off. Look, if that intruder was diabolical enough to plant Devora's glasses in your nightstand, they'd have no qualms calling the sheriff's office with a tip that you were concealing evidence. It could go as simple as them telling Hickman they overheard you talking about hiding the glasses until the transfer station opened for garbage drop-off."

"Are you serious?"

Theo's voice got louder. "Do the words *search warrant* mean anything to you?"

"Yeah. They're right up there with the words *bail money*."

"Call him. And let us know what happened."

"Fine."

In spite of the fact I had told Charlie I intended to check for clues when it got light out, I changed my mind. The snow had stopped but the ground was covered with enough of that thick, mushy stuff to make it impossible to find footprints in the once muddy area under the window. Ugh. I had no choice. It was Deputy Hickman or no one.

Gladys Pipp was off for the day, or at least I thought she was off when another woman answered the non-emergency line and connected me immediately to Deputy Hickman. Usually Gladys chitchats for a while and lets me know what kind of mood the deputy is in. The new woman threw me to the lions without a clue.

"There's no easy way to explain this," I said to Deputy Hickman, "but I seem to have come across the victim's wingtip eyewear in my house."

"You hadn't mentioned Mrs. Dobrowski having been inside your house, Miss Ellington."

"She wasn't. Only her glasses."

There was an inordinately long pause at the other end of the line, and for a minute I thought he'd hung up on me. "The glasses. Help me understand this. You found Mrs. Dobrowski's glasses in your house."

"Yes. In my nightstand. By the bed. Under some wadded-up tissues. I found them last night."

"Let's take a step back, Miss Ellington. Was there any sign of a break-in?"

"Not last night. I mean, I didn't find a sign of a break-in last night and I had Don and Theo from the Grey Egret come over to check out the house with me."

"I see. You called them when you discovered the glasses."

"Um, no. At that point, I hadn't discovered the glasses."

"I'm quite confused. Why were the owners of the Grey Egret checking out your house if there was no sign of a break-in and you hadn't yet found the glasses?"

"I went to Wegmans and took the dog with me. When I got back, it felt like someone had been in the house. The dog felt it, too. He sniffed the air."

"Miss Ellington, dogs are constantly sniffing the air. And you said there was no sign of a forcible break-in?"

"Yes. No sign. Until late last night. After Don and Theo left, I rechecked the windows and one of them was unlocked. A living room window. Facing the back of the house. Maybe there are footprints under the snow. A good forensic team would know."

"Miss Ellington, allow me to backtrack for a moment. Are you absolutely certain those glasses belonged to the victim? Maybe your sister owns a similar pair."

"Francine? Bejeweled glasses? Not on your life. They're Devora's all right. She was wearing them when she came into our winery to complain about the noise during the first day of filming."

"Hmm, according to my notes, that's when you threatened her."

"It wasn't a threat. More like a retort. And I'm the one who's feeling threatened. The dead woman's eyewear was in my nightstand."

"I have another call to make this morning. As soon as I'm done, I'll stop by to pick up the glasses. Don't touch them."

"Will you be bringing a forensic team?"

"Miss Ellington, consider yourself lucky I'm not bringing a search warrant."

Chapter 24

It was too early to mosey into the tasting room and spread my tale of woe to the staff so I made myself some toast while I waited it out for Deputy Hickman to arrive. I kept telling myself it's a pair of glasses and not a murder confession, but I wondered how Grizzly Gary would interpret my find.

Too antsy for screenwriting, I tackled a project I should have done days ago—drawing up the suspect map. I wasn't totally unfamiliar with the process, but this time I needed to approach it differently. I needed a way to visualize the connections among the suspects as well as some space for background information. That meant coming up with a graphic that looked more like a humungous analog clock rather than a whiteboard with my usual crisscross lines.

After mulling it over for a few minutes, I finally had an epiphany. Well, not exactly an epiphany, but an idea. If I were to tape construction paper over the large oval mirror in the guest bathroom, I could draw a stylized clock face with suspects instead of numbers. Counting the film crew and the actors, plus Gerard and Gordon, that would make eight. Plenty of room. And plenty of room for their side connections as well. Devora, of course, would be smack dab in the middle. My arrows would replace clock hands and I could color-code them as well according to what we knew and what we needed to know.

Without wasting a second, I dredged up sheets of construction paper from the pantry. Jason apparently used them for whatever the heck he did with his entomology work. With transparent tape and scissors, I had completed my bathroom masterpiece in a half hour. As far as guests were concerned, they didn't need a mirror to wash and dry their hands.

One by one, I added the names, clockwise from the right—Stefan, Skylar, Mickey, Rikesh, Gavin, Priscilla, Gerard, and Gordon. Then I wrote Devora's name in the center of my suspect clock.

Under each name, I wrote what Stephanie, Theo, and Cammy had found out. That was the easy part. Under Priscilla's name, I added, "Petrified Devora would ruin her career," and under Gavin's, "Threatened Devora having been blacklisted by her." I only needed one word under Gerard's—*money.*

Then I scribbled a secondary link. The first of many if Stephanie, Cammy, and Theo continued to dig. I wrote Bailey Wagner's name under Devora's with the note "Put her career on ice according to Priscilla," and again under Mickey's with the note, "Linked with Bailey on Facebook." I also added an asterisk that read, "Small part in one of my screenplays."

If nothing else, I was beginning to fill in the clock face. I paused for a moment, wondering whether or not to link Priscilla with Gordon since they appeared to be rather cozy both times they came into the winery, but I decided not to. Not yet anyway.

Just then I heard three loud raps on the door. For the life of me, I wondered why no one, especially our vineyard workers, ever used the bell. Granted, it was small and located to the left of the door instead of the right, but it *was* visible.

I knew it had to be Deputy Hickman and I immediately shut the bathroom light off and closed the door before racing to the kitchen to let him inside. The morose look on his face, coupled with the dismal gray sky, made for a most unwelcoming sight.

"Um, come on in," I said. "Thanks for picking up the eyeglasses."

"Thanks for picking up the eyeglasses?" I'm making it sound as if he stopped by to get the laundry.

Before he could answer, I added, "I know this seems preposterous. I mean, the eyeglasses in my nightstand and no real sign of a break-in except for an unlocked window. Please don't think for a minute I had anything to do with Devora's death and that I was withholding evidence. Why would I withhold it? If I killed her, I'd certainly dispose of those ugly wingtips and not call attention to myself. And then again, why would I have told Stephanie Ipswich there was a body in her pond if I was the one who put it there?"

For some inexplicable reason, I couldn't stop talking. I was digging myself deeper and deeper into an abyss with no way to climb out. "Uh, you can stop me at any time," I mumbled, "I think I've said enough."

Deputy Hickman stepped into the kitchen and closed the door behind him. "Indeed. Frankly, Miss Ellington, that story of yours is so outrageous, so unbelievable, and so, well, impossible to fathom, that I genuinely do believe you're not fabricating it."

"What? You believe me?"

"Much as I hate to admit it, I do. Even with your particular skill set for writing screenplays, I doubt you could come up with something like this. Let's not waste time, show me where those eyeglasses are."

Charlie, who didn't bother to get up from his dog bed, watched as the deputy and I tromped up the stairs to my bedroom. I pointed to my nightstand from the doorway and stepped back to let him go through.

"Um, there are some yucky wadded-up tissues in there so you may want to use gloves or something."

"I'm collecting evidence, Miss Ellington. Donning gloves is protocol, as is placing the object in question in a special self-sealing plastic bag."

I didn't say a word while he picked up the glasses and put them in the bag. Then, as he turned to face me, the sides of his mouth formed a smile. "I see what you mean. Knowing your sister, these do not appear to be something she would have selected for eyewear."

"Go ahead and say it. They're horrible. Tacky and ostentatious. And I'm positive they're Devora's."

"Identifying the eyewear may be the easiest part of this investigation. The enigma, however, of how someone could have gotten into your house without leaving as much as a single clue defies reason. Are you sure nothing was disturbed?"

I nodded. "You can see for yourself. Come on, I'll show you the window that I accidently left unlocked."

Deputy Hickman thundered down the stairs in front of me.

"It's over there," I pointed. "In the living room."

He placed the plastic evidence bag on the kitchen table and proceeded to follow me into the living room.

"You've got hardwood floors. The kind that show every bit of dirt and wet spots if you don't wipe your shoes or take them off at the door. It was snowing yesterday, well into the evening. Are you certain you didn't see any wet footprints when you came inside?"

My God. He sounds like Francine.

"Um, I wasn't exactly looking."

"You would have noticed. The change in the wood's color is obvious."

"I didn't notice anything. And neither did Don and Theo. Don's very observant. Very particular. Theo, not so much, but Don—"

"I get it, Miss Ellington. There must be something else going on."

With that, he walked over to the window in question but remained a good yard or so away. "I wiped my boots when I came through the door. Your mat is the kind that absorbs water. Must be your sister and brother-in-law are a bit more, shall we say, discerning."

As opposed to my slovenliness?

"And look in front of that doggie door. It has one of those mats as well."

Terrific. Francine and Jason get the Good Housekeeping Award of the year.

Deputy Hickman rubbed his chin and took a step closer to the window. Then he reached into his pocket and pulled out a small flashlight that he shone on the floor.

"Aha! Seems there was an intruder after all."

"Huh? What? I don't see anything."

"Don't get any closer or you'll destroy the evidence."

"What evidence?" I asked, although it came out more like a whine. "I don't see any evidence."

"Whoever opened that window and crawled inside was either a thoughtful intruder or a cunning one. He or she placed a small mat or maybe even a towel on the floor so as to hide any evidence of footprints. Look closely. There's a rim of dust and grime around the edges of where such a mat or towel had been placed. Very cunning indeed."

In that entire batch of suspects, there were only two people whom I thought would be so fastidious—Stefan and Priscilla. Stefan practically reeked of obsessive compulsivity and Priscilla was, well . . . kind of prissy in a girly sort of way. No so much personality, but mannerisms. And choice of personal care products like the pink tissue. It was perfectly folded when she pulled it out of her pocket the first day of filming.

"Does this mean you'll be sending a forensic team over to dust for prints?"

"Yes, Miss Ellington. I'll call my office and we'll have them send someone over. I'm not optimistic, however. If our intruder was mindful enough to use a mat or a towel for footprints, he or she most assuredly wore gloves. And as for any evidence outside the house, I'm afraid the wet snow took care of that. We wouldn't even be able to see footprints leading back to the road."

"Now what do I do?"

"Keep your windows locked and your doors as well. I noticed you've got a sturdy double bolt on both entrance doors. Good. And I'd keep that dog fence of yours locked as well. No sense taking a chance someone could crawl through the doggie door."

Charlie's going to hate that if he's fenced in. Bad enough he goes nuts during hunting season.

"It would have to be someone really petite," I said. "Hmm, when I went to Wegmans I pulled the plastic lid over the doggie door, so even if someone thought to use it, they wouldn't have been able to. Oh, well. It doesn't matter. They got in anyway."

"If that's all, Miss Ellington, I need to be on my way. I'll have the forensic team phone you when they're on the way."

"Uh, you have my cell number, right? Have them call that number or the winery. I have to head over there."

"Understood. And one more thing. Try to stay out of this investigation. I know how tempting it may be for you to play juvenile sleuth or whatever they call it these days, but we're dealing with a killer."

• • •

I gave a nod and walked Grizzly Gary to the kitchen door. The minute he left I pulled it shut and bolted the lock. All in all, it was a pretty decent visit. Without him saying it out loud, I was pretty positive I was no longer a person of interest. Then again, I could have been delusional.

Chapter 25

Glenda gasped and covered her throat with her free hand when I told her and Cammy what I had discovered next to my bed. She placed the pitcher of water she was holding on one of the tasting room tables, bent down, and spit on the floor three times. I'm not sure she actually spat as much as made the motions.

"Unsettled spirits or vengeful spirits find a way to communicate from the beyond," she said. Her voice was softer than usual and it quivered.

I wanted to inform the tasting room staff of the latest intrigue in Devora's murder so I made the trek across the wet snow to share the news. However, judging from Glenda's reaction, I should have held off.

"It's not a spirit from the dead," I said. "Deputy Hickman found evidence of an intruder in my house."

At that point, the two customers from Sam's table headed to the gift racks and he immediately hustled over to where Cammy, Glenda, and I stood. "This I gotta hear," he said. "I only caught bits and pieces. What's this about finding a dead woman's glasses in your drawer?"

"We might as well let Lizzie in on it, too," I replied. "And one of you can tell Roger when he comes in tomorrow. As for Fred and Emma, they'll get an earful when I grab something to eat."

We moved to the cash register, where Lizzie stood, but before I could say a word, Glenda spoke. "Devora's evil spirit is lurking in Norrie's house. Leaving remnants of the earthly world."

Sam cocked his head and laughed. "Give me a break. Someone's messing with Norrie. If you ask me, Devora struggled with an attacker and her glasses fell off. Probably right before she got strangled and dumped in the pond."

"I get that part," I said, "but why stash the glasses in my house, in a place where I'd be sure to find them?"

"To cast suspicion on you," Lizzie remarked. "Nancy Drew would have come to that conclusion instantly. I wouldn't be at all surprised if the sheriff's office receives an anonymous call telling them someone overheard you bragging about having those glasses."

"Hmm. Theo said something similar but I wasn't convinced."

Glenda shook her head. "It's Devora's spirit. Can't any of you sense the unrest and turmoil in the air?" Then she looked directly at me. "I know you don't want to burn sage sticks for a ritualistic cleansing, but will you at least consider a warding-off-evil chant? Zenora can perform one this afternoon. She's quite accomplished with that ritual."

"Absolutely not. She'll frighten the customers away from the winery."

"Not the winery, Norrie. Your house. You need to purify your house."

How good is Zenora with vacuuming?

"Okay, fine. I give up. Send her over. After six. And tell her to make it a quick chant, not a Broadway production."

I couldn't believe I had just invited one of Glenda's lunatic cronies to come to my house in order to purify it from a nonexistent evil presence. Still, if that's what it would take to get Glenda off my back, I'd put up with Zenora.

"By the way," I asked, "has any of the film crew been in?"

"In and out this morning," Sam replied. "They downed their coffee as if they were chugging beers and out the door they all went. Lots of black coffee to go as well. I was sitting off to the side of the bistro when they got here. Overheard the director say something about 'needing to finish up quickly.' At first I thought he was referring to the filming and the hype about that storm. Next thing I know, Priscilla started to cry. Not loud sobs or anything, but crying is crying. And then she said, 'I did everything I could to speed things up.'"

Cammy crossed her arms and glared at Sam. "You heard all that and didn't tell us?"

"You were all busy. Besides, what was I going to tell you? Black coffees and a loosely strung actress?"

"Never mind," I said. "You guys better get back to the tasting room tables. Looks like more customers walked in while we were talking."

Glenda and Sam took off for their tables but Cammy hung back. She took me by the elbow and motioned for the kitchen. I gave Lizzie a quick wave and followed Cammy.

"Don't tell me what you're thinking," I said, "because I already know how ridiculous it is to have Zenora at the house."

"Not that. Zenora's harmless as can be. Nuttier than a fruitcake at Christmas, but benign. I'm worried about who really *was* in your house."

We plunked ourselves at the table and I propped my head on my elbow. "I've got it narrowed down to Priscilla and Stefan. The person who snuck in was extremely tidy."

Cammy listened as I spelled out the details. Listened and groaned at the same time. "Bummer. Too bad Sam couldn't have heard the rest of Priscilla's conversation."

"No, but Zenora might."

"Huh? Now you've lost me."

"Honestly, if Glenda hadn't mentioned Zenora, I wouldn't have thought of this. Zenora reads tea leaves. *And heaven knows what else.* All I need to do is find a way for her to read Priscilla's tea leaves and get Priscilla to open up about the murder. Deep down I don't think she's our murderess, but she may have had a role in protecting the culprit. Like sneaking into my place with those hideous glasses."

"Why would she do a thing like that?"

"To protect someone who may be protecting *her* career. Have you noticed how cozy she and Gordon are?"

"Suppose that is the case. How are you going to get Zenora to read Priscilla's tea leaves?"

"I'm not sure. If you haven't noticed, I'm not the best with details, but I'll come up with a plan."

Again, Cammy groaned. "What about Stefan? Didn't you say you thought he might have been responsible?"

"And then some. Which reminds me, I need to call Godfrey. He's checking on something else for me."

"Holy cannoli, Norrie. I've seen squid with fewer tentacles than the ones you've got going with this snooping around of yours. And please don't tell me you plan to have Zenora read Stefan's tea leaves as well."

"Good grief, no. I plan to outright ask Stefan if he snuck into my house. After all, I did see him sneak out of that Mercedes."

"Good luck with that. And by the way, pick a public place. Like the winery. Not the vineyard."

"Don't worry. I have no intention of becoming the next pond victim."

I ordered a roasted turkey on brioche bun at the bistro and shared the information about Devora's glasses with Fred and Emma.

"Make sure you keep that house locked as tight as could be," Fred said. "Whoever snuck in was downright brazen. Too bad you couldn't have Charlie swap places with Alvin. That goat wouldn't put up with any nonsense."

"And *I* wouldn't put up with that goat. He still spits at me whenever I walk by."

Fred's roasted turkey sandwich all but melted in my mouth and I seriously considered ordering a second one when my phone vibrated. It was a text from the forensic department informing me that a lab technician was on the way to my house.

"I've got to get back to the house, guys," I said to Fred and Emma. "Deputy Hickman sent a lab tech to check for prints. Maybe we'll get lucky."

We didn't. I knew I was in trouble when the technician rubbed the back of his neck after attempting to find fingerprints on the window using colored powder and a black light. I was intent on watching his technique in case I ever wanted to try it myself. The guy looked like a taller, thinner version of Godfrey Klein but without the receding hairline. Same light hair and round face though.

"Sorry to inform you," he said, "but I can't seem to pull a single print. Frankly, I didn't expect to find an obvious one but I hoped to secure a latent print or a partial. I'll tell you what's odd, though, whoever opened your window and got inside not only wore gloves but must have used one of those window cleaning cloths to make sure no residue of any kind was left behind."

"Window cleaning cloths? Like towels?"

"No, those have fibers that would give us some evidence. I'm talking the streak-free microfiber cloths that you can get on Amazon or at any hardware store. I take it you don't clean the windows much, do you?"

Oh, brother. What is it with these guys and housecleaning? First Grizzly Gary, now this guy.

Then, if that wasn't enough, the man walked to the adjacent window and ushered me over. "What do you see?" he asked.

I shrugged. "A window."

"Look closely. You can see specks of dust and some smudges. Nothing out of the ordinary, but compared to the window we presume the intruder used, it's absolutely teaming with filth. Too bad it wasn't the one in question or I would have had a field day."

Wonderful. A window teaming with filth. I'll need to get a cleaning service in here before Francine and Jason get back.

"Um, yeah. So, uh, now what?"

"I'll look around outside but don't hold your breath. The ground's covered with wet snow. I'll let you know when I'm done."

With that, the technician gathered the materials he'd used on the window, returned them to a small black suitcase, and slipped on his jacket. He was out the kitchen door before I had the chance to ask him if he was able to pull any prints from Devora's glasses. I mean, how long could that possibly take? Grizzly Gary had left with that hideous monstrosity hours ago.

While I waited for the lab guy to examine the exterior window, I played the two messages that were left on the landline. I was so preoccupied with the forensic house call, I had completely forgotten to check the message center for the phone.

The first message was Renee's, brief and devoid of emotion. "Gordon called. They've completed the filming. He's going to review the video with Skylar but he doesn't expect any redos. The crew is still officially retained in the area until they can be cleared. Thanks, Norrie."

Terrific. Now how am I going to get Zenora to read Priscilla's tea leaves?

The next message was from Godfrey, and the animation in his voice made up for Renee's monotone. "Forget Uncle Joe's. You owe me a five-star dinner. I'm thinking steakhouse in Canandaigua. I found out who owns that black Mercedes. Call me."

I never picked up a phone receiver faster in my life and I had all but one of Godfrey's numbers punched in when the lab tech knocked on the kitchen door. "I might have found something. It's a note that got stuck to some branches in one of the berry bushes by the window. It could have blown in from anywhere but it's written on a memo pad that says 'Ramada Inn.' If I'm not mistaken, isn't that where the victim was staying?"

"Hold on!" I shouted. I flung the door open and held out my hand. "Show me."

"I can't do that. It's evidence now. Or it could be."

"Is it in one piece? Does it have a date? Is it signed?"

He held up a clear plastic bag and smiled. "It's wet but it's in one piece."

Chapter 26

"Well? Don't just stand there. Come back in and read it to me. For all we know, the tidy obsessive-compulsive intruder who broke into my house might not have been so careful after all."

The lab guy took a step inside and closed the door. I snatched the plastic bag out of his hand before he knew it and looked at the bold print on the top. "Yeah, it's a Ramada Inn room memo pad all right, but any of the tourists on Seneca Lake could have written it. We just held the Wine and Cheese weekend. A zillion people. Give me a second."

The lab guy shifted his weight from foot to foot. "Are you satisfied? Whoever wrote it underscored it with a lipstick. We can have a field day with that in the lab. Lipstick is one of those substances that absorbs everything it comes in contact with."

One look at the lipstick and I froze. "I've seen that crimson color before. On the murder victim's face. When she was alive." *Alive and accosting me at the winery.* "Oh, my gosh. It had to have been written by Devora. That's the dead woman. Did you read what it said?"

"'Meet me at the watering hole' or something to that effect."

I handed him the bag and all but gave him a hug. "No doubt in my mind. This was written by Devora. The victim. Not a random tourist. Holy cow! Did you read it carefully? It says, 'Agreed. Pick the time. It better be a scenic watering hole for a reshoot.' Reshoot! Scenic watering hole! The Ipswiches' irrigation pond! Whoever had Devora's note in their possession is the killer. You have to call Deputy Hickman right this minute."

"He'll get my report. There are procedures, you know."

"Look, whoever killed Devora lured her to that pond. She probably didn't want anyone else in the film crew to know she was reconsidering the location for the shoot. She couldn't say anything out loud so she wrote a note on a memo pad. Heck, everyone takes those things from hotel rooms. I think it's included in the price."

The lab guy rolled his eyes and started to say something but I kept talking. “Don’t you get it? Most likely the killer stuffed the note in a coat pocket and it fell out. Take a good look at it. It wasn’t wadded up like trash.”

“Uh-huh. I need to get going. I only gather the evidence.”

“If you must know,” I said, “Deputy Hickman and I aren’t exactly on the best of terms. I think he considers me to be nosy and intrusive.”

The lab guy rubbed his chin and stared at me. “Uh-huh.”

“And he doesn’t like me speculating or theorizing.”

“Uh-huh.”

“So you’ll call him, right?”

“I’ll follow the protocol outlined by the Yates County Sheriff’s Office. Don’t worry, he’ll get a full report.”

On what? The brand of lipstick?

“You have to call him. Like now. Like right now. You need to compare the lipstick on that note with Devora’s. I guarantee it’ll be a match. Not many women can get away with wearing vampire red lipstick. Listen, I know Devora’s purse was in the van. It’s got to be in some evidence locker by now. Get the purse, find her lipstick, and do whatever it is you do in order to make the comparison. Hurry.”

“I’m the only technician in the lab today and right now my immediate concern is writing that report.”

“To hell with the damn report. Do something useful. Find the killer. Do I need to hunt you down and make sure you do that? ”

I’ve seen people run during all sorts of sprints and relays, but the lab guy had them beat by a mile. He raced to his car without even a simple, “See you” or “Bye.” In retrospect, I may have been a bit overly zealous.

I didn’t hold out any great hope that he or any member of the forensic department would immediately process the evidence, but I was sure of one thing—that note came from Devora Dobrowski and not her restless spirit, as Glenda would profess. Like it or not, that part of the puzzle would have to wait, unlike Godfrey’s discovery.

I picked up the landline and dialed his number, anxious to find out who was behind the wheel of that Mercedes and what possible connection they could have to Stefan. Drat! The call went to Godfrey's voicemail, directing me to leave a message or to call the entomology department's main line if it was an emergency.

What kind of emergency? Stink bugs in the pantry? Been there.

I groaned and, trying not to sound too whiny, asked Godfrey to please call me the minute he got my message.

Zenora wasn't due for another couple of hours so I used that time to boil spaghetti for dinner, work on my screenplay, and review the suspect clock I had completed in the guest bathroom. Under Devora's name I added, "Left cryptic note with time and place for killer."

True, I wasn't a hundred percent certain it was Devora's note, but honestly, who else could have written it? Not Priscilla. Her shade of lipstick was more peachy. Pinkish even, but certainly not blood-spattering red. And as far as I could tell, none of the men were into crossdressing. It had to have come from Devora. Maybe Deputy Hickman would run a handwriting analysis but I didn't count on it.

Meanwhile, I had to find an unobtrusive way for Zenora to read Priscilla's tea leaves and find out if the actress was the one who snuck into my bedroom. And if so, who was she protecting and why? With the filming over, there was no reason for her to return to the winery, unless, of course, I could come up with one. And if I did, it would have to be convincing.

I added Ragu sauce to my spaghetti and opened one of Francine's packets of soy-a-meal meat-like crumbles. I was too lazy to prepare a meal that took more than two or three steps, and I was way too tired to head back to the bistro. With enough sauce and grated cheese, the soy crumbles could almost pass as meat.

With the dishes done, I returned to my screenplay and waited it out for Godfrey's call and Zenora's visit. Outside, wet snow began to fall with more intensity than it had during the earlier part of the day. It was that heavy, yucky stuff that called for studded snow tires, or at the very least newer treads. I figured by Sunday we'd be socked in if the hype about Neville turned out to be true.

Sometimes we'd get forecasts predicting record snow, only to wind up with a few inches and feeble excuses about changes in the jet stream. I wondered if Neville would hold up.

I returned my gaze from the window back to the laptop when two things happened at once. I heard a weird screeching noise from the front of the house at the exact moment the phone rang.

"Probably an owl," I said to Charlie as I got up and walked to the landline. No sooner had I answered than the outside noise got louder.

"It's Godfrey. Are your bird-in-distress machines running, because I can hear them in the background."

"Um, I hear it, too, but it's not our machines. We only run those during the harvest to prevent anything with feathers from eating the grapes before we can pick them. Give me a second. It's still light out. I'll take a peek and see what's going on."

I put the receiver on the table and walked to the front window. A few yards away, a woman clad in a long yellow cape with bizarre renderings of suns, moons, and stars was circling the house, lifting her arms in the air and spreading them out as she continued to walk around the building. She paused at intervals and assumed what looked like yoga warrior poses.

That wasn't the worst part. The worst part was the chant. It sounded like a combination of keening, screeching, and yowling. I stood by the window with my mouth wide open until I remembered Godfrey was still on the line. I hurried to the phone and took a breath. "It's Zenora. Glenda's friend. Doing a ritualistic house cleansing. Apparently she decided to start outside."

"Yeesh. Zenora. I remember her from that reading of your wine distributor's will. Is her hair still whirling around her face like a giant tumbleweed?"

"I can't really tell. She's wearing some sort of bizarre head covering. Looks like a turban that started to unroll."

"Why on earth is she there in the first place? You don't believe in that stuff."

"True, but Glenda wouldn't let it go so I figured what would be the harm to have Zenora come over." Just then, the most horrific, bone-chilling wail cut through the walls of the house like a blade. "Hang on, I better go check this out."

Back to the window I went, only Zenora was out of my sight line. I ran to the kitchen window, and sure enough there was Zenora, only this time in a pose that would defy the most accomplished yoga instructor. I opened the door and shouted, "What happened?"

Zenora rose from the ground and walked toward me. "The darkest energy field imaginable. I need to complete my protective circle before I can enter your house."

"Okay, but can you do it quietly? Alvin's not too far away and he has a tendency to go berserk when he hears strange noises."

Zenora nodded and returned to her position on the snowy ground.

"Everything's fine," I told Godfrey. "Protective chant, that's all. Tell me, who owns that black Mercedes? How did you find out?"

"The car's owned by Brouse Candies out of Toronto. Good thing you were able to get the plate number. I contacted a friend at the agricultural department and asked him if he knew anything about a visit from Brouse Candies. Honestly, Norrie, I really wasn't up for sifting through all that boring departmental correspondence."

"Did he know who was in the car?"

"He works with food additives, not law enforcement. The only reason he knew the car belonged to Brouse Candies was because they have to register the license plate number with security so they can park the car in a reserved section on campus. All my friend did was call and confirm that the car was on campus the day you spotted it. He already knew that Brouse Candies had meetings with representatives from the agricultural department and told security as much."

"Then the rumors were true. About Gerard Dobrowski being in the area during the time of Devora's murder. I can't put it off any longer.

I've got to force the truth out of Stefan and get him to admit why he was in that Mercedes. It wouldn't surprise me if Gerard paid him off to kill Devora. Gerard certainly didn't want his estranged wife to get her hands on his candy fortune. What better way than to use someone she trusted?"

"I'll give you this much, money and greed are strong motivators, but how would Stefan have managed it?"

"The note! The note was meant for him!"

"What note? You lost me."

"Oh, my gosh. So many things keep happening at once that I'm losing track myself. I need to add a time line to my suspect clock."

"Suspect clock? Now I'm really baffled."

I inhaled, relaxed my shoulders, and proceeded to tell Godfrey about the lab tech and the murder notes that had now taken over the guest bathroom. When I finished, the only thing he could say was, "Whoa." Well, *that* and "Let Deputy Hickman deal with it. If Stefan is the killer and you go after him, you're likely to be his next victim."

"You sound like Bradley and Theo," I said. "The three of you should team up. I wanted to confront Stefan days ago but everything else got in the way. I can't put it off."

"Aargh. Francine warned me about how impulsive you were. Look, if you must speak with the guy, make it a public place. Better yet, a crowded public place. And maybe you shouldn't go alone."

"Is that an offer to help?"

"It's an offer to keep you out of trouble. Don't do anything rash without calling me. Fair enough?"

"Uh-huh. And thanks, Godfrey. I really do owe you."

Just then I heard three raps on the door followed by a singsong wail, "It's meeeeeeeeeee."

Unless banshees had moved to the west shore of Seneca Lake, it had to be Zenora.

Chapter 27

I put the receiver in its cradle and went to the kitchen door to let Zenora in. The sky had gone from murky gray to pitch black in a matter of minutes. The second she set foot in the door, she recoiled and pulled a small vial of who knows what from the pocket of her black gauchos.

"Hyssop oil for combating negativity. I ran out of myrrh."

She said it matter-of-factly, as if she had run out of milk or sugar.

I held up my palm and widened my eyes. "Don't drip it anywhere. Um, maybe you'd like to put your cape over one of the chairs."

"Good idea. Don't worry, all I plan to do is wave the vial of oil in my immediate vicinity until a sense of calmness takes over and I can begin the interior chant."

With that, Zenora removed what was left of the turban and flung the solar system cape, for lack of a better description, over one of the kitchen chairs. She proceeded to wave the glass vial across her chest. Her long grayish black hair fell in waves across her back and shoulders. Up close, I could see small crow's-feet and the start of marionette lines around her mouth. With the dark hair against her pale skin, I guessed her age to be late forties or maybe even early fifties. I was pretty certain the contrast in coloring made her look older and more severe.

"I can begin now," she said.

"Um, sure. You can—"

"Yeeowl! Yeeaw! Yeeyee habamana, habamana." The words flew out of her mouth like a primordial scream. Charlie raced up the stairs and most likely hid under the nearest bed. Zenora continued her protective chant while I stood speechless in the middle of the kitchen before venturing into the other rooms to watch. She moved about the house, staying close to the exterior walls. Occasionally she'd pause, take out that vial of hers, wave it around, and then continue with her mantra.

It was hard to believe that the woman I watched was formerly known as Mabel Ann and still made her living as a file clerk for one of the university libraries. *Most likely in a remote part of the building.*

Finally, I took a seat at the kitchen table, leaned my elbow on the flat surface, and rested my head in the palm of my hand. The loud screeching, grinding noise penetrated my eardrums and I wondered if I'd ever be able to decipher human speech again. Finally, after what seemed like hours, Zenora walked into the kitchen and said, "I used an elemental dispersion technique to send the cleansing spirits to the upper level of your house."

"Dispersion technique?"

"A special waving motion to capture the energy in the air."

I swallowed. "Good. Very good." I figured if nothing else, the dog would appreciate her remaining on the ground floor.

"I need to do the same thing with your basement. Can you point me to the door?"

"Over there," I said, pointing to the latched door. "If you need the light, there's a switch on the other side of the door."

"No light needed. Only energy."

I watched from my seat at the table as Zenora opened the door, waved her arms and mumbled something that sounded like "habanero peppers." When she completed her ritual chant, she returned to the table and sat down.

"I'm exhausted," she said. "Cleansing a house takes so much spiritual and physical energy."

"Would you like a cup of coffee? Or some tea? I've got peppermint and green tea."

"Green tea would be lovely."

I walked to the Keurig, selected the appropriate K-Cup pod and plopped it in.

"Automatic tea?" Zenora gasped. "You're making automatic tea?"

I nodded. "Is something wrong? It tastes fine. I think it's just dehydrated tea leaves compressed into these tiny pods."

Zenora looked as if she'd dropped a priceless heirloom. "But there won't be any tea leaves to read."

Suddenly I had my moment. My opportunity to request the favor of all time from her. I added bottled water to the Keurig and turned on the machine. "Zenora, would you be willing to read Priscilla McCoy's tea leaves?"

"The actress? The one who was filming in your vineyard? Glenda told me all about her. Does she want her tea leaves read?"

"No. I do."

"I'm not sure I understand."

The blue light came on the Keurig and I plopped the green tea pod into position. "Okay. I'm not sure how much Glenda's told you exactly, but Priscilla might have been coerced into sneaking in here to leave the victim's eyeglasses in my nightstand."

"Glenda mentioned the glasses. Thought it was Devora's doing."

"Yeah, well, I'm more inclined to believe it was someone who could actually hold them, as opposed to . . . oh, I don't know. Teleporting them?"

"Glenda and I understand the powers that the restless dead may have. It's a gift."

I tried not to roll my eyes but it was tough. "If it wasn't Devora's doing, it might have been Priscilla. I thought maybe if you read her tea leaves, you could say something that would convince her to tell the truth. Priscilla's kind of high strung and one Kleenex away from a full-blown sobfest."

The machine stopped its chortling noises and I handed Zenora the cup of tea. "I have sugar and honey."

"I like my tea as is." She took a sip and held the cup in her hand. "You know, reading someone's tea leaves could take hours. And from what I sense, having cleansed your house, Priscilla might not have acted alone. I felt more than one undesirable presence in here."

Most likely Deputy Hickman.

"So you won't do it?"

"Not the tea leaves, something more profound. If you really want to find out who was in your house, you'll have to accept the fact that it may have been the murderer. In order to do that, I will need to read everyone's auras."

Auras. At least I won't have to go to Wegmans to buy loose-leaf tea.

"The entire film crew? All seven of them?" I swore I could hear my voice crack.

Zenora placed the cup on the table and covered her mouth. For a moment I thought she was going to be sick. "Seven. The number seven. Glenda didn't prepare me for this."

"What's wrong with the number seven? It's a prime number, sure, but there are lots of those."

Zenora pressed her fingertips into her temples and took a breath. "Seven is a biblical number and a mystical number. Its associations are far-reaching and incomprehensible."

"So I guess the answer is no?"

"On the contrary. One murder victim and seven auras is a sign I can't ignore."

"Great. Auras. Um, not to sound dismissive, but isn't aura reading about personality traits? How's that going to help me find out the truth?"

"Auras can change with a person's current circumstance. Think of them like flickering lights. And some colors cannot be ignored. Brown for confusion. Deep red or purple for sudden change, and black, the most toxic of all. A black aura can mean someone is harboring anger, or worse yet, hatred. Once revealed, the puzzle pieces you've toiled over will suddenly fit. Names and information will be like tiny pieces of metal drawn to a powerful magnet."

For a minute, all I could think of were those silly magnetic games we played as kids, putting hair on a cartoon character's face. I knew Zenora didn't go into the guest bathroom because I watched her as she did her chant. And yet, I had the most unsettling feeling she knew exactly what was on the oval mirror.

Like it or not, Zenora had given me the plan I needed. Granted, it was loosely woven and would take some solid planning to put it in place, but still, it was better than anything I could come up with.

"That's wonderful, Zenora. Give me a few days to work things out."

"You won't have a few days."

"What do you mean?"

"The storm that's coming isn't like the other spring storms we've had."

"It's media hype. Probably to get everyone to spend money at the supermarkets."

"Not this time. My bones can feel the difference in the air. Heavier pressure. Like a force grounding all of us to the center of the earth until it passes."

"Can you be more specific?"

She shook her head. "I have no control over the forces of nature, but I'd make it early in the week if I were you."

"Fine. Tuesday or Wednesday. I'll let you know when we can meet at the winery."

"Oh, no. Not the winery. It has to be here. In your house. I have everything cleansed. We can't take a chance holding it elsewhere."

I looked around the kitchen and living room, mentally trying to figure out where to place everyone. With the seven-member film crew, not to mention Theo and Don because I wouldn't dare do this hocus-pocus without them, that would be nine. Then Zenora and I would make it eleven. Of course, I'd have to have Glenda here, not to mention Cammy, and I couldn't very well leave Godfrey out of the mix, so all in all, I'd need to squeeze fourteen. And what about Bradley? Would he really feel like doing this after work? *Or any other time?*

While I rearranged furniture in my head, I wondered how I'd break the news to him. The guy was about as straight as could be, and even though my plan was destined to get results, I wasn't convinced he'd go for my approach. Then there was the film crew. I couldn't very well tell them I was having a psychic dabbler read their auras. Aargh. Words like *manipulation* and *coercion* came to mind but I wasn't that sneaky. Or skilled, for that matter. And if Neville was going to make an appearance, then time was running out.

"Um, one more thing, Zenora. You'll have to read the auras without them knowing it. Mill around. Be inconspicuous."

Who was I kidding?

Zenora clasped the palms of her hands together. "I can't read auras while people are in motion. They have to be still. Calm. As if they were meditating or enjoying Savasana, the yoga corpse pose."

Terrific. How am I going to get a room full of people in corpse poses? They'd have to be—

"I think I have a way. I'll let you know."

I thanked Zenora and told her I'd call the next day. Then I picked up the phone and dialed the only person who could force the film crew to come to my house and to sit perfectly still—Renee.

Unfortunately, the call went to voicemail, but I left her a very compelling message:

"If you want your film crew to return to Toronto instead of lingering in Yates County Sheriff's limbo, you need to insist they come to my house for a film screening on Wednesday. I think I can root out the killer. Call me."

No way was I going to tell her it was for an aura reading with a would-be mystic who also categorized academic files in order to pay the rent. Renee had enough to worry about. Since I knew film directors always reviewed the footage before sending it off to the editing department, I figured if Renee could convince Gordon Wable that the screenwriter needed to see it as well, it would be the perfect ploy to get him, the actors, and his crew into the house. Then Zenora and I could take it from there.

Chapter 28

With the wind howling and Charlie repositioning himself on the bed all night, I woke up with a dull headache and a stiff neck. Looking out the window, I guessed we had gotten three or four inches of new wet snow but nothing to be concerned about. I washed up, opened the cover to Charlie's doggie door, and made myself a cup of coffee. Two or three sips in, the phone rang with a frantic Theo on the other end.

"Did you watch the breaking news? It's on all the channels. They interrupted the cartoon hours to announce it."

"What? Announce what?" I'd forgotten it was Saturday and that all the local stations ran cartoons from six to noon.

"There may be a break in the case. Priscilla McCoy and Stefan Olinguard were taken in for more questioning. It must be a big deal or the news stations wouldn't be covering it. There's footage of them being led out of the Ramada Inn by Deputy Hickman."

"How would the news media get wind of that?"

"Really? You have to ask? Everyone's on *social* media, including the TV stations. Someone probably caught the action and posted it."

"Devora's eyeglasses. That has to be it. I'll bet the forensic crew found fingerprints that matched theirs. Skylar mentioned something about their prints being on file with a national Canadian database since they're required to provide them to certain countries upon filming. No doubt our law enforcement contacted them for a copy and found a match. Or, in this case, two. I'm calling Gladys Pipp right after I watch the news. Holy cow. This changes everything."

"Huh?"

"I'll tell you later. Thanks, Theo."

I immediately turned on the TV, and sure enough, Channel 10 had breaking news. It seemed one of the guests at the Ramada saw Priscilla and Stefan getting into a Yates County Sheriff's car and posted it on Instagram and Facebook. No wonder it caught the attention of the news media. It was like waving a lollipop at a two-year-old.

According to the broadcaster, Priscilla and Stefan were taken in for further questioning. End of story. But that didn't stop the broadcaster from speculating with her partner.

"The sheriff's office must have new evidence," the woman said. "Why else would two prominent figures in the Devora Dobrowski murder be taken in for questioning at such an early hour? Were you able to find out the specifics, Sean?"

"I'm afraid not, Sherry. All they would say was that actress Priscilla McCoy and assistant film director Stefan Olinguard were brought in for further questioning. We'll keep our viewers apprised of the situation as we learn more. Now on to the latest forecast for spring storm Neville. It appears our guy has stalled over the Ohio River Valley and isn't expected to reach us for a few more days. That should give our viewers plenty of time to fill up their gas tanks and stock their pantries."

As soon as the announcer said *Ohio River Valley*, I cringed and momentarily forgot about the murder case. If I was lucky, Roger hadn't turned on his TV yet. The Ohio River Valley was the major source of contention in the French and Indian War, and if Roger caught the news, it would be enough fodder for him to regale our customers with a lengthy discourse about the relevance of that valley.

My coffee was now cold and I gave it the thirty-second nuke job in the microwave before picking up the phone to call Gladys. Three more sips in and she was on the line.

"Hi, Gladys. It's Norrie. Is it true? What's on the TV about Priscilla McCoy and Stefan Olinguard being taken in for more questioning?"

"That's right. The office is open on Saturdays until five," she said.

"I take it you can't talk. Yes or no? Was it the fingerprints on Devora's eyeglasses? I can't believe Deputy Hickman got the results so quickly."

Glady's voice sounded like a recording. "Indeed. Our office is quite efficient on all matters pertaining to the county and the safety of our residents."

"So he did get a match on the prints?"

"Yes. One p.m. would be fine for you to stop by and pick up neighborhood watch signs."

"One match. Is that correct?"

"Yes, that's right."

"Has the person been arrested?"

"No. It's no trouble whatsoever. Under the circumstances, I'd suggest the earlier you get here, the better. That wet snow is beginning to pile up."

"I get it. Thanks a million, Gladys. Next time I'm in, I'll bring jam."

My next phone call was quicker and without innuendo.

"Theo! It's Norrie. Either Priscilla or Stefan's prints were found on those glasses, but it's circumstantial evidence, and whoever's prints they are isn't under arrest. Not yet. Gladys couldn't really talk. Anyway, I need to go toe-to-toe with Stefan about him getting out of that Mercedes belonging to Brouse Candies. That's the only way I'll get some answers."

"Or some lies. Look, for all we know he could have been hired by Gerard to get Devora out of the picture. If he killed once, doing it a second time won't make a difference. Whatever you do, don't see him alone."

"I know. I know. Godfrey volunteered to play Joe Hardy with me this time."

"Hey, that's my role. Tell him to play Frank."

"First I need to figure out when and where to pull Stefan aside for a chat. I imagine he and Priscilla will be stuck at the public safety building for at least an hour or two. And darn it all, Renee still hasn't gotten back to me about my aura-reveal plan to expose the killer."

"Your what?"

"Yikes. I should have told you last night but it was late and I was exhausted." I took a breath and went on to explain about Zenora and the auras.

Halfway through, I heard Theo gasp. "That's the most ill-conceived, half-baked, lunatic scheme you've come up with yet. And with Zenora, no less. Good grief. Fifteen people in your house and one of them a possible killer? Thanks for putting Don and me on the list. It's like the Agatha Christie novel *And Then There Were None*, but instead of an island off the coast of England, they'll be in your kitchen."

"Only if I can't get anywhere with Stefan. I suppose the best-case scenario is to wait it out in the lobby at the Ramada and catch him when he and Priscilla get back."

"It's the safest, if you ask me."

"I suppose. Godfrey and I could always be there under the guise of having seen the TV footage this morning and asking them if they had heard from Renee."

"Sounds benign enough. Then what? Godfrey takes Priscilla aside and you go after Stefan guns a-blazing?"

"It works in the movies, doesn't it?"

"I refuse to answer. I'd tell you to be careful, but with Godfrey there you won't have any choice."

When I got off the phone with Theo, I called Gladys back. Given her demeanor on the phone, I knew Deputy Hickman was in earshot. I asked her to call my cell phone when Stefan and Priscilla were released. That way I wouldn't waste any time getting to the Ramada.

Then I showered, got dressed and shared microwaved eggs and toast with Charlie while I waited for Gladys's call. Using the landline, I touched base with Cammy regarding the morning news and told her my aura-revealing plan.

"I know," she said. "Glenda couldn't wait to tell me this morning. She had a long talk with Zenora last night and the two of them believe they can channel enough of their own energy to compel the killer to come forth."

"Really?"

"Norrie, even on a good day Glenda can't channel enough energy to move the boxes around in our storage room. Do you honestly think she and Zenora can pull this off?"

"I'm banking on peer pressure. The kind that involves giving people the look that makes them think you know something when you don't have a clue."

"Oh, brother."

I could hear a slight panic in my own voice. "But you'll be there, won't you?"

"Yeah. It should be entertaining if nothing else. Do you want me to arrange snacks with Fred?"

"Thanks but I'll take care of it. I've got to run. I'm expecting a call from Gladys Pipp at the safety building. I'll be in touch."

"Just be careful."

My next call was to Godfrey and he agreed to meet me at the Ramada once I knew for sure Stefan and Priscilla had been released. Since Two Witches and the Experiment Station were closer to the Ramada than the public safety building in Penn Yan was, we'd beat them to the Ramada by at least fifteen or twenty minutes. Not a terrific amount of lead time, but enough for us to get ourselves seated at their café, which fortunately had floor-to-ceiling windows that faced the entrance.

"We could be waiting five minutes or fifty," I said to Charlie. The dog looked up from licking his paws and then resumed gnawing at the hairs that separated each of his black pads. If nothing else, the dog was pretty fastidious about cleaning himself once he'd been outside. Almost as fastidious as the intruder who left us Devora's eyeglasses.

Rather than sit around getting edgier by the minute, I took out my laptop and continued with the edits I had promised Renee. Focusing on my screenplay allowed my mind to drift into another place and time. And one that I could control. An hour and a half went by and I stood for a much-needed stretch. It was odd that Renee hadn't gotten back to me, so I decided to phone her again.

No sooner had I dialed her number than my cell phone rang, and I immediately put the receiver down on the landline and picked up the cell call. It was Gladys. Again in her I-can't-talk-now voice. "Thank you for your kind words about our office. We received your message a few minutes ago. We are always pleased to serve the public."

I immediately called Godfrey, put on my winter jacket, grabbed a scarf, and raced to the car. Charlie had ample kibble and water to last well into the day. To be on the safe side, I kept his doggie door open but the fence gate shut. No sense worrying that he'd return to the Ipswiches' pond for further investigation.

Godfrey was already at the Ramada when I arrived. He ushered me to a table next to the windows and told me he'd ordered coffees for us. "That's the beauty of being centrally located," he said. "I was out of my office and down here in less than ten minutes."

"It's Saturday. You've got to get a life, Godfrey," I said. "You can't be stuck in that office all day."

His face practically beamed. "It *is* my life. Notice of a new grant arrived this morning for the study of Madagascar hissing cockroaches. I couldn't wait to read it."

"Ugh. I can't think of anything more repulsive. Don't tell me you're considering applying for it?"

"Me? No. I can see why you might think that, considering cockroaches are in the same subclass as vineyard pests, but I much prefer working with the Coleoptera class and not the Blattodea class. Hmm, as I recall, Jason did his thesis on an insect in the Blattodea class . . ."

"Oh, hell, no. Don't even think it. Last thing I need is for him to apply for another grant that will take him and my sister to another godforsaken place for a year while I deal with the dead-body-of-the-month club."

Godfrey reached across the table, grabbed my wrist, and gave it a slight shake. "Relax. I won't say a word. Promise."

At that moment, a lanky blond waiter appeared with our coffees and asked if he could bring us anything else. My stomach was in knots and it felt like hours since I'd gobbled up those microwaved eggs. Tempting as it was, I couldn't afford to waste time eating when Stefan and Priscilla were about to walk in the door. "Um, maybe later," I said. "We'll enjoy our coffee for now."

I added cream to the steaming cup and was about to reach for a sugar packet when Godfrey gave my ankle a kick. "Look out the window. A Yates County Sheriff's vehicle just pulled up to the entrance."

My hands suddenly felt clammy and all moisture seemed to have left my mouth. I took a sip of the hot coffee sans sugar and watched out the window. "I owe Gladys. She's right on the money. That's Stefan now, getting out of the car."

I eyeballed the entranceway from our table and watched as Stefan walked toward the door. "No one else is getting out of the car. Uh-oh. No sign of Priscilla." I watched as the vehicle pulled past the entrance and turned left onto the road.

Godfrey widened his eyes and let out a slow breath. "Maybe Gladys got it wrong. Maybe they made an arrest and it's Priscilla."

I stood and shoved my chair into the table. "Only one way to find out. Too bad I didn't think to order some Bailey's Irish Cream for this coffee. I may need it."

Chapter 29

As I raced to the entrance, I thought about a screenplay I'd written a few years ago in which one of my characters accused another of cheating. She acted impulsively, ruining a burgeoning relationship but at least she got her answer. I figured I had nothing to lose where Stefan was concerned.

No one was at the doorway when he stepped through and brushed some wet snow from his coat. The reception desk was way off to the side of the lobby so I was positive no one could hear us. And while I wouldn't exactly say I accosted him, I kind of overwhelmed him. Then again, he had it coming. "Did you set Priscilla up to take the fall for you?" I huffed. "To be charged with Devora's murder? I saw the news this morning. Is she under arrest? And by the way, thank you for being so considerate when you broke into my house. Nice present, by the way. If you have tacky taste in eyewear."

Stefan jerked back as if I was about to pull out a lance and do some serious damage. "I didn't kill Devora if that's what you're implying."

"Implying? I thought I was more direct. Look, if you want the whole world to know what's going on, we can stand here and I can get louder. Or, you can join me and a friend of mine in the café. It's on your left."

"I guess I don't have a choice, do I? Lead the way."

Stefan and I didn't say a word to each other until we reached the table where Godfrey was seated. I motioned to an empty chair and plopped myself in front of my now ice-cold coffee. "Stefan—Godfrey. Godfrey—Stefan." I glared at Stefan before continuing. "Godfrey is an entomologist at Cornell. He has access to all sorts of deadly insects. In fact, he was just returning from a symposium on the snake fly. Nasty bite. Makes the skin swell before necrosis sets in. Good thing he has his specimens carefully concealed in a specialized container under the table."

Godfrey turned beet red and all but choked on his coffee. I smiled and reached for a sugar packet. "Stefan would like to share some information with us."

"Look," Stefan said, "I don't know what this is about but I had a horrid morning at the public safety building in Penn Yan. If you must know, I sent word to Renee to have our production company's barrister make the drive here."

"Barrister? Not solicitor? So it *is* true. Priscilla is under arrest for murder."

Stefan shrugged. "The evidence is circumstantial at best. Her fingerprints were found on Devora's glasses, but that's easily explainable. Priscilla said Devora asked her to hold them for a minute while she got something out of her eye. It was during our shooting before . . . before her body was found the next morning."

"Did anyone see Priscilla holding the eyeglasses?"

Stefan shook his head. "Once we got to the public safety building in Penn Yan, I made some calls and asked everyone on the crew. No one remembered. Not surprising. We had a lot of things going on."

"If Priscilla was the person in question, why were *you* at the public safety building?" I asked.

Stefan leaned back in his chair and stretched his arms. "Priscilla didn't want to go alone. She called Gavin and Gordon but they didn't answer their phones. Then she tried me. Right now, no arrest has been made and she refuses to answer any more questions. They have the right to detain her for another twenty-four hours. Or is it forty-eight? I'm not that familiar with the laws in your country."

"Twenty-four hours," Godfrey and I chimed in at once. Then he went on. "They do have the right to apply for up to ninety-six hours if it's a serious crime like murder."

I gave him a funny look and he grinned. "Insects aren't my only life. I do watch TV, you know."

At that moment, our waiter reappeared and Stefan ordered coffee and a croissant. I leaned my elbow on the table and stared directly at his eyes. Pale hazel eyes. "You orchestrated all of this, didn't you? You knew her prints were on those eyeglasses. You were never more than a foot away from Devora at all times so you had to have seen something. You were the one who planted them in my house. In my nightstand. So I'd find them and notify the sheriff's office."

Stefan slipped out of his coat and let it rest on the back of his chair. "That's ridiculous. Why would I do a thing like that? To set the record straight, I like Priscilla. I have no ill will directed at her. And while Devora is an entirely different story, I certainly would not have resorted to murder."

I kept my gaze fixed on his eyes. "Then why were you in cahoots with Devora's estranged husband? And don't lie. This past Tuesday, I saw you getting out of the Brouse Candies Mercedes in front of the hotel. And yes, it *was* the Brouse Candies Mercedes. I had the license checked."

Stefan squirmed in his chair and for a minute I thought he'd break. No such luck.

"That's right. This past Tuesday. Early. I spoke with Skylar because he was checking out something in the vineyard and told me he thought you were sleeping in. Even though it wasn't like you. Then I had a chat with Renee, which led me to believe something may have happened to you. So, out of concern more than curiosity, I drove to the Ramada and had Housekeeping check to see if you were in. Sure enough, the room had been slept in and the shower was used, but you were long gone. And don't even think of fabricating some story about using the fitness center or eating an early breakfast because I saw you plain and clear getting out of Gerard Dobrowski's car. It was for your payoff, wasn't it? You met to collect the money he owed you. What else would you be doing in his car?"

"It's not what you think."

"Oh, please. Give me a break. That's the most overused line in creation. Want to know what I think?"

Just then, Stefan's coffee and croissant arrived, complete with a tray of flavored butters and jams. The waiter refilled Godfrey's and my coffee cups while he was at our table and all conversation paused while we were being served.

I added a new sugar packet to my coffee, took a sip, and continued as if I was having a pleasant conversation about gardening or some other benign topic. “Gerard Dobrowski needed to get his estranged wife out of the way for good so the Brouse Candies fortune wouldn’t be divided in two. Especially since their new venture in New York would bring scads of money his way. It was serendipitous. Devora was directing a film smack dab in the middle of wine country and only minutes away from the industrial park where Gerard’s new manufacturing plant would be built.”

Stefan didn’t say a word but Godfrey widened his eyes and tapped his fingers on the table. I clasped my hands together, rested my elbows on the table, and pushed my coffee cup aside. “Money is one hell of a motivator. How much did he offer you to make sure Devora would never get her share of the fortune?”

“I wouldn’t, I mean I didn’t—”

“And using Priscilla . . . that was the easy part. You had the perfect situation when she lost her necklace and you found it. Then you had a conversation with Devora about using a different location for the final scene. It was perfect. Except for one thing. I saw you get out of that Mercedes.”

Stefan’s face flushed and his hands began to tremble. “I know what it must look like but—”

“The Yates County Sheriff’s Office has the note to confirm what I said. About the new location. And as far as breaking into my house to frame Priscilla, not many intruders are, shall we say, anal-retentive? Who else would place a mat, or in this case a towel, on the floor to conceal muddy footprints. I’ll wager the one you used came from this very hotel. I’ll give you this much, you’re a good planner.”

“I may be a good planner but I’m no murderer. And yes, using a towel to absorb dirt is the decent thing to do, I suppose, if one is breaking into a house. But I wasn’t that person. The real reason I was in that Mercedes in the first place was at the request of Gerard Dobrowski, but not to collect money for Devora's murder. I met with him to plan her damn funeral arrangements. No one else would do it. And yes, I will be getting paid for that job. In fact, I have a signed and dated contract to prove it. Witnessed by his driver."

If my mouth could have opened any wider, it would have absorbed the entire room. I was so positive I had Stefan dead to rights that his explanation took me totally off guard.

"You still can't prove you weren't the person who climbed into my house late Thursday," I mumbled.

Stefan scratched the back of his head and crinkled his nose. "Late Thursday?"

"Uh-huh."

"Then it's a good thing I have an alibi for that time. One that's easy to verify. I suffer occasionally from gout and my big toe swelled up that afternoon. I suffered with it as much as I could before driving to the Finger Lakes Urgent Care late in the day. In retrospect, I should have taken a Tylenol and waited it out. Do you have any idea how many sniveling, coughing, and spewing children were in that waiting room? I probably contracted something far worse than a case of gout."

In that instant, I felt genuinely sorry for Stefan. Not only was he stuck planning a funeral for a woman he despised, but he had to defend himself from my accusations as well.

I bit my lower lip and let out a slow breath. "Um, I'm not quite sure what I can say, except *Oops*. And sorry. I really am sorry, but you should have told the crew where you were going on Tuesday so none of this would have happened."

"What? Tell them I was in charge of Devora's funeral arrangements? That certainly wouldn't have endeared me to them."

"Yeah, I see what you mean. So, uh, would you like to stick around for lunch?"

Stefan shook his head, stood, and motioned for the waiter. "I'll just pay for my food and get going."

"It's on me," I said. "It's the least I can do."

Stefan grabbed his coat and exited the restaurant without saying another word. I smiled at Godfrey and leaned forward. "Well, that could have gone a lot worse, I suppose."

"Compared to what? And deadly snake flies? Really? They're perfectly harmless."

"You mean to say they're real? Snake flies are a real thing? I made that up on the spur of the moment."

"From now on, stick to screenplays, okay?"

Chapter 30

"I guess I can cross Stefan off the list for now," I said. "I mean, his alibi adds up and it kind of makes sense about the funeral arrangements. But that doesn't mean Gerard Dobrowski's off the hook. He had a hell of a motive. And you know what I'm thinking?"

Godfrey rubbed his temples and gritted his teeth. "I'm almost afraid to ask."

"Gordon Wable, that's what. The guy outright lied about flying in from Vancouver. I found his ticket stub and it was from Toronto. Toronto! Drivable distance to do the deed and get home. What if Gordon teamed up with someone else? Like Gavin, maybe. He would have gone along for the ride considering Devora all but blacklisted him."

"There's no evidence, Norrie. Unlike Priscilla. Look, I know you don't want to consider it, but in my line of work we evaluate an insect's physical characteristics coupled with its diet and capabilities before accusing it of, let's say destroying the wood in someone's home. I wouldn't want to work under the premise that I'm dealing with termites when in fact it could be woodworm, powderpost beetles, woodborers, carpenter ants—"

"Arragh. I get it. I get it. But Gordon Wable isn't a carpenter ant, and in all honestly, I'd rather find a way to get the truth out of him and the rest of that crew before resorting to Zenora's aura reading. To be honest, it terrifies me, but I'm running out of ideas."

"Whoa. Slow down. What aura reading? What are you talking about?" His wispy light brown hair seemed to stand on end but I attributed that to the static in the room from dry indoor air rather than his reaction to my comment. I groaned and rolled my eyes. "Sorry. Lately I can't seem to remember who I told what to. The aura reading is kind of like a grand reveal, à la Miss Marple or Hercule Poirot."

Godfrey sat poker-faced while I explained the plan that would ultimately compel Devora's killer to fess up. Then he rubbed his eyes, clasped his hands, and bent his head over them as if he was about to pray. “Fifteen of us, huh? During a possible snowstorm if the Neville predictions are right. I can’t think of a worse scenario.”

“Maybe we won’t have to. I can always confront Gordon with that ticket stub, although these guys seem to be better actors than the ones in front of the screen. Too bad I can’t bug his room.” I tapped my fingers on the table while Godfrey reached across it to grab the menu.

“Oh, my gosh!” I announced. “I think I can. They sell all sorts of mini surveillance cameras at Walmart. Stephanie Ipswich mentioned it a few weeks ago at one of the WOW meetings. She set one up in her twins’ bedroom. Said it was teeny tiny and not at all like those old-fashioned nanny cams. Said it had a sound feature, too, so she could hear everything.”

“Let me get this clear in my head. You intend to purchase a surveillance device and somehow sneak it into Gordon’s room in a place where he won’t notice it.”

“Uh-huh. Of course, I may be running out of excuses for Housekeeping to let me into the rooms, but I’ll figure something out.”

Godfrey started to say something when all of a sudden I saw another Yates County Sheriff’s vehicle pull up to the entrance and drop off Priscilla McCoy. Even with a white scarf draped over her head and the collar of her black car coat pulled up above her neck, she was unmistakable. She slammed the door shut, tucked her bag under an arm and tromped into the building as if her knee-high boots were made for combat and not style.

“You saw that, didn’t you?” I asked Godfrey. “Priscilla slammed the car door. Stay here. I’m going to catch her before she gets on the elevator. Oh, and order me a BLT, will you?”

I was out of the café and in the corridor when Skylar and Mickey left the elevator and found themselves face-to-face with Priscilla. I took a step back and watched the elevator door close behind them. Fast, so as not to waste a second, I wedged myself into an alcove and turned sideways so I wouldn’t easily be seen. The good news was that I could hear every word being said.

"I can't believe the two of you hung me out to dry," Priscilla said. "Backstabbers!"

"Hey," Skylar replied, "I don't know about Mickey, but I wasn't about to lie. I didn't see you holding Devora's eyeglasses."

Priscilla crossed her arms, her handbag dangling against her thigh. "We were standing right in front of you."

"But I wasn't looking at you. I was concentrating on the footage we took. To see if the lighting was okay or if we needed a reshoot."

Then Mickey spoke. "He's right. I wish I had seen you hold the old bat's eyewear, but I didn't. I was busy threading the film."

"It doesn't matter," Priscilla said. "I only held those glasses for a few seconds, but that was all it took for my fingerprints to get on the temple. A big fat thumbprint. I should have put on my gloves but I'd taken them off for the scene."

"So now what?" Skylar asked. "They released you so that must mean they don't have evidence to make a conviction stick."

"Not yet. Stefan sent word to Renee to have our company's barrister drive here. If Stefan fears the worst, then I'm afraid I'm doomed. Even if the real killer comes forth, I'm afraid it's going to be too late for me to meet the terms of the contract I have with Light-Star Pictures. I'm supposed to be in Los Angeles Friday. That's six days from now. Light-Star Pictures. My first big break for international stardom, and where am I? In a Podunk little town watching my career circle the drain."

"I'm sorry, Priscilla," Mickey said. "Honestly, I am. But you'll have other opportunities. It's not as if you're a struggling actress anymore, taking on bit roles or understudying."

Priscilla brushed the hair away from her face and looked around. "Where's Gavin? What's he doing?"

"Last I heard," Skylar said, "he was in his room going over the new script Renee emailed him. Another cozy mystery in his favorite locale—Toronto. This one food-themed. Right up his alley."

"That's right. I remember him saying something about it. Uh, speaking of Renee, have either of you heard from her?"

I could see Skylar and Mickey shake their heads just as the elevator door opened and a couple walked out.

"We're going around the corner for a pizza," Skylar said to Priscilla. "You're welcome to join us. Rikesh plans to come as well but Gordon decided he'd take a drive and stop by a few wineries."

"I couldn't eat anything. Not now. Maybe another time. Looks like we'll all be stuck here for a while."

"Stuck, but still on payroll," he said. "Consider that a good thing."

I held still and watched as the guys left the hotel and Priscilla pushed the button for the elevator. Overhearing their conversation had given me the answers I needed without stressing Priscilla any further. I walked back to the café and waved to Godfrey.

He reached over and pulled out my chair. "You didn't tell me what kind of bread so I ordered your BLT on white toast with mayo on the side. That's how I like it, so if you don't, you can have my grilled cheese."

"Two of my favorites. I'm good either way. In case you're wondering, Skylar and Mickey got out of the elevator just as Priscilla walked in. I huddled in a corridor alcove and caught the entire conversation. She's pissed at the both of them for not coming to her defense about holding Devora's eyeglasses and she's crestfallen about losing her role in some major production with Light-Star Pictures."

"So where does this leave you? Bugging Gordon's room? Because if so, I may be able to help."

"Really? You're willing to do that?"

"I gave it some thought while you were away from the table and I came to the conclusion that it was better than that aura-reveal catastrophe in the making."

"The aura thing may still be our only viable option."

"Not if Gordon's hiding something. What do you say we hit Walmart after lunch and do some serious shopping?"

• • •

This time it was Godfrey who talked the housekeeper into letting us enter Gordon's room. It was surprising how fast she ushered us in when he showed her his entomology identification and explained he'd received a complaint about bedbugs. She stopped midway through her cleaning, having only a bit of dusting left, when she said, "Can I wait until I know for certain the room is safe?" Godfrey assured her that if any problems were detected, he'd report them immediately to management and the occupant would be given another, presumably bedbug-free, room.

We'd gotten back from Walmart with an anti-theft mini voice and camera recorder for under twenty bucks, not including batteries. It took Godfrey less than ten minutes to conceal the device on a decorative wall sconce, one of two that hung on either side of the king-sized high-profile bed. We figured we'd have plenty of time since Gordon was taking in a few wineries and those visits are never fast.

He put his coat back on and walked to the window. "Still snowing. I don't know about you but I want to get the heck out of here before—"

"Shh. Do you hear that?" I whispered. "Crap. It's a click from the door's card insert. Gordon's back. The bed! Hide."

I grabbed my jacket from the back of the desk chair and tossed it under the bed. Then I took a nosedive so fast I felt as if I'd crushed my ribs. The pain seared me—a stabbing pain in my chest that disappeared once I realized I had landed on top of my bag, complete with wallet, hairbrush, and all sorts of implements of torture. At least the floor was carpeted, even if it was that short, dense carpeting.

Godfrey made his move by ducking to the floor and rolling carefully under the bed, but not before throwing the mini-cam box under the bed. Thankfully he was on the opposite side of the bed from me. I lifted the bed skirt and moved an inch or so in order for him to scooch next to me. We were nose to nose and my chest was pressed against his.

I took shallow breaths and prayed he'd do the same. I moved

slightly and turned my head toward the door. The half inch or so between the bed skirt and the floor gave me enough room to see Gordon's brown lace-up winter boots as he approached the bed and sank into it.

The salty saliva that had built up in my mouth tasted awful when I swallowed it. I clenched my fists and tried to remain perfectly still. This was, by far, one of my worst ideas ever.

Chapter 31

Please don't let my cell phone go off. Please don't let my cell phone go off. The ringer is set on high.

While I fumbled in my pocket to retrieve my phone and push the mute button, Godfrey was already two steps ahead of me. He shifted his body so he was no longer on his side, but instead was stretched out on his back holding his phone above his chest. I could see the screen and watched as the line across the ringer image turned to mute. Meanwhile, one of Gordon's boots thudded to the floor a foot or so from my head. I waited for the second one to drop, but nothing. I felt like yelling, "Drop the damn boot already," but all I could do was wait it out.

Hell. What if the guy decides to take a nap? There's no way Godfrey and I can sneak out of here without being heard.

Then, two things happened simultaneously. Godfrey gave my elbow a squeeze at the exact moment I heard a knock on the door. Make it three things. Gordon's other boot dropped. This time even closer to my head.

Seconds later, a stocking-footed Gordon got up from the bed and opened the door. "I got back here as fast as I could," he said. "Honestly, I had no idea you were brought in for more questioning. I was asleep at the time, and when I woke I ordered breakfast in and decided to check out a few of the wineries. I never would have knowingly let you face that alone."

My field of vision was limited to the knees down but my hearing was a hundred percent accurate and Priscilla McCoy's damsel-in-distress voice was unmistakable. "It was horrible. Absolutely horrible. Stefan was there for a while but then he left because they wouldn't let him stay in the room with me while I was being questioned. He promised he'd call Renee and insist she send our company barrister here."

"Come here. You could use a good hug and a shoulder to cry on."

Terrific. I stared at two different sets of feet pointing at each other while I waited for the hug to end. It didn't. Well, not right away it didn't. I wondered if perhaps the hug might have turned into a different kind of embrace that included the usual smooching, but no matter how hard I tried to adjust my view, all I could see were feet.

Godfrey returned to his original position, sideways against my body, only by now I had shifted so that we were in a spooning position. Surprisingly, it felt comfortable, like being tucked into bed with a familiar blanket. *This can't be happening. That kiss we had was eons ago and I can't possibly become involved with two men. It's bad enough I write that stuff.*

No change as far as Priscilla and Gordon were concerned and I wondered how long they could possibly remain in that embrace. I could feel Godfrey's breath on my neck and I detected a subtle citrus scent. Lemon maybe? The warmer his breath got, the more intense the citrus. I could feel my pulse quickening. *Damn. This is not good. Not good at all.*

Suddenly, Gordon's voice jolted me out of whatever it was I was feeling and I all but sat up at attention.

"No sense standing here when the bed's far more comfortable."

Holy crap. Did he really say that? My God, it's the second oldest line in creation. The one that replaced, "Would you like to go upstairs to see my etchings?" I gave Godfrey's ankle a slight kick, then nudged him with my elbow.

Next thing I knew, Priscilla and Gordon were sitting at the edge of the bed. I felt a bouncing movement as someone's weight sank into the mattress. It was followed by the next person's weight and a rocking motion. It didn't take Zenora's psychic abilities to figure out their vertical embrace was now horizontal.

I didn't want to be close to the edge of the bed in case Priscilla decided to slip off her shoes and tuck them beneath the bed skirt so I used my arm to shift my weight, but the end result was that I was practically on top of Godfrey.

He pressed an arm on my shoulder and rolled me forward, but not so far as to be free from the proximity of his body. The citrus scent got stronger as I heard the movement above me and realized Priscilla and Gordon were no longer talking.

Unfortunately, my attention boomeranged back to Godfrey, and in an instant I was afraid we'd be doing the same thing under the bed that those two were doing on top of it. I tried to take slow, deep breaths but all I managed to do was inhale an intoxicating scent of lemons and oranges.

Just then, the room phone rang and Gordon and Priscilla were off the bed as if someone had shouted "Fire!"

By now it felt as if every muscle in my body was about to spasm and it took Herculean strength to remain still. It didn't help matters that my bag was still underneath me, causing me more physical anguish than a medieval rack. I held my breath and listened as Gordon took the call.

His voice couldn't possibly have been any louder. "You're kidding? She wants the screenwriter to review the footage? Seriously? Did she say anything about sending a barrister our way? Priscilla's on thin ice in case no one bothered to notice. Her necklace was the murder weapon and her prints were found on Devora's eyeglasses. What? Yeah, I know. Someone could have planted them, but right now she's the patsy."

There was silence for a second or two and then Gordon continued. "Fine. Downstairs in ten."

I heard the receiver thud back in its cradle before Gordon spoke. "Sorry, sweetie, but that was Stefan. We need to go over a few things. Look, I'm sure they're not going to place you under arrest any time soon or they would have done it. The evidence isn't strong enough."

"*They* think the evidence is strong. The coin on my necklace had her fingerprint on it when the damn witch just *had* to come over and see for herself what coin of the realm it was. If I had known I was going to lose that necklace and it would wind up being the murder weapon, I would have wiped that coin clean with professional solvent."

"Try to relax. I won't be long. We can talk things over at dinner. Everything appears to be walking distance from here and the sidewalks are clear even if the snow is piling up."

"Last thing I feel like doing is eating. I'm going to lose my role with Light-Star Pictures and some up-and-coming bimbo will probably walk off with it *and* an Oscar."

Then she broke into hysterical sobbing while I tried to remember if chiropractic care was included in my health plan.

After what seemed like an eternity, Gordon and Priscilla left the room. Godfrey and I remained under the bed for a good two or three minutes just to be on the safe side in case one of them returned.

"I look like Lurch," Godfrey mumbled when he got up from under the bed. "If they ever do a remake of the *Addams Family*, I'll be hired on the spot."

"Not if I beat you to it. My body's so stiff it's like rigor mortis set in. And talk about the fear factor. I was petrified we'd be outed."

"Oh, I'll talk about the fear factor all right." He rubbed his arms and legs and shook his head. "Do you have any idea the kind of insects that are found in hotel carpeting? Fleas, dust mites, bed bugs, carpet beetles, and the occasional spider."

"Ew. That's disgusting."

"I don't know about you, but I'd like to make a quick exit and call it a day."

"Are you kidding? And miss out on our only opportunity to search the room? I guess I should have mentioned that sooner, but honestly, this is our chance to see if we can find any incriminating evidence Gordon may have stashed away."

"I hate to tell you, but the sheriff's office already has the evidence they need."

"Maybe. Maybe not. If Gordon lied about his plane flight, what else is he covering up? How about you open the closet and check the pockets of his shirts, pants, and jackets while I do the same with the drawers?"

Godfrey ran a hand through his wispy hair and walked to the armoire. "Like I have a choice."

"Ugh. This is too much information," I said. "The guy wears Hanes boxers in assorted colors."

"Hey, this was your idea. Keep going. So far I've pulled up zilch."

The other dresser drawer held two sweatshirts and a gray cardigan and the only items in the nightstand were Bibles. I walked to the counter/desk and opened the long drawer. Pens, a pad, and a thick envelope from the hotel with Gordon's name and room number on it. My first thought was that it was a copy of his bill, but they don't put bills in envelopes, they shove them under the door the night before checkout. Besides, it was too thick for a bill, unless the guy ordered nonstop room service and indulged in more than one spa treatment.

"I may have something," I said. "Hang on."

The envelope had already been opened so it wasn't as if I was tampering with mail. And is it really mail if it's not delivered by the postal service? I pulled out the contents and stared at a fax.

"Godfrey! Check this out. It's a fax from Renee, our producer. It's dated two days ago, after he arrived here." I flipped the pages without reading her note and realized I was looking at a contract. Then I went back to her note. *"Gordon, I've emailed you the full contract. Sign and date the electronic facsimile and return it to me ASAP. As discussed, it's a three-movie deal for the Edna Lowery Librarian Mysteries, to be filmed outside Toronto with one sequence in the Caribbean. The series is our most lucrative to date, and although the contract was originally assigned to Devora, we are confident your direction will exceed our expectations. Hope the local authorities can wrap up that nasty matter soon. Any questions, reach out to me. Best, Renee."*

I handed Godfrey the envelope and he studied it for a minute before he spoke. "You know what this means, don't you?"

"Yeah, Gordon got himself some job security for at least a year or so. Not to mention beach time in the Caribbean. Too bad the protagonist in the Edna Lowery Mysteries is in her sixties. That leaves Priscilla out of the game unless, unless . . ."

"Unless what?"

"Unless she gets a role in one of the Edna Lowery movies. In fact, if she loses out on that Light-Star production, I'll bet the farm Gordon casts her in one of his. You saw how cozy they were."

"I didn't *see* anything and neither did you. We were *under* the bed. Hell, the fleas, ticks, and carpet beetles probably had a better view."

"Ticks? You never mentioned ticks."

"I didn't want to upset you."

"Oh. And like fleas or mites wouldn't upset me?"

"Forget the siphonaptera and ixodida for a minute and think. You said Gordon lied about his flight. Now you have a motive for murder. What if he wanted, or needed, to direct that Edna whatever series."

"Lowery. Edna Lowery."

"Okay, fine. Her. Edna Lowery. Suppose he wanted that three-movie deal and the only way to get it out of Devora Dobrowski's hot little hands was to make sure it never got there in the first place."

"Oh, my gosh. I was so wrapped up thinking about his movie deal that the whole evidence thing blew by me. If Lizzie ever found out, she'd make me reread the entire *Nancy Drew Handbook* again. Of course, we can't pin anything on Gordon. It's a contract, not a smoking gun, but it does make him one heck of a suspect."

"It gives him motive. But you'll have to figure out how he came by the means, and what opportunity he had. The film crew certainly would have mentioned seeing him."

I folded the contract and put it back in the envelope. "Not if he kept his distance. And not if he was working with one of them."

"Hurry up. Put the envelope back and let's get going before we overstay our welcome. We can have this conversation in your car or mine."

"Mine," I said. "It's closer. You lost your good parking spot when we got back from Walmart."

"Yeah. No good deed goes unpunished."

Neither of us said another word as we closed the door behind us and took the stairwell down to the main floor. No sense taking chances. A crowd of tourists entered the hotel as we left, making it easy for us to blend in. Once outside, we wasted no time getting into my car, and I wasted no time pulling out of there.

"I know a quiet spot where we can talk," I said. "Rosinetti's Bar and Restaurant. Cammy's family owns it."

"Good. That means they serve hard liquor."

Chapter 32

Rosinetti's had been a Geneva fixture since the end of the Second World War. And while its décor had changed over the years, its ambience didn't according to Cammy. With ever-changing posters and mirrors on the walls, a long wooden bar, rectangular tables that sported red, white, and green tablecloths, and dim lighting, the place exuded a combination of warm hospitality balanced by a certain amount of privacy for its patrons.

The rich aroma of herb-infused tomato sauce coupled with the lingering odor of beer hit our nostrils the moment we set foot inside the doorway. It was late in the afternoon and most of the tables were full. Godfrey and I grabbed the nearest one by the doorway and perused the menu while we waited for the waitress, a college coed who looked as if she was still in junior high.

"Cammy's aunts are probably cooking back there," I said. I pointed to the kitchen while I let my eyes adjust to the dimness of the room. "Sometimes her brother bartends, when he's not on duty with the fire department," I added.

Godfrey's eyes never left the menu as he spoke. "I didn't even realize this place existed. Wow. Three-cheese calzone with sausage. And look—garlic calzone with olives."

"Guess we might as well order a calzone, huh? And like I was saying before, you need to get out of your office more often."

"Um, speaking of getting out, isn't that Gordon Wable sitting at the bar?"

"Oh, my God! It *is* him. And Stefan's the guy to his right. Oh, my gosh. I've got to send a text to Cammy."

"Huh?"

"It has to be a text because I can't speak out loud. Cammy knows all the bartenders. She needs to tell whoever is on duty to listen in to Gordon and Stefan's conversation. Then they can tell her and she can tell me."

"And it will all be lost in the process. Like that old game of telephone we used to play when we were kids. Look, we've got his room bugged and you'll be able to hear his conversations on your phone. That's what we set out to do in the first place, wasn't it?"

I shrugged. "Crime solving is an evolving process."

At that moment, the waitress arrived and took our order for a sausage, garlic, and cheese calzone. It sounded heavenly and I was thankful I wasn't seeing Bradley that night or I'd have to forgo the garlic and sausage. The following weekend was another story. We'd made plans to dine in Skaneateles and poke around the town, figuring Neville would be long gone by then.

For some reason, nerves most likely, I fidgeted with the two jars of parmesan cheese and dried peppers that were on the table, and that's when something occurred to me. Something that didn't register earlier.

I shoved the jars away from me and leaned closer to Godfrey. "Stefan's phone call to Gordon. You heard Gordon, didn't you? He complained about having to show the footage to me. Renee got my message and came through. You know what this means, don't you?"

This time Godfrey picked up the two jars and shook them. His voice was as dry as the Sahara. "An impending disaster with Zenora. Maybe we'll get lucky and Gordon will slip up by then and you'll hear the conversation. That is, *if* he had anything to do with Devora's murder and *if* he talks about it while he's in his room."

"What I can't figure out is why he's at the bar elbow to elbow with Stefan. Stefan had decent alibis for that Mercedes business and the break-in. Gordon's whereabouts are sketchy at best, but you can't lie about an airline ticket stub."

While we waited for our calzone, I went over my suspect list with Godfrey, pausing now and then to gauge his reaction. It ranged from lukewarm to tepid with one exception—Priscilla.

He made a weird clicking noise and finally sighed. "Of all the players, she had motive, means, and opportunity. She could have easily convinced Devora to scope out the Ipswiches' pond, and, well, you know what happened from that point."

I shook my head. "I don't think Priscilla had the brute strength to overtake Devora. Even if she caught her off guard."

"Maybe you're not looking close enough at Priscilla. Did you see those calves? Every muscle is toned. And her arms, too. That woman's no slouch."

Muscle tone? Calves? Hmm, maybe insects aren't on the top of his list after all.

Just then, a scalding hot calzone with a peppery aroma was headed to our table. In the minutes that followed, there was no discussion about suspects, calves, Zenora, or spring storm Neville. In fact, the only sounds emanating from our table were the not-so-subtle chewing noises followed by a few *mmms* and *ahhs.*

Lucky for us that Gordon and Stefan were still deep in conversation at the bar, because they never noticed us when we paid the bill, tipped the waitress, and exited Rosinetti's. We walked back to my car without saying much of anything. Then Godfrey groaned. "I know how this is going to turn out. It always does. The reading of your wine distributor's will a few months ago . . . that catastrophic chocolate extravaganza . . . and now the aura reveal. I might as well brace myself. When did you plan to launch the *Hindenburg*?"

"If you're referring to my *Grand Reveal*, Zenora wants to hold it on Wednesday. So much for earlier in the week. She has a quilting class on Tuesday and doesn't want to miss Monday's TV lineup. So you'll be there, won't you?"

"If it will get you to stop ruminating about my office hours, the answer's yes. Getting there shouldn't be an issue, but do me a favor and make sure you have plenty of candles and water."

"Zenora didn't say anything about candles or water."

"Not Zenora. Neville. If the power goes out, you can kiss your well water goodbye and hang out in the dark. Not the best predicament with a murderer in the house."

"Yeesh. Come to think of it, I could use a few things at Wegmans even though I'm in and out of there all the time. I'll pick up the pace so we're not followed by Gordon and Stefan. So far so good, huh?"

"I'll save my opinion until Thursday morning."

• • •

When I finally got home and dumped the Wegmans bags on the kitchen table, Charlie shoved his food dish at my feet and looked up. It felt like hours since I'd last filled it with kibble. In fact, it *was* hours. "Sorry, guy," I said. "I'm tracking a killer and we all have to be flexible."

I poured the kibble and watched as he devoured it. Then I hung up my coat, slipped off my boots and glanced at the landline to see if it had registered any messages. Sure enough, the light was blinking. The caller ID said *Ipswich* and I knew it was Stephanie. I pushed the Play button and stood still.

"Hey, Norrie, it's me. Stephanie. Before you get your hopes up, the answer is no. I couldn't find anything else on Skylar. Only work-related stuff. I did see a cute photo of him taken a few years ago on some set. I sent it to your email as an attachment. Sorry I couldn't be more help. By the way, have you heard anything more from Hickman? He hasn't been back here since his department interviewed our staff. Derek thinks it's a good sign for us. What about you? Call me when you get a minute."

It was late and I was way too exhausted to gab, so instead I put away the stuff I'd bought at Wegmans. *Thank you, Godfrey, for spooking me.* I'd purchased a few power-outage candles and four LED power-failure lights as well as two twenty-four-bottle cases of spring water that I still had to retrieve from the car. If nothing else, Francine and Jason would be ready for the first storm in the fall.

Not taking any chances, I'd also added chocolate chip cookies to my emergency supplies as well as more crackers, chips, and a bag of apples. We had more than enough bandages and a first aid kit in case someone fell in the dark and got scraped up. The thought of antidotes for poisons crossed my mind while I wandered down aisle sixteen but Devora wasn't poisoned, she was strangled. With a necklace, no less. I made a mental note to hide my jewelry box.

Once I finished stashing the stuff, I went into the guest bathroom and had another look-see at the oval mirror/suspect clock. No revelations. Then I moved to the couch, booted up my laptop and found Stephanie's attachment.

Sure enough, Skylar Randall flashed a grin at the camera as he stood behind a tripod. I recognized the movie set immediately. It was one of Conrad Blyth's Amish love stories. Before he got kicked to the curb with no explanation given. In the background, a long-haired girl had her arms draped around some guy's neck and she was in Amish attire. He, on the other hand, wore a leather motorcycle jacket, complete with epaulet chain on one shoulder and torn jeans. Obviously not one of the actors. All I could see were their profiles and a large camouflage bag at the guy's feet. I couldn't make out the writing on the bag but it didn't matter. Cute picture or not, it was absolutely no help. I exited the screen and was about to close the laptop when I noticed an email from Renee. It was longer than her usual emails, and once I read it, I was sorry I'd told her I could deliver results in the first place. What was the matter with me?

> *I trust your judgment, Norrie. That's why I directed Gordon to share the film footage with you. I'm not sure how that's going to help. It's not as if the murder was caught on tape, but maybe there's something in that film that will point you in the right direction. God knows, we're getting nowhere here. I'm holding off sending our barrister since Priscilla hasn't been charged yet. If the roads are bad, he can always hop a flight. Keep me posted. Gordon tells*

me the crew is restless. At least Gavin can work on his lines. Best, Renee.

I flipped the lid on the laptop and leaned back on the couch. Renee trusted my judgment. What judgment? I was all over the place with my own cockeyed investigation. At least Nancy Drew followed the clues with precision and thought. I jumped around from would-be suspect to would-be suspect with more ill-conceived action plans imaginable, including my version of a Hail Mary pass as far as getting covert info from the mini-cam in Gordon's room.

With no choice but to finalize the details of the aura reveal with Zenora, I picked up the phone and called her. I kept telling myself that we had three days, possibly four if I counted Wednesday, to nab Devora's killer before resorting to some sort of hocus-pocus, but I wasn't optimistic. What I *was* sure of was that if I got too close to the killer without thinking things through, I could be the next one with something wrapped around my neck.

After mindless channel surfing, I called it quits for the night and followed Charlie up to bed. For the first hour or so, I slept the sleep of the dead. Then I heard voices. I was positive two people were downstairs and immediately reached for my phone, only to realize it *was* my phone. Godfrey had programmed it in conjunction with Apple's Live Listen program and it was picking up a conversation in Gordon's room.

I moved closer to the phone, petrified that if I picked it up I'd lose the connection. For a relatively inexpensive system, the audio was pretty clear and I recognized the voices—Gordon's and Priscilla's.

Without her usual sniffling and sobbing, Priscilla enunciated every single word. "Like I was saying, I went down the hall to get some ice and who did I see? Skylar and Mickey at the vending machine. Traitors. Bad enough they hemmed and hawed about what had happened when I ran into them at the elevator, but now they even went so far as to say I was overreacting. Overreacting? My fingerprint was on those horrid tortoiseshell glasses of Devora's. That's enough to have the deputy slap handcuffs on me."

A few garbled noises followed and I couldn't determine if they were kissing or if they moved farther away from the recording device. Then, all of a sudden I heard Priscilla again.

"But I got even. I told them the deputy called to inform me I was no longer a suspect and was free to return to Toronto. I wanted to see the expressions on their faces."

Gordon's voice practically boomed. "And?"

"Humph. Mickey tugged on that ratty Toronto Maple Leaves sweatshirt that's all but glued to his skin and Skylar adjusted the collar of his stupid sweater for the umpteenth time. If you ask me, they were both nervous. Skylar had the nerve to ask if the deputy said anything about anyone else and I shrugged. That'll show them."

Then a loud knock in the background. Gordon yelled, "Hold your horses. I'll be right there." His voice got softer and I strained to hear it. All I could make out was the word *bathroom* and I knew that's where Priscilla had gone.

Chapter 33

I was glued to my spot on the bed intent on hearing every word and even more intent on finding out who Gordon's night visitor was. Within seconds, I got my answer.

"Hell, Skylar," Gordon said. "Do you have any idea what time it is? This better be important."

Skylar must have been too close to the door for his part of the conversation to be picked up but I got the gist of it from Gordon's response. "If that's what she said, I'd take her word. Why would she lie?"

More muffled sounds. I guessed Gordon must have moved toward the doorway to keep Skylar from walking more than a foot or two into the room. Then, for some reason, Gordon's voice picked up. "No, she didn't say anything to me. Look, I doubt she'll drive back on her own or even catch a flight out of Rochester. Not with all that snow. Add it to the lake effect stuff and it's a nightmare. That's why I'm stuck here. Priscilla may be free as a bird as far as the authorities are concerned but she'll be forced to wait it out with the rest of us."

Somehow, Skylar's voice came in range and I heard him say, "Mickey's pissed as can be about her news. He practically freaked out when she told him. And you should have seen her face. Smug as anything. Still, I wasn't buying it. I had to get out of the room and find out for myself. She seems to be pretty tight with you."

"We go way back. That's all."

"Was she always a loose cannon?"

"If you mean *emotional*, that's what makes her such a good actress."

"I'm sure that will put Mickey's mind at ease."

"Tell him to leave it alone and go to sleep. Nothing he can do about it anyway."

"I suppose. Hey, is it true what Stefan told us about screening the footage for Norrie? That's a first."

"I simply go with the flow. If that's what Renee wants, that's what she'll get. So what are you, Mickey, and Rikesh doing for the next few days while we're cooped up here? We don't have enough money in the budget for a bar tab."

"We plan to shoot some footage in town. Small-city life. The college campus. Everything in walking distance from the hotel. Who knows? The film editor and post-production supervisors might decide to use some of it in the movie. At least it will keep us from going stir-crazy."

"Sounds like a plan. And speaking of which, mine includes some sleep. So if you don't mind . . ."

"Hey, sorry to bother you."

The next sound I heard was the door closing. Then silence for at least thirty seconds followed by Priscilla's voice. "I thought the SOB would never leave. And he's not the worst of the lot. I can't believe Mickey thinks *I* killed Devora. Honestly. At least Rikesh seems to be staying out of it."

Yep, Priscilla must have had her ear to the door. Or better yet, she was smart enough to grab one of the glasses on the sink and press it against the bathroom door. A regular Nancy Drew feat. I took a breath and kept listening. This time it was Gordon who spoke. "Come on, I'll rub your back and get rid of some of that tension."

Then silence. Then a few moaning sounds. Ew. There was a fine line between eavesdropping for the purpose of solving a murder and listening in to someone's intimate goings-on. To be on the safe side, I turned off my phone and went back to bed. If Priscilla was guilty of anything, it was being in the wrong place at the wrong time. Wearing the wrong necklace. How could I have possibly thought she was the one who climbed in my window?

• • •

The next morning I walked into the winery covered with sticky wet slush from my hat down to my boots. Lizzie mentioned something about getting used to it but that would never happen. I hated wet snow. Especially the heavy kind that clogs up snow blowers and makes everyone's life a misery. And this wasn't even Neville. Neville was alleged to be so heavy that it would make it impossible for cars to move down the road unless the plows were running nonstop.

If I was lucky, Neville would be too slow to get here by Wednesday or he would pick up speed, arrive early by a day or so, and get the heck out of here. Unfortunately, that wasn't the case. But Neville was the least of my problems. Deputy Hickman was another thing.

No sooner had I thrown my coat over the chair behind my desk than I heard him clear his throat. He stood in the doorway of my office with his arms crossed in front of his chest. One of them held a manila folder. "This is a courtesy call, Miss Ellington."

"Huh? What?"

He walked toward my desk and held out a piece of paper. "Eugene, the lab technician whom I sent to your house on Friday, was quite adamant the lab compare the lipstick on a note found by your window with the tube of lipstick from Ms. Dobrowski's purse."

Before I could say a word, Deputy Hickman went on. "Eugene was also quite adamant we do not send him to your residence again unless, and I quote, 'the place is teeming with dead bodies.' Miss Ellington, Eugene is one of our most dedicated and capable forensic technicians, but at the mere mention of your name, the poor young man recoiled. What on earth did you do or say to him?"

"I, um, er . . . Well, maybe I was a bit too zealous. I may have given him the wrong idea."

"See to it that it doesn't happen again."

I nodded. "The lipstick was a match, wasn't it? That note was written by Devora. If you want my opinion, I don't think it was written in response to Priscilla. That leaves—"

"The Yates County Sheriff's Office to do its job."

He removed a photo from the folder and showed it to me. "Do you recognize this man? Do you remember seeing him at your winery?"

Not the winery, but on my suspect list. "Is that from today's *Finger Lakes Times*? Is it an official announcement about the candy manufacturing plant?"

"I take it you recognize the gentleman in the photo."

"Not personally, no. But I do recognize him. It's Gerard Dobrowski, Devora's estranged husband and CEO of Brouse Candies. I'm really good with internet searches."

"Miss Ellington, our office is also quite adroit with internet searches. We are also in contact with Canadian immigration and customs. Mr. Dobrowski was in the area during the time of the murder and has since returned to Toronto, where he is being questioned by Canadian authorities."

"Aha. I've been saying all along that the husband had a motive to kill her. Believe me, if he was in our winery, I would have shouted it from the roof."

Grizzly Gary moaned. "Maybe one of your staff noticed him. One of your staff who had the restraint not to shout anything from a roof, a rafter, or a loading dock."

"Feel free to ask them but I don't think he was here."

"What makes you say that?"

I didn't want to get Bradley in trouble for sharing information with me so I sort of fibbed. "The tabloids. According to the latest gossip, Gerard and Devora had such a tempestuous relationship that if he was here, we would have known about it. You know, like Elizabeth Taylor and Richard Burton in *Who's Afraid of Virginia Woolf*?"

"I'm not sure I understand, Miss Ellington, but it doesn't matter. Now, if you don't mind, I need to show this photo to your staff."

"Because you think the husband was the killer? Personally, I pondered the idea of him hiring one of the film crew to pull off the murder in exchange for a whopping amount of payola. Gerard had the resources, you know. What do you call that? Motive, means and—"

"I call that conjecture. Mr. Dobrowski may possess information that can corroborate what we already have on file regarding the existing suspects. That's why he's being questioned in Canada."

"What? How can he *not* be a suspect? The divorce . . . the money . . . really? Greed is like a really, really strong motivator."

Deputy Hickman turned and walked to the door. "Thank you for your time, Miss Ellington. As usual, it's been most enlightening."

"Give my regards to Eugene," I mumbled, but he was already out the door.

Too furious to peruse winery emails or tackle the written stuff on my desk, I thundered into the kitchen and plopped myself at the table. A few seconds later, Cammy walked in. "Trouble in paradise? Grizzly Gary is making the rounds."

"Ugh. Can you believe it? The one person who has the most compelling motive isn't even a suspect. What's wrong with these people? Devora was a witch on wheels but that wouldn't have sent her into the pond bobbing for air. I guarantee, money had to be a factor."

Cammy pulled up a chair and leaned toward me. "Aside from Gerard not wanting to part with his money, who else may have needed to fill their coffers?"

"Beats me. All of the crew members are paid well and the actors certainly are. But maybe one of them is so deep in debt that doing away with Devora seemed like the only option."

"If that's the case, it's a well-kept secret. Stephanie, Theo, and I scoured the internet and couldn't find anything that would lead us to believe one of those guys was in over their heads. They all appear to be solid workers. Steady, stable, and focused."

"Damn it! Too bad one of them didn't have a gambling problem."

There was an opened box of crackers on the table and I reached in to grab a few. "Oh, crap. Deputy Hickman has all the resources known to local law enforcement and he can easily pull up their bank accounts. Meanwhile, I'm stuck with Glenda's crazy friend Zenora and the even crazier aura reveal."

"Remember, that was your idea. If it fizzles like a bad sparkler, you can't point a finger at anyone else. Not to get you even more nervous, but have you followed the weather reports lately? The unpredictability of spring storm Neville has got all the meteorologists baffled."

"I'm sure it won't be as bad as they say. They always exaggerate to get viewers."

"Um, have you looked outside in the past hour? It's continuing to come down."

"It's that wet stuff. The road crews are keeping up with it."

"Unless it turns colder. I wish they'd tell us when that secondary front is supposed to come through but no one knows."

I laughed. "You know what they say about the weather in the Finger Lakes? If you don't like it, wait five minutes. It will change."

I had no idea how prophetic my statement was until later in the day when all hell broke loose. The wet, heavy snow continued to fall and it kept our vineyard guys pretty busy shoveling walkways instead of tending to their usual duties. In addition, we needed to run a plow through the parking lot every few hours so our customers wouldn't wind up stuck at Two Witches. Since Sam and Roger lived the farthest away, I sent them home along with Lizzie, and told Fred to close down the bistro. He showed me where he kept a few premade sandwiches just in case and thanked me. Only Cammy and I remained at the winery, and she wasn't too worried about driving home. With an all-wheel-drive car, studded snow tires, Bluetooth, and Hum motor assistance, Cammy was pretty confident she'd make it back to Geneva in one piece.

Then, at a little past five when the last of our customers had finished tasting wine and were idling by the gift items, Don called from the Grey Egret.

"Hey, Norrie. Theo was out shoveling the steps in front of our winery when he saw car lights that suddenly disappeared. He thinks maybe a car slid off the road into that long ditch on Route 14. Impossible to tell with the snow coming down so fast. Before we call the sheriff, we really need to be sure. Our snowplow guy left about a half hour ago but we were hoping yours was still there and could take a swing by the base of our driveway. If there is a car stuck in the ditch, it would be visible from the road."

"Hang on, I'll check."

Sure enough, Casey Robson, who owned a trucking and plowing service in Penn Yan, was still working his way around our parking lot. I threw on my hat and coat and charged out the door without stopping to tell anyone what was going on. The minute I flagged Casey down, he rolled down the window of his Dodge Ram. "What's up? Got a car stuck in this heavy muck?"

"Not in our lot, no, but Theo and Don next door think one may have slid off the road just past Gable Hill Road before the turnoff to our driveway. Can you check?"

"On my way. I'll call nine-one-one if it looks like someone's hurt or trapped in the car. Otherwise, I'll get one of my men to come by with our tow truck."

"Good deal. Let me know, huh?"

"You got it. Hey, you may want to send your crew home before this gets any worse. Geez. And this is only the warm-up."

I went back inside and let Cammy know what was going on. "Everything's tidied up and anything else that needs to be done can be done in the morning. Let's lock up and call it a night, unless you want to spend quality time with Charlie and me overnight," I said.

Cammy laughed. "Much as I adore that Plott hound, I'd like to sleep in my own bed. Yeah, it's coming down for sure, but it's those big, heavy flakes. Not the wind-driven icy ones. I'll be fine. The trick is to go slow. The roads get slick. If Theo really did spot a car in the ditch, I'll wager the driver was speeding."

Under normal circumstances, Cammy would have been right. Unfortunately, these weren't normal circumstances and the last thing the driver was doing was speeding.

Chapter 34

I had barely turned the lock to the winery building when I heard sirens.

"Uh-oh," Cammy said. "That can't be good."

Then my cell phone rang with Casey on the other end. "Good thing Theo noticed those lights. It was a car all right. Nearly flipped over. The driver's conscious but I can't get her out. The closest fire rescue is in Geneva and they're on their way along with the Penn Yan sheriff's deputies. I'll stay on the scene until they arrive."

"Thanks, Casey. Anyone else in the car?"

"Nope. Good thing, too. From the angle of the car, a passenger may have been killed. I hope for the driver's sake she wasn't texting or drinking."

I thanked him again and ended the call. Then I looked at Cammy. "Drive slow. Like really, really slow."

"How bad was the accident?"

"Bad enough, I suppose. According to Casey, only one woman in the car and he doesn't think it's life-threatening."

Cammy tightened the scarf around her neck. "The spring storms are the worst. They start out like nothing with nothing and then boom! Next thing you know you're putting your windshield wipers on high speed and hoping no one decides to pass you."

"That's why I like Manhattan. Mass transit. It's someone else's problem. Anyway, I'll call you later tonight. After I catch the forecast."

"Sounds like a plan. Have a relaxing evening."

The last thing I had was a relaxing evening. For the second time in one day I got to be visited by Deputy Hickman, only this time he didn't stop by to show me photos.

It was about an hour and a half past the time when Cammy and I locked up the winery. I had eaten a bowl of premade chili while staring at my suspect clock in the guest bathroom. I know. I know. Not the most inviting place to dine, but I was hungry and perplexed at the same time. I figured I could easily do two things at once—eat food and theorize about Devora's killer.

The sudden knock on the door caused me to drop the empty bowl on the floor and watch as the spoon rolled behind the toilet. Not wanting to keep someone waiting in the cold, I shut the door to the guest bathroom and made a mental note to return for my stuff.

When I opened the kitchen door and found myself face-to-face with Grizzly Gary, I wasn't quite sure what to think but I knew it wasn't a social call.

"I'm here on a matter of the utmost urgency," he said when I motioned for him to come inside. "I'm sure you're aware there was an accident on the road in front of your driveway."

"I know. One of the guys from the Grey Egret thought he saw a car going off the road and I asked my plow guy, who was clearing our parking lot, to go check on it. He was the one who called nine-one-one. Listen, if the driver was drinking, it wasn't at our winery. The car hadn't even gotten here yet. Casey, the plow serviceman, said the driver was a woman and she appeared to be okay. Please don't tell me she died from shock or something."

"The driver only sustained minor injuries and a possible concussion. They're keeping her overnight at the hospital as a precaution in case of internal bleeding. As for drinking and driving, those test results are still pending. The driver claimed she was run off the road by another vehicle; however, she could not provide a description. But that's not the reason I'm here."

"I don't understand."

"The driver is Priscilla McCoy and she claims you called her hotel insisting she drive to your winery."

Priscilla? Holy cannoli!

"What? That's ridiculous. I'd never ask anyone to get behind the wheel of a car when there's a boatload of snow falling. Maybe she had a concussion and she's delirious."

"Actually, Miss Ellington, she had a note in her possession written by the desk clerk at the Ramada. It seems the phone call was made to her hotel, and when she didn't answer, the caller, a female who identified herself as Norrie Ellington from Two Witches Winery, asked the desk clerk to take the message and give it to Miss McCoy."

My face felt warm and I swore my heart was beating faster than usual. "Well, I certainly didn't call her. Do you have the note? What does it say?"

By now, Deputy Hickman was leaning against the refrigerator and was less than a foot away. He reached in his coat pocket and pulled out a small piece of paper. Then he proceeded to read what was on it.

> *Priscilla, I know who Devora's killer is. It's urgent that we talk in person. Don't call me. Don't email me. And whatever you do, don't tell anyone. Drive to the winery. I'll wait inside for you. Norrie.*

"And that, Miss Ellington, I believe is the reason Miss McCoy was on the road in such hazardous driving conditions."

I felt like screaming but kept my voice low. "You've got to believe me. I'm not the one who called the Ramada."

Deputy Hickman put the note back in his pocket and clenched his teeth. "Miss Ellington, if I understand correctly, Miss McCoy is the only female member of that film crew. Am I correct?"

I knew what he was getting at and it wasn't pretty. "Um, yeah. I suppose. I mean, with Devora dead and all . . ."

He cleared his throat and continued. "The desk clerk was certain it was a female voice and I have no reason to believe otherwise. Therefore, I can safely conclude the message was not sent by a member of the film crew."

"Well, it wasn't me!"

Suddenly, I had a horrible thought. The only other female who would be acquainted with Priscilla was Renee, and why on earth would Renee do a thing like that? It was ludicrous. Unless Renee wanted to prevent Priscilla from taking on that major motion picture role. Still, it didn't sound like something Renee would do.

I crossed my arms and huffed. "I don't know what to tell you but I find this as disturbing as hell. Maybe the killer thinks he or she is about to be found out and is desperate to send the investigation in another direction. That happens in crime shows all the time."

As soon as I said that, I regretted it. For the next two or three minutes, Grizzly Gary kept reiterating this was a real investigation and not "an exaggerated screenplay."

"I don't suppose one of your employees would have placed the call?" he asked when he finished his dissertation.

"Absolutely not. Other than Cammy and me, everyone else had gone home for the day. And besides, none of them, including Cammy, would have had a motive to drag Priscilla McCoy from her hotel to our winery. It's preposterous."

"I must admit, Miss Ellington, you make a point. No doubt, my office will need to pursue this matter further."

He stepped away from the refrigerator and walked toward the door.

"Wait! Whoever left that message might have been the person who ran Priscilla off the road. My God! Maybe they were trying to kill her. Oh, no. Maybe they'll try again. In the hospital. With a lethal dose of who knows what. I've seen all those movies where the killer pretends to be the nurse and administers something toxic in the patient's IV tube. You need to call the hospital."

"Slow down, Miss Ellington. This isn't an episode of *Grey's Anatomy*. However, given Miss McCoy's celebrity status, I spoke with Ontario County since she's at Geneva Hospital and they have a deputy posted at the door to her room."

The muscles in my neck loosened and I let out a slow breath. "Good. Good."

By now, Deputy Hickman had his hand on the doorknob and was about to leave. "Whatever you do, Miss Ellington, do *not* call the desk clerk at the Ramada and badger her. Given the conversation between you and me, I intend to ask if perhaps the desk clerk might have heard background noises during the call. Anything to bring us closer to identifying the caller."

"If there's anything I can—"

"The answer's no. And one more thing—Don't badger the hospital either. Let us do our jobs."

I nodded and locked the door once he had left. It was still coming down in big wet flakes and I wondered if we'd get a reprieve before Neville actually made his appearance. When I was positively certain Deputy Hickman had made it down our driveway and onto Route 14, I called Don and Theo to let them know what I'd found out.

"Priscilla McCoy?" I thought my eardrums would burst when Don shouted her name over the phone. "And Hickman thought you were responsible for calling her?"

"He doesn't know what to think. It was a woman's voice on the phone, and face it, how many women are directly involved? And thank goodness I'm posing this question to you and not Glenda or she'd be convinced it was Devora's evil spirit back from the dead."

"Hmm," Don said. "You've got a point. Two points actually, if I count Glenda. Which reminds me, are we still on for Wednesday? Snow and all?"

"Yeah, we're on all right. I'm not sure if it was Cammy or Emma who told me, but there's supposed to be a break in the snow for a day or so before it gets really bad. Besides, Zenora's tied up with other things until Wednesday, and we can't very well have an aura reading if Priscilla's in the hospital."

"Penn Yan?"

"No, Geneva. It was closer and their EMTs were the ones at the scene."

"Did Hickman tell you what happened?" he asked.

"Priscilla told the EMTs she'd been run off the road. She thought it was deliberate. Too bad she couldn't give the deputies a description of the other car. Anyway, Grizzly Gary also told me her car wasn't badly damaged. Only dented a bit and scratched up. A deputy drove it back to the Ramada." *Add that repair bill to the production costs and this film will be in the red before it's on-screen.*

"Hang on," Don said. "Theo is clinging on my shoulder. I'm putting you on speaker phone. Okay, you can keep talking."

"Hi, Theo. Listen, Priscilla herself may have set the whole accident thing in motion when she lied to the camera crew. She told them she was cleared to return to Toronto and they were really ticked. I overheard that conversation from the mini-cam Godfrey and I put in Gordon Wable's room. Maybe one of them wanted to prevent her from leaving."

"Mini-cam?"

"Uh-oh. I might have forgotten to tell you about that."

Theo groaned. "Is there anything else you might have neglected to tell us about your widening investigation, Miss Marple?"

"Nah. At least I hope not."

"Ditto on that!"

Chapter 35

The snow had slowed down considerably the next morning, and if I didn't know for sure spring storm Neville was on his way, I would have sworn we'd see crocuses and daffodils by midafternoon.

According to Deputy Hickman, the hospital was to keep Priscilla McCoy overnight for observation and then discharge her if she didn't show any signs of a complication. Having been through similar situations in the past, I knew that hospital discharges take longer than the surgeries they perform. That meant I had enough time to get washed up, feed the dog, and drive to the hospital in order to offer Priscilla a ride back to the Ramada and find out what really happened.

I introduced myself to the Ontario County Sheriff's deputy who was seated by her door and explained that I was an acquaintance of Priscilla's. He asked me to spell my name and checked it off a list he had on a clipboard. "I'd knock first if I were you. Miss McCoy is adamant the press not be allowed in her room."

As soon as he said that, I pictured the worst. Heavy bruises, a cut lip perhaps, swollen eyes, and mangled, tangled hair. What I saw instead was hardly cause for alarm. Priscilla's ash-blond hair was fanned out on the pillow behind her head and gave me the impression I was looking at a celestial being instead of an actress.

There were no cuts or bruises on her face, although one of her hands was bandaged and there was an ice pack on her shoulder.

"Norrie," she said the minute I entered. "You didn't have to come here. That gruff-looking deputy told me the message I got yesterday didn't come from you. I can't believe I was such a fool as to get in my car and drive to your winery without calling you first. All of this could have been avoided. Now I'm saddled with a miserable headache and a bunch of bumps and bruises. Don't get me wrong. I'm not complaining. It could have been so much worse."

"Do you have any idea who ran you off the road?" I moved closer to the bed and sat in the chair opposite the machinery that monitored her vital signs.

"It was a blur. The car lights off to my right were blinding. Someone had their brights on and they aimed their car directly at mine. It was deliberate. Who drives with the bright lights on in a snowstorm? It makes the visibility a hundred times worse. What an idiot I was to get in that car, but when I got your message, well, *the* message, I simply had to find out for myself what you knew. Then to learn it was all a ruse . . . You can't imagine what's going on in my mind right now."

"I may have some idea."

"I doubt it. Want to hear the worst? Gordon came here late last night with Skylar and I heard them whisper to each other when they thought I was sleeping. Gordon was fit to be tied because Skylar and his two buddies were convinced *I* was the one who left the message with the desk clerk and . . . Can you believe it? That I fabricated the whole story about being run off the road in order to make it look as if I was the next victim in order to cover up my culpability."

"Uh, yeah. That does seem a bit extreme."

"Not if you follow their reasoning. Those camera guys are convinced I was the one who lured Devora to that pond, got into a tussle with her, and somehow managed to wrap my necklace around her neck, tug on it hard enough to kill her, and then give her a shove into the water. I'll admit, I work out and I'm in good physical shape, but I'm no Holly Holm."

The vital sign monitor made a strange beep and I jumped.

"It does that all the time," Priscilla said. "At least it lets me know I'm alive. For the time being anyhow. Listen, this is a horrible thing to say but I doubt Skylar, Mickey, and Rikesh are all that broken up over Devora's death. So even if they think I killed her, I seriously doubt they'll want to seek revenge on her behalf. But someone wants me out of the way. Or spooked at least. Well, they got the last part right."

"I don't blame you. If they believe you killed her and you're about to get away with it, they may be tempted to do whatever they can to make sure that doesn't happen. Why? Because they're suspects, too."

"Gee. I never thought of it that way. Oh, my God. This really is my fault. I led them to believe I was exonerated. I brought this on myself."

"Only if that other driver was one of them."

"Norrie, do you have any idea how the investigation is going? I know you speak with that deputy all the time."

"Oh, I speak all right. The trouble is, he doesn't. I have no idea whatsoever."

"I need to be in LA by Friday. Light-Star Pictures starts filming and this is the break I've been waiting for. Shh. Don't say anything. I was set to be released this morning but I told the doctor on duty that my headache was a real pounder and got him to extend my stay by another day. They'll run more brain scans. Meanwhile, if someone *is* trying to kill me, at least I'll be safe in here for another day. After that I intend to lock myself in my room at the Ramada. That's why I asked you if you knew how close those deputies were to finding the killer. I'm down to the wire."

"It's only Monday. You can always catch the red-eye to LA on Thursday night if the sheriff's office returns your passport. The storm's stalled for now but by then it will have done its damage and moved out of the area."

"The storm, maybe. But unless that deputy apprehends the person who strangled Devora and then returns my passport to me, I may be stuck in Renee's stable of romance actors until I'm too old to kiss."

I stood and stepped back from the bed. "I should get going. Oh, before I forget, Renee asked me to review the footage from the filming. I invited the cast and crew to my house Wednesday around seven so we could all watch it together. Before you say anything, I already spoke with Don and Theo from the Grey Egret and they promised they won't let you out of their sight. In fact, one of them even offered to drive you there and back."

"That won't be necessary. Gordon already told me and I made him swear he'd be my bodyguard for the duration. I should have mentioned it."

"Then it's settled. I'll see you Wednesday night. Our bistro chef is preparing the food so no one has to worry about my cooking, or the storm, for that matter. It isn't expected until after midnight."

At that moment, a nursing assistant stepped into the room and I slid the chair away from Priscilla's bed. "Um, guess that's my cue to get a move on. Get some rest."

"I will when I'm on that plane to LA."

• • •

The next two days were an absolute bust in terms of getting any further with my so-called investigation. Other than constant phone tag games with Stephanie, Theo, and Godfrey, not to mention quick conversations with Cammy, all we were left with were the same two questions:

"Did you hear anything?"

"Was anyone arrested?"

Stephanie was chomping at the bit to be part of Zenora's aura reveal but understood that my kitchen and living room could only hold so many people. "Besides," she said when I spoke with her from my winery office, "I can't leave Derek and the boys in the house if that storm decides to sock us in tonight. Not only will the place look as if a demolition crew showed up, but they'll stuff themselves full of frozen pizzas, pop, and more candy than most manufacturers can produce in a year."

I told her it was a good thing Brouse Candies was moving into the area when I literally had an epiphany and rushed to end the call so I could phone John Grishner. It was right in front of me all the time but I never gave it much thought. John had mentioned ordering Concord grape root stock in December and being one of the last vineyards to do so. That meant the other wineries must have known the candy company was a done deal. And if so, Gerard Dobrowski had to have used his and Devora's monies to finance that venture. It wasn't only the fortune he wanted to acquire, but the one he used without Devora's knowledge. Even more reason to get her out of the picture.

"John, it's Norrie. Listen, remember when you said you were the last vineyard manager to order Concord root stock? Well, do you know who the first one was? It's important. I need to find out how they knew the candy company was coming long before everyone else did."

"They didn't do anything wrong, if that's what you're concerned about."

"Not them. The CEO of Brouse Candies. Can you find out?"

"Give me a few minutes to sift through the papers on my desk. By the way, we're bringing Alvin into the big barn this afternoon in case Neville dumps too much snow for us to handle. Alvin hates the barn but we've got a nice stall all fixed up for him and he can ride it out with the farm equipment we've got stored. Your brother-in-law was insistent we have a backup plan for his goat in case of emergencies."

Heaven help the farm equipment. That goat will spit all over it.

"Um, good idea."

John cleared his throat. "Oh, yeah. The root stock. If I remember correctly, someone mentioned it late last summer during a Cooperative Extension meeting. I've got those notes in one of these piles. Hang on and I'll call you back."

Less than forty minutes later I had my answer, only it wasn't a winery that knew about Brouse Candies relocating to the Finger Lakes well before the rest of us, it was our own Cooperative Extension. It seemed Brouse Candies had contacted them regarding the availability of Concord grape juice in the coming years.

My original theory began to take hold. Gerard Dobrowski paid someone on that film crew to murder his estranged wife. That's why he was in the area, not to check on a manufacturing plant location that he already had in place. But who did he pay off ? Who was the conniving rat on that film crew? And how did Priscilla fit into any of this?

I crossed Gordon off my list even though he lied about his plane flight. For all I knew, he could have been canoodling with another woman in Toronto before rekindling whatever was going on with him and Priscilla. No matter what, he was off the hook as far as Devora's note was concerned. Whoever Devora responded to had obviously approached her about a new location for the shooting and it certainly wasn't Gordon. That left the usual suspects—Gavin, Stefan, Skylar, Mickey, and Rikesh. It was enough to make my head spin.

I shook my head and stared at the blank screen on my computer. Then I decided to have another look-see at all the players. I perused their Facebook and Instagram pages until I developed an annoying twitch in my left eye. I closed the laptop and was about to chat with Fred regarding tonight's refreshments when something occurred to me. It was regarding a photo I'd seen before. Call it instinct, call it a gut feeling, but whatever it was, I was pretty certain I knew who killed Devora and why.

The only way I could be sure was to set a trap. And if I expected it to work, I couldn't very well tell the whole world about it. So I decided to share my devious little plan with the two people whom I knew wouldn't blow it—Don and Theo.

"It's kind of risky if you ask me," Don said. "Kind of like waving a red cloak in front of a bull."

"If you mean my plan is going to set the killer in motion, you're right. But we'll be on guard. Poised to watch every move that's made."

"Do you think we need to worry about Glenda and Zenora?" he asked.

I gulped. "I always worry about those two but they'll be safe. They don't pose any threats."

Don's voice sounded softer but maybe it was the phone connection. The wind had picked up a bit and that always did a number to landline reception. "I hope you're right about this, Norrie. I'm already wishing the night was over and it hasn't even started yet."

Chapter 36

Fred drove to my house at a little before five with trays of ready-made sandwiches. Assorted breads, cheeses, cold cuts, and veggies. In addition, he had made a scrumptious-looking egg salad and an equally impressive imitation crab salad. Emma had baked fruit tarts and cookies for the screening and he delivered those as well.

"So far it's only the wind picking up," he said. "The real deal's not supposed to start until after midnight so your aura-reveal-catch-the-killer shindig should be done by then. By the way, what are you going to do once you ferret out the culprit?"

"Um, call the sheriff and hope he's not out issuing a traffic ticket or something."

Fred chuckled. "Good plan. I hope it works."

"Me, too. If not, Priscilla will have lost her chance for international stardom and the killer may literally get away with murder."

"About tomorrow—"

"If that storm does what it's supposed to, then all the roads will be closed for a while. Best bet is to check a news app from your phone. Satellite and cable may be iffy. I sent an email to everyone telling them the same thing. Seriously, what tourists are going to hit the wine trail when it's buried under snow?"

"The same ones who do in the winter?"

"Yikes."

I put the trays of food in the fridge, moving my half-full jars of mayo and ketchup to the crisper drawer. The pastries were fine on the kitchen counter and would stay there until I came up with a better idea. Then I did the one thing I'd meant to do since I last spoke with Don and Theo. I wrote a sign that read *Keep Basement Door Shut* and posted it.

Zenora and Glenda were to act as food servers while Zenora did her aura-reading thing. I must have used the word *inconspicuous* at least a hundred times when I last spoke with the two of them. In addition, I made them a list that included: *don't chant, don't touch anyone, don't wave herbs around,* and lastly, *don't set anything or anyone on fire.* Glenda assured me that Zenora would be six to eighteen inches away from her subjects as per the protocol for aura reading, but still, I was worried.

Earlier in the week Skylar had informed me that I needed to clear a large enough area for him to set up a six-foot tripod screen for his HD projector, which needed to be on a table across from the screen. He mumbled something about two to three thousand lumens and how a larger screen would have been better, but theirs was back at the studio in Toronto. I assured him it would be fine no matter how many lumens there were. Then he went on to explain about sound systems and channel mixers.

It was worse than listening to Herbert, our winemaker intern, talk about fermentation and definitely worse than listening to Godfrey babble on and on about some species of insect. In a fit of exasperation I told Skylar that even if he brought a 1970s boom box, it would be fine. The guy groaned and our call ended. Now I had to figure out exactly how much space he'd need for the speakers and all those wires that came with it.

Godfrey was the first to arrive, having left the Experiment Station early. I offered him a sandwich but he insisted on waiting until everyone got here.

"At least have some juice or wine," I said.

"Juice. I think I'm going to need all my wits about me tonight."

Cammy and Glenda showed up at a little before six and parked their cars along the driveway. In the distance I could see the dim security lights in the tasting room. Theo and Don were the next two people who arrived. They, too, had locked their winery and parked along the driveway. Then Zenora made her appearance. If I didn't know better, I would have sworn she'd just left the stage following a performance of *Cats.* The only things missing were the cutesy cat ears and whiskers.

What part of inconspicuous did she not get?

I couldn't take my eyes off of her tight-fitting black body suit complete with a silver fur bola. She slipped into matching silver slippers the minute she took off her boots by the kitchen door. My water-absorbing boot mat resembled a rummage sale table with everyone's footwear piled on top of it. The standing coatrack was full but the large deacon's bench next to it compensated by taking on a mound of outerwear.

Don, who was seated at the kitchen table, took one look at Zenora and poured himself a large glass of Chardonnay. Yep, no doubt about it. It was going to be one hell of a long night.

Bradley and I had already spoken about the evening and I knew where I stood. That left the film crew and the actors and I was beginning to get antsy.

"Relax," Theo said. "They'll come." As if to prove it, he walked to the window, looked out and announced, "Was I right or what? A van is headed up the drive. It has to be them."

Sure enough, Skylar, Mickey, and Rikesh were at the kitchen door complete with enough film equipment for me to open my own studio. Not to mention a box of streak-free microfiber cloths that Mickey had tucked under his arm. Once inside, I directed them to the living room, where I had cleared off space for their setup.

"Gavin, Gordon, and Priscilla should be here any minute," Skylar said. "They're driving together."

I looked past him at the door. "What about Stefan?"

"He told us he'd drive here separately. Said he had a few things to finish up. Go figure."

The crew immediately got down to business setting up the screen and the rest of their equipment, when Gavin, Gordon, and Priscilla showed up.

"My hair hasn't looked this bad in years," Priscilla said. "That wind made a tangle of it. Can you tell me where your guest bathroom is?"

Oh, my God! The guest bathroom!

In all my rush to make sure everything was set up for the filming and aura reveal, I had completely forgotten that my suspect clock was in full view over the mirror. I all but shoved her out of the way as I made a mad dash to get to the room. "Toilet tissue!" I proclaimed as if I'd discovered some rare mineral. "I need to replenish the toilet tissue. Give me a minute and then you can go in."

I ripped the suspect list from the mirror and wadded it up in a ball that I stuffed under my sweatshirt. From there, I raced past the living room and upstairs, where I tossed the paper wad into the guest bedroom and closed the door. Seconds later, I directed Priscilla to the guest bathroom.

"My goodness, Norrie," she said. "You didn't have to rush on my account. All I needed was the mirror."

As Priscilla headed to the bathroom, I noticed Don was now seated next to Gavin on the couch with Theo across from them in a wingchair. The three of them appeared to be deep in conversation, with Don hanging on Gavin's every word while Theo kept readjusting his position in the chair.

Gordon, unfortunately, was trapped at the kitchen table by Godfrey, and when I walked past them to find Cammy, I heard Godfrey say, "I'd be happy to forward you a copy of my study on the Mediterranean flour moth. You know, it isn't only grain stores that are faced with that pest. The Plodia interpunctella can be a nuisance in the home as well."

Before I could interrupt Godfrey, Zenora crept up behind me and tapped me on the shoulder. I nearly jumped out of my skin. "I have to fixate on someone's presence to get a good reading," she whispered.

I pulled her aside and whispered back, "What do you mean *fixate*?"

"You know. Stare at them. Look deeply at their faces."

"Try to look deeply without creeping them out. Maybe they'll take their time when they select a sandwich."

"Should I start now?"

"Yes. Now."

"Hey, everyone!" I announced. "Stefan should be here any minute, but meanwhile, my friends Cammy, Glenda, and Zenora will be serving sandwiches and assorted salads. Wines and juices are on the dining room table so help yourselves. Also, take a plate, utensils, and napkins. Once everyone is here, we'll get a sneak peek at the film."

"Can you tell me again why we're doing this?" Gavin asked.

Gordon immediately seized the opportunity to extricate himself from Godfrey and walked toward me. "Because Renee insisted the screenwriter view the footage. Said she wanted to make sure the film was in keeping with the tone of the story."

"Geez," Gavin replied. "We've never had to do that before."

I had to think fast before everything unraveled. "Um, maybe it's because of the change in directors. Continuity and all that."

A few people grumbled but once Cammy, Glenda, and Zenora moved about with the sandwiches they quieted down.

"What the hell's keeping Stefan?" Skylar asked. "Don't tell me he decided to buff his boots or something. Heck, it's not like we're screening this thing in Hollywood."

"Are you all set?" I asked him.

"Uh-huh. We're good to go. The sooner we show it, the sooner we can get out of here. No offense. The food looks good but that wind is getting stronger. The windows are rattling."

Another joy of living in an old farmhouse in the Finger Lakes.

"I'm sure he'll be here any minute."

I kept my eye on Zenora and prayed she was able to do whatever it was with the auras. Just then, the lights began to flicker and the already strong wind got even more intense.

"Maybe something happened to Stefan's car," Priscilla said. She was now seated next to Gordon in the living room and a good distance from Godfrey.

"I'm sure he'd call," Mickey said from the other side of the room. "I'd give it another ten minutes and let's get this show on the road. All we need to do is turn down the lights."

Zenora let out a gasp that took all of us by surprise. "Turn down the lights? You mean dim them?"

"Yeah. Dim them," Mickey said. "We need ambient lighting to view the film. Why? What's so earth-shattering about dimming the lights?"

"Vision problems!" I announced while grabbing Zenora by the elbow and ushering her to the kitchen. "The poor woman has vision problems."

Once in the kitchen and out of earshot, I whispered, "What's the matter?"

Zenora wrung her hands. "In order to read the auras, I rely on peripheral vision. I need light. And a calm, soothing atmosphere."

Too bad she didn't take a course on speed-reading for auras because the film crew was getting restless and I could only put off the screening for so long.

"Um, do the best you can. Improvise."

Apparently that's exactly what Zenora did because for the next thirty or forty minutes, I watched her maneuver around our guests, but more importantly, I watched our guests maneuver themselves as far from her as possible. She did, however, manage to corner me near the staircase.

"Bunch of perfectionists if you ask me. Mostly yellow and oranges," she said.

"Who? Which ones?"

She pointed out Skylar, Rikesh, and Gordon.

"What about the others? Could you get a reading?"

Zenora closed her eyes and inhaled. "That actress's aura was practically screaming. I've never come across such a brilliant red color."

"Red? What does it mean? Don't tell me I was wrong about her."

"I don't know what you thought, but given her aura, she's competitive and, well, let's just say she enjoys her sexuality."

I looked over to where Priscilla was standing and noticed she kept touching Gordon's arm. "Uh, yeah. That's about right."

That left Gavin and Mickey, but before I could say anything Zenora told me she was having trouble reading their energy centers. Something about cloudy chakras. Or was it murky chakras? Anyway, it didn't matter. The landline rang and I rushed to pick it up from the extension in the kitchen. "It's Stefan!" I shouted.

"Tell him to get a move on," Skylar yelled back. He walked to the kitchen and stood in the doorway.

I held the phone next to my ear and didn't say anything. Finally I ended the call with two words—"I'll try."

"What was that all about?" Skylar asked.

"Stefan's at the Yates County Public Safety Building. He's been arrested for Devora's murder and wants me to call Renee. He called here because they'd only allow him a local call."

"Wow. It's always the ones no one suspected. Stefan. Of all people. That's terrible. I knew that woman was going to push him off the edge." Then Skylar bolted to the living room and announced, "Stefan's under arrest for murdering Devora."

"Is that true?" Priscilla asked. She was now a few feet from me in the kitchen with Gavin, Gordon, and Mickey standing right behind her. Her back was toward the basement door and I noticed the eye-latch was undone.

As I moved toward her to refasten it, Gavin bumped her elbow. "Time to start packing, eh?"

I bent down to pull up one of my socks, and while still hunched over I said, "Wow. What a night."

At that moment, the lights began to flicker and I heard someone ask, "Do you have any candles?" Before I could respond, everything went black.

Chapter 37

"So much for the damn screening," Skylar announced when all of a sudden Priscilla let out a shriek followed by the sound of plates, tins, and God knows what crashing to the floor.

"The basement!" Mickey shouted. "She fell down the cellar stairs!"

"More like shoved, you stinking scoundrel! And I'm right here, so deal with it."

The lights flickered for a split second before coming on. Priscilla leaned back on one of the pantry shelves for leverage and pushed herself up. Then she lunged for Mickey's throat.

"You thought you could get me out of the way by forcing my car in a ditch, and when that didn't work you tried to throw me down the stairs into Norrie's basement. Well, the joke's on you because I fell into the pantry door, not the basement. Norrie switched the sign."

"It's okay, Priscilla," Gordon said. "He's not going anywhere. You can back off." He put his arm around her waist and moved her closer to him but not close enough apparently.

Priscilla broke free and was on top of Mickey like a wild woman. "What were you hoping for? That I'd break a leg? An arm? Because if you wanted to kill me, you would have done it the same way you did to Devora. What did I ever do to you anyway?"

Then, out of the blue, because things weren't crazy enough, Glenda waved some sort of aromatic stick in the air as she muttered, "Cleansing negative energy. One with the universe."

Zenora, who was a foot or two away from Mickey, Priscilla, and Gordon, held out her arms and stared straight ahead.

"Is she going into a trance or something?" Cammy asked. "I got in here as fast as I could from the living room."

Zenora spun her head around and looked directly at me. "A murky brown aura is taking hold. I sense confusion and toxic thoughts."

Gee, you think?

The door to the basement flung open but I seemed to be the only one who noticed. Everyone else appeared to be too busy grasping the scene in front of them. Priscilla hammered Mickey with fist punches and a wallop to his chin. Then, the pièce de résistance—she grabbed his shirt by the collar, causing it to rip. And when it did, I gasped. There, resting on Mickey's bare skin, was a double-looped chain that resembled the kind found on motorcycle jacket sleeve epaulets. Like the one I'd seen in that Facebook photo Stephanie showed me. The exact kind of double-looped chain used to kill Devora.

It took me a minute, but it sank in. I was right all along. The real murder weapon used on Devora's neck wasn't Priscilla's necklace. Behind me, from the basement doorway, I heard a familiar voice. Bradley Jamison stepped away from the threshold and said, "It's over." Then he gave me a quick hug and said, "Good thinking about having me in the basement to turn the breakers on and off. If this wasn't an old house with the circuit board in the cellar, it wouldn't have been as easy to pull off."

"Yeah, and the open floor vents made it even better. I knew you'd hear me."

"Forget the floor vents," Gordon shouted. "Someone give me a hand with Priscilla."

Godfrey rushed over and together, he and Gordon wrestled Priscilla away from Mickey, who held a hand over his chin and didn't say a word. Meanwhile Cammy did her best to shoo Glenda and Zenora out of the kitchen. "Cleanse the air somewhere else," she said.

"From across the living room I heard Rikesh shout, "Don't let those two near this equipment. It's really expensive."

As Gordon and Godfrey eased Priscilla farther away from Mickey, Skylar took a step toward him and glared. "I don't get any of this. I don't get why you strangled Devora and I damn well don't understand what Priscilla's got to do with any of it. Were you in cahoots with Stefan and let him take the fall?"

Mickey pulled his collar up and swallowed. "Stefan had nothing to do with any of this."

"What then? Did Devora's husband offer to pay off your motorcycle in exchange for making her disappear permanently? Their impending divorce is tabloid news, for crying out loud."

"Not Gerard Dobrowski," I said. "It had nothing to do with him or his candy fortune." *Or the fact we're now about to plant enough Concord grape root stock to get us into the next millennium.*

The house had suddenly quieted down, making the wind outside sound even more forceful.

"What then?" Skylar asked. He crossed his arms and remained inches away from Mickey. "You might as well tell us the truth because you're not going anywhere."

Priscilla must have wielded one hell of a punch because the flesh on Mickey's chin swelled up. I walked to the refrigerator-freezer and grabbed a bag of frozen peas. Organic frozen peas that I'd probably never consume. "Here," I said to him. "This may be the last nice gesture you'll get, so talk fast."

Mickey put the bag on his chin and eyeballed the crowd that had now surrounded him. "Fine. Like Norrie said, it had nothing to do with Gerard. Or his money. Devora had a dislike for my girlfriend, Bailey Wagner. And dislike is putting it mildly. She used her connections and saw to it Bailey got passed over for a number of roles. With no recourse, Bailey did what she could. Miniscule parts, commercials, and understudying. She was the backup actress for Priscilla's lead role in Light-Star's major motion picture. That's when I got the idea to rid the world of Devora Dobrowski once and for all while at the same time framing Priscilla for the murder so that the lead role would go to Bailey."

Priscilla broke free from Gordon and Godfrey, who each had a hand on either arm, and charged Mickey like a linebacker. "You monster! You were going to let me rot in prison for a crime you committed! I've got news for you, buddy. There aren't enough peas in Norrie's freezer to save you from what I'm about to do."

"He's not worth it, Priscilla!" I shouted. Thankfully, Bradley got an arm around her waist and moved her away from Mickey.

Skylar, who still hadn't budged from his spot near Mickey, glanced at Priscilla and then back to Mickey. "Hmm, so when there wasn't enough evidence to charge Priscilla, you decided to crank it up a notch to get her out of the way."

Mickey nodded. "I never intended to kill her. Only put her out of commission for a while. It wasn't personal like it was with Devora. Priscilla simply stood in the way of Bailey getting her big break."

"I'd like to give you a big break," Priscilla said. "Starting with one of your arms. But in a way, some of this was my own fault, I suppose. I let everyone believe I was exonerated for the murder and that I could leave New York any time I wanted, but it wasn't true. My passport's locked up with all of yours."

"I don't understand why you'd lie about that," Bradley said to Priscilla.

"Because I wanted to see Skylar and Mickey's reactions when I told them. If either of them thought I killed Devora, they would have been really ticked that I got off free as a bird. And that would have meant they weren't involved in her murder. Unfortunately, those two keep their emotions close to their chests."

"Yeah, like that epaulet chain." I moved closer to Mickey until we were face-to-face. "Tell me, how did you pull off the murder?"

"Like clockwork," Mickey answered. "And a stroke of luck. I found Priscilla's lost necklace and pocketed it. Careful to wear my winter gloves to avoid fingerprints. It was similar to the chain on my jacket but not as strong. Still, I figured it would be believable under the right circumstances."

"Wrapping it up in a cattail and putting it by the edge of the Ipswiches' pond where it was bound to be discovered?"

"Uh-huh. But that came much later. I had already approached Devora the day before about scouting out a new and better location. She handed me a note back at the hotel and underlined it with that hideous lipstick of hers. So, when Skylar and Rikesh went to the van to check on the sound feed the next day, I knew I had everything I needed to get Devora out of the picture for good. Once we trekked up to that little pond, I caught her off guard, and, well, the rest is history. Not wanting to have the evidence in plain sight, I decided to wear it around my neck rather than put it back on the jacket."

"But you forgot one thing," I said. "Devora's handwritten note. The lab tech found it in the bushes under my living room window. Let me guess. It slipped out when you retrieved her eyeglasses. You couldn't very well leave them at the scene when they might come in handy later. Tsk-tsk. Should have waited until you got inside before reaching into your pocket."

"Hey, I'm really sorry about that. All I meant to do was—"

"Scare the living crap out of me?"

"No. Cast suspicion on you and scope out your house just in case."

Just then, the lights began to flicker for good and we were plunged into darkness. All I could feel were bodies pushing against each other and enough scuffling to make me wonder if I'd need to have Francine's floors refinished.

"He's getting away!" Gavin shouted. "I had him in my grip but he broke loose."

"We're on it!" Theo shouted back.

More scuffling, pushing, crashing, and bumping. Someone must have opened the kitchen door because a blast of cold air swept through the place. Outside, in the dim grayish light, I could see a figure running toward one of the cars.

"Hurry!" I yelled. "Before it's too late."

In retrospect, I should have called Deputy Hickman and let the sheriff put out a BOLO. Instead, I ran shoeless, headfirst out the door, only to trip on the slick steps and fall into cold, wet snow.

Chapter 38

"Are you all right?" Godfrey asked. He was the first one out the door after me and pulled me up. "I don't know whose boots I grabbed," he said, "but they fit."

"I'm fine, but Mickey's getting away. He probably has another pair of shoes stashed in that van. He'll be on the thruway in a matter of minutes. The wind isn't going to stop him."

"No," Godfrey answered, "but someone else will. Take a look."

Another figure emerged from the murky darkness and within seconds had knocked Mickey to the ground.

"Quick! Call the sheriff! Call nine-one-one."

The melee that ensued was over before I knew it and all I could see was Mickey on the ground with someone's foot resting on his stomach. Killer or no killer on the loose, my guests each had the good sense to grab a pair of boots, no matter who they belonged to, and put them on before running across the lawn to see what happened.

"It's Stefan!" Rikesh yelled. "I thought he was in jail."

"You thought wrong," Stefan shouted back. "It was all a trap to get the killer to let down his guard and it worked. I was never arrested. I hung out at the hotel like Norrie and I planned it. Then, at nine, I drove over here. Good timing, I'd say."

Off in the distance I heard sirens and I knew Godfrey had made the call.

"You can get your damn boot off my chest," Mickey said. "I'm not going anywhere."

"You can say that again." This time it was Skylar's voice and the edge to it was sharper than most cutlery knives.

"I'll step back," Stefan said. "But you better get your sorry butt up and walk straight ahead to the house."

Not that Mickey had much choice. Gavin, Gordon, Rikesh, and Bradley had him pretty much corralled so all he could do was walk directly to the house and into the kitchen, where Priscilla apparently had also been corralled, only in her case by Glenda and Zenora. Cammy, meanwhile, worked frantically to clean up the mess of plates and assorted kitchenware that landed on the floor during the melee.

"Inhale the aromatic scent of my special passionflower and lemongrass mixture," Glenda said. She handed Priscilla a small tin but not before removing the lid. "Go on, take a whiff. These herbs were recently dried. A few good inhalations and your anxiety will dissipate."

Zenora put her hand on Priscilla's shoulder. "If that doesn't work, I have valerian root in my car. I never travel without it."

"Forget the herbs," I said. "Everyone's anxiety will dissipate once Deputy Hickman gets here and slaps a pair of handcuffs on Mickey's wrists."

Well, almost everyone's. Mine hit the ceiling the moment Grizzly Gary set foot in the kitchen three or four minutes later. "Good Lord! Please don't tell me you made a citizen's arrest, Miss Ellington. The last thing I want to do is deal with the paperwork for New York Penal Code section 35.30."

"No, we didn't. I mean, I didn't. But we've got Devora's killer. It's Mickey Permutter, one of the cameramen. He also broke into my house and hid her glasses, not to mention running Priscilla McCoy off the road. And if I'm not mistaken, got his girlfriend to pretend to be me on that phone call to the Ramada. Oh, and before I forget, he pushed Priscilla down the basement stairs, only it wasn't the stairs, it was my pantry."

Deputy Hickman gave me the funniest look. "Exactly how much of Two Witches wine did you consume?"

"I can explain."

With the help of Theo, Don, Godfrey, and Bradley, Deputy Hickman was able to piece together the details surrounding Devora Dobrowski's demise. Then he read Mickey his rights and carted him off. Just like that.

"Someone call Renee and get a barrister," Mickey shouted, but Skylar slammed the door shut.

"Holy cow," Rikesh said. "Too bad we weren't filming tonight's screening party. It may have won an award in one of those indie film festivals."

Skylar glanced at me from where he was standing and rubbed his chin. "Geez, in all the hubbub I forgot we're supposed to show the footage to Norrie."

"Um, that's not exactly necessary," I replied. "Showing the footage was a ploy to get everyone over here. Renee was desperate to get all of you back to Toronto. Deadlines and all."

Then, out of nowhere, Priscilla started to cry. Softly at first, then louder sobs. "That storm will sock us in for days and I'll never make it to LA. That bouncing bimbo Bailey will get what she and her boyfriend wanted after all."

"Another whiff of the passionflower and lemongrass?" Zenora asked, but Priscilla sobbed into her hands until Cammy grabbed a paper towel and handed it to her.

"Listen, I don't know about anyone else," Gavin said, "but I'd like to get back to the hotel before that storm really hits."

Stefan gave a nod and edged toward the door. "Way ahead of you. I'm just glad this is over with."

Moments later Gavin was out the door with Gordon and a sobbing Priscilla. It was surprising how fast Skylar and Rikesh packed up their equipment and loaded it in the van before taking off.

"Gosh, Norrie, I hate leaving you here to clean up," Cammy said. "I can stick around a bit longer."

"Nah, we've got it," Theo told her. "We're just down the driveway. The rest of you really should get a move on. Come on, Don, we'll start in the living room."

With that, Glenda, Zenora, and Godfrey headed out the door, but not before I pulled Godfrey aside and gave him a hug. I caught that citrus scent as I brushed his cheek and hurried to end the hug. The night didn't need any more drama.

A few seconds later I could hear Godfrey telling the ladies about natural herbs used for pest control but I think it wafted over them. Bradley stood by the kitchen window and looked out. I reached behind him and threw my arms over his shoulders. “Thanks for believing in my plan.”

The hug turned into a kiss and then another. “I believe in you, Norrie. Everything else comes with the territory. Listen, I really should get on the road or you may be stuck with me until the weekend.”

“There are worse things to be stuck with.”

Still, Bradley put on his coat, gave me another kiss and promised we’d dine at Port of Call on Saturday even if we had to dig ourselves out of the snow. From sweeping up broken plates to vacuuming crumbs, Theo and Don zoomed through the house like nobody’s business.

“Hey,” I said, “we’ve got all the desserts. We never got around to serving them. What do you say we make a dent in them?”

“Only if you promise not to get more crumbs on the floor,” Don replied.

“Relax. That’s why we have Charlie.”

“Yeah, speaking of which, where is he? I haven’t seen him all night.”

“Uh, that’s because I shut him in my bedroom. Not only would he beg for food with so many people in the house, but he’d pass gas and asphyxiate all of us.”

“Yeesh. All Isolde does is groom herself and toss up the occasional hairball. That’s the beauty of owning a cat.”

We spent the next hour eating Fred and Emma’s pastries and congratulating ourselves for catching Devora’s killer.

“You know,” I said, “I was almost positive her estranged husband was behind it. I’m really not cut out for this sort of thing and yet, ever since I’ve been here it’s one dead body after the next. Thank goodness Francine and Jason will be back in two months. Two months. What can possibly happen in two months?”

Theo and Don looked at each other and didn’t say a word. They didn’t have to. I could see it on their faces. Two months was a heck of a long time.

Epilogue

As it turned out, the forecasters were right. Spring storm Neville arrived at a little past midnight and stayed for two whole days. Roads were closed on Thursday and Friday but Saturday brought us one of the biggest crowds of wine tasters we'd seen since the Wine and Cheese event. Two days of being cooped up can do that to you.

Gordon Wable managed to pull some strings and got Light-Star Pictures to push back the start-up date for Priscilla. She took an early morning flight to LA on Saturday and arrived in plenty of time for her filming on Monday. Good thing, too, or the Ramada would have run out of tissues.

Mickey was arrested for the murder of Devora Dobrowski, and last I knew was still in the Yates County Public Safety Building awaiting the arrival of his barrister. The rest of the film crew drove back to Toronto on Saturday, Skylar and Rikesh in the van, Gordon in his car, and the others in the production company vehicle.

Stephanie was relieved the whole ordeal was over with and that the only thing they had to worry about was weeds in their irrigation pond and not bodies.

A major announcement regarding Brouse Candies' new manufacturing plant hit the Finger Lakes airwaves like a haboob. Lots of job opportunities from technical support to hourly positions. I imagined the local dentists were pleased, too. As for the six wineries in our little WOW group, we were relieved our vineyard managers had the foresight to order Concord root stock and clear acreage for planting.

Only one thing plagued me and I wouldn't learn the truth until weeks later when I happened to pick up a tabloid newspaper as I stood in line at Wegmans. As I thumbed through it, I spotted a photo of Gordon Wable seated in expensive box seats at a Toronto Blue Jays game on Jackie Robinson Day in April. During the exact time when he was supposed to be in Vancouver. The caption read, "Film director

Gordon Wable cheers the home team." No murder, only runs, hits, and errors. I placed the magazine back on the rack and smiled. As far as I was concerned, our winery team hit a home run.

About the Author

J. C. Eaton is the pen name of husband-and-wife writing team Ann I. Goldfarb and James E. Clapp.

A New York native, Ann spent most of her life in education, first as a classroom teacher and later as a middle school principal and professional staff developer. Writing as J. C. Eaton, she and James have authored the Sophie Kimball Mysteries, the first book of which, *Booked 4* Murder, took first place in the 2018 New Mexico-Arizona Book Awards in the Cozy Mystery category. They are also the authors of the Wine Trail Mysteries and the Marcie Rayner Mysteries. In addition, Ann has published nine YA time travel mysteries under her own name.

When James E. Clapp retired as the tasting room manager for a large upstate New York winery, he never imagined he'd be co-authoring cozy mysteries with his wife. Nonfiction in the form of informational brochures and workshop materials treating the winery industry were his forte, along with an extensive background and experience in construction that started with his service in the U.S. Navy and included vocational school classroom teaching.

You can visit Ann and James at www.jceatonmysteries.com, www.jceatonauthor.com, www.facebook.com/JCEatonauthor/, and www.timetravelmysteries.com.

www.ingramcontent.com/pod-product-compliance
Lightning Source LLC
Chambersburg PA
CBHW022106240626
47153CB00007B/2257

* 9 7 8 1 9 5 0 4 6 1 4 8 6 *